DEAD WRONG

DEAD WRONG

PATRICIA STOLTEY

FIVE STAR
A part of Gale, Cengage Learning

GALE
CENGAGE Learning·

Farmington Hills, Mich • San Francisco • New York • Waterville, Maine
Meriden, Conn • Mason, Ohio • Chicago

GALE
CENGAGE Learning·

LIBRARY OF CONGRESS CATALOGING-IN-PUBLICATION DATA

Stoltey, Patricia.
    Dead wrong / Patricia Stoltey. — First edition.
        pages ; cm
    ISBN 978-1-4328-2986-5 (hardcover) — ISBN 1-4328-2986-6 (hardcover)
    ISBN 978-1-4328-2979-7 (ebook) — ISBN 1-4328-2979-3 (ebook)
    1. Abusive men—Fiction. 2. Runaway children—Fiction. 3. Murder—
Fiction. I. Title.
PS3619.T6563D43 2014
813'.6—dc23
                                                                2014025066

First Edition. First Printing: November 2014
Find us on Facebook– https://www.facebook.com/FiveStarCengage
Visit our website– http://www.gale.cengage.com/fivestar/
Contact Five Star™ Publishing at FiveStar@cengage.com

Printed in the United States of America
1 2 3 4 5 6 7 18 17 16 15 14

For my mom
Sylvia T. Swartz

ACKNOWLEDGMENTS

Many thanks to all of the members of my critique group, Raintree Writers. I am especially grateful to April Moore, Bev Marquart, Brian Kaufman, and Ken Harmon.

And last but definitely not least, a big thank you to Five Star senior editor Deni Dietz for teaching me more than I ever learned in writing classes.

CHAPTER 1

Glades, Florida
Wednesday, January 22

Lynnette staggered backward from the hall into the kitchen until she bumped against the table. She gripped a chair with one hand and raised the other to her face, an automatic response to the pounding in her head. Her knees buckled. Using the chair back to steady her balance, she sat down hard.

Her tongue felt sticky, the taste salty. She had to breathe through her mouth. Sharper pain shot through her nose when she touched it. She raised her head and stared at her fingers, now smeared with red streaks. Liquid oozed down her throat when she tilted her head back. She gagged and coughed.

"Carl," she whispered as she raised her head. Tears stung her eyes. She wanted to run out the door, but he leaned against the wall and watched her, his eyes narrowed and his hands clenched at his sides as though waiting for another reason to strike.

"Don't start with me," he said. "And don't ever tell me what to do."

"I didn't—"

"The hell you didn't. Go clean up your face." Carl went to the refrigerator, took out a beer and popped the top. He returned to the living room without waiting to see if she did as told. A few seconds later, the volume on the television increased.

Lynnette braced one hand on the table and the other on the chair seat before standing on spongy legs that threatened to col-

9

lapse and dump her on the floor. She pulled a dishtowel from the drawer by the sink and shuffled to the freezer for ice. Gently holding the compress to the bridge of her nose, she returned to the kitchen chair.

What the hell just happened? Lynnette glanced at the wall clock. Two-thirty in the morning. She'd been asleep when Carl got home thirty minutes ago, but he'd slammed a door and yelled a string of obscenities that jolted her awake. A sharp clatter followed, as though he'd thrown his car keys against the wall.

Alarmed, Lynnette had jumped out of bed and hurried down the hall. "What's wrong? Are you okay?"

"Hell, no, I'm not okay. The bastards put me on desk duty." He yanked off his badge and tossed it on the table. His gun belt dangled over his arm.

"Why?"

"We heard a ruckus from behind the old mall and drove back there to check it out. Gang of Puerto Ricans smoking and drinking, looking for trouble. We tried to break it up. They gave us a load of shit, so I jerked one kid aside and kicked his ass. Punks. They deserve what they get."

"They reported you?"

"Yeah. Right after they dragged that kid off to the hospital." Carl snorted. "I know damn well he wasn't hurt that bad."

"What'll happen now?"

He grimaced. "I have an appointment with my supervisor after lunch."

"Then what? Will they suspend you?"

"I don't want to talk about it anymore." Carl had moved toward the refrigerator, then seemed to remember the gun belt over his arm. He muttered, "Damn," and stuck the belt on top of the refrigerator before opening the door and grabbing a beer. A few seconds later he had settled into his easy chair in the living room in front of the television. Lynnette had watched him, all the while wondering what kind of man would beat up a kid just for smarting off.

"Damn it, stop staring at me. Go back to sleep."

She'd turned on her heel and headed for bed. After listening to the television blasting loud music and gunfire for fifteen minutes, she'd returned to the living room.

"Carl, babe, can you turn the volume down? I can't get to sleep with—"

"God damn it!" In four long strides, he'd reached Lynnette and punched her in the face.

Now she sat in the kitchen with the ice pack pressed to her face, trembling, trying not to cry, trying not to scream, trying to be calm. She had no idea how to react. Would she trigger another outburst if she went to the bathroom? What if staying in the kitchen made him mad? Should she go to bed? Call the cops? Walk out?

One thing was certain. If he tried to hit her again, she would fight back . . . and that would not end well for her. Her cop husband was six feet two inches tall and weighed two hundred twenty pounds. No contest. He'd hear if she called the police. Her hands shook as she considered and rejected the idea. What about making a run for it? Her car keys were in her purse, and the purse was in the bedroom. He'd see her go down the hall and come back with luggage. He'd know. He'd stop her.

She removed the ice pack. The towel was bloody and smelled faintly of bleach. She tipped her head back again and pressed the ice to her nose. It hurt. It hurt even more that her husband of less than five days had hit her with his fist.

My husband. Not for long, baby.

In a small ceremony at city hall with only two witnesses, Lynnette had agreed to love, honor and cherish Carl Foster. She had made a terrible mistake, one her stepmother, Ramona, had warned her against.

"Lynnette, darling," Ramona had said after meeting Carl for the first time. "You're not seeing the man clearly. He's too possessive, too demanding. He was rude to me, as though he wanted to make me mad so I'd leave. You're twenty-eight, old enough to know better. What would your father say?"

"You don't know Carl the way I do, Ramona. Please give him a chance."

A couple of days later, before the wedding, Lynnette walked in on Carl and Ramona yelling at each other. Ramona grabbed Lynnette's arm and tried to pull her out of the room, but Lynnette had jerked away and stepped to Carl's side. Carl ordered Ramona out of his house, and that was that.

Thinking about the blinders she'd been wearing a week ago made her head hurt worse. She heard a noise and then a sigh, so she took the ice pack away from her face. Carl stood by the table in the kitchen, less than three feet from her chair. He stepped toward her. She held up her hand in warning.

He stopped and bent his head, then rubbed the heel of his hand against the corner of his eye. His jaw clenched. He stuffed his hands in his pockets and stared at her, his glare taking her breath away. A picture of a boy, crumpled on the ground, flashed and disappeared. She thought about Carl hitting the kid as hard as he'd hit her. What to do? Treat him like a mean dog? Cower?

"This was your fault, you know," Carl said. "You shouldn't have messed with me. Not this morning."

"My fault?" *What an asshole.* But she couldn't say anything more. He was a very dangerous asshole. She stared at his shoes to avoid eye contact.

His tone hardened, almost as though he rebuked Lynnette for her lack of forgiveness. "What do you want from me?"

To see you dragged off to jail, you creep. She pointed to her nose. "I think you broke it."

He took a step closer and squinted as he studied her face.

She held up her hand again. "Stay back."

Carl ran his fingers through his hair, rubbed his jaw, and peered at her nose from where he stood.

He shrugged. "I can't tell from here. Looks okay to me."

"I should go to the emergency room."

"Don't be a baby. You're not going anywhere. Don't even try."

He took another beer from the refrigerator, snapping the top open as he strolled out of the room. Then the television blared even louder than it had before.

Lynnette stood, still shaky, and used the edge of the table as support while she tested her ability to walk. In the bathroom, the mirror reflected a battered woman—a woman Lynnette didn't recognize. After gently probing her nose and cheekbones, she decided she didn't need a doctor. The bleeding had stopped. One eye was going to be a shiner for sure, the right eyelid more puffy than the left. She washed down a couple of aspirin with water from the tap.

Slumped on the floor, her back propped against the door, she ran her fingers absent-mindedly across the plush bath mat. She wanted to walk out right now, but not in her nightgown, not without her papers and her laptop. There was no way to pack without getting caught.

Patience, Lynnette. Wait until he leaves.

Until then, she didn't dare piss him off.

Carl rattled the doorknob. "I'm going to bed. I need to get in there."

"Yeah, okay." She struggled to her feet and flushed the toilet, then opened the door and slipped past him without a word.

After fixing a new ice pack in the kitchen, she stretched out on the living room couch to think.

Why didn't I see the signs? Ramona had tried so hard to tell her. The way he'd pressured her about marriage so soon after

13

they started dating. Insisted she spend all her free time with him. Discouraged her from making new friends. He claimed his possessive nature was all about love, but she wasn't stupid. She should have known better.

I fell for this guy's line. He looked great in his uniform, and the sex was incredible. I let him talk me into getting married because I . . .

Lynnette shook her head. What did it matter? She tried to shift her busy brain into neutral while she took deep slow breaths. "Quiet, quiet," she muttered.

After dozing off and on until mid-morning, Lynnette gave up on sleep. She sat on the edge of the couch with her head bowed and wished her father was still alive. He had been her anchor, the one person she could always talk to. Without him, living in this new town, she felt completely alone.

Thoughts of her father would have to wait. It wouldn't be wise to dwell on her grief, not if she wanted to maintain her anger and resolve. She sat up straight and whispered, "Bullshit. I will not live like this."

She returned to the bathroom and examined her face in the magnifying side of her hand mirror. That only made the bloom- ing bruises look worse. She combed her dark hair forward around her face, but it was too short to hide the damage. She dabbed liquid foundation around her nose and right eye. The swollen eyelid was going to attract attention. Using the ice pack a couple more times might help. There was plenty of time before she could leave.

She went out the kitchen door that led to the garage and retrieved her big-ass pair of sunglasses from the car's console.

Back in the kitchen, she made a pot of coffee. A half hour later, when she heard Carl moving around the bedroom, the pot was nearly empty. She did her best thinking over coffee, its dark roast aroma and warmth both comforting and energizing.

Focused now, she made a plan. Fixing Carl's lunch on schedule seemed wise, even if she didn't want to see or talk to him. Not now. He'd become a stranger in an instant, and she didn't know what he might do next.

As she made sandwiches, she thought of all the things that might go wrong, her mind throwing out one question after another. Would she make too much noise if she used the food processor? Would he notice she'd picked a patch of mold off one corner of the bread crust? She hadn't brewed a pot of tea for iced but used instant instead. Would he taste the difference?

It shocked her to be so afraid in her own home—the one place she thought would be a safe haven.

A handful of chips and an apple, peeled and quartered the way he liked it—surely he would be satisfied with that. After Lynnette set Carl's plate on the table, she rinsed off the paring knife and left it beside the sink.

The screened patio off the living room seemed like a good place to eat her lunch while she stayed out of Carl's way. Juggling a plate with her own sandwich and glass of iced tea, she struggled briefly with the security lock on the sliding glass door. Outside, the pink stuffed cushions on the patio furniture smelled of mildew. It no longer mattered. She sat in the chair across the table from the glass door so she could see Carl when he entered the living room. After a few minutes he approached the door, made eye contact, watched her for a moment, and walked away. The garage door rumbled open and then closed.

CHAPTER 2

Miami, Florida
Wednesday, January 22

Sammy Grick rang the mansion doorbell twenty times, but Mrs. Ortega never answered. Hired to pick up a package from Mr. O's house and deliver it to him in Los Angeles, Sammy didn't want to screw up a good thing. Pleasing the boss was the only way to keep this job making big money. Mr. O paid his best gofers well. Paid a lot better than collecting insurance from property owners and kicking the shit out of the skims.

Sammy banged on the door with his fist loud enough to wake the fucking dead, even though the doorbell had echoed from inside each time he jammed his thumb on the button.

No one answered.

Sammy pulled his cell phone out of the computer case he carried and called his boss.

"Mr. O, she's not here."

"What?"

"Mrs. O isn't answering the door. I don't think she's home. Should I pick the lock?"

"No, that'll set off an alarm. There's a key in a jar under the bush by the garage door. When you get inside, if the light on the alarm pad is green, enter 7329 to turn it off. Then I'll tell you what to do."

Two minutes later, with only a brief glance at the hoity-toity furniture in the dining room and the glassed-in wine closet that

16

ran the length of the hall to the restaurant-sized kitchen, Sammy climbed the winding staircase to the master bedroom to loot his boss's wall safe according to his new instructions. Fucking screw-ups. Why did it always happen to him? Like the time he hijacked someone's baby by mistake.

He was supposed to pick up Mr. O's Lexus from a hotel parking lot and take it to the airport. The key wouldn't work, and Sammy panicked, scared he'd be late picking up Mr. O. He rigged the ignition, thinking he had the right car and the wrong key, and took off. Six blocks later, he heard the noise in the back.

In any other situation, Sammy would have fingered the son of a bitch who'd messed him up, taken him down and kicked the bastard until nothing but a pile of bloody gunk remained. But Sammy couldn't blame a baby for sitting in the car seat where his whore of a mother left him. He sped back to the hotel parking lot, screeched the car to a stop at the rear of the lot, and backed it hard into a concrete post. Twice.

The baby wailed.

"That's what your fucking stupid bitch mother gets for leaving you alone!" he had yelled as he struggled to free himself from the seatbelt. Then even louder, "Why do they put the son-of-a-bitching buckle under your ass?"

It was a good thing Mr. O never heard about that one. Mr. O would have fired him, right after he'd built Sammy a new asshole. This new courier job was his best chance to make good and get more responsibility, do something more respectable than smashing fingers with a ball-peen hammer or hoisting bodies into dumpsters that reeked of rotten meat. "Do this job right and you'll make a bundle," Mr. O had told him. "Fail me and you're fucked." So what happens first thing on this new job? Sammy has to call in and admit something had gone wrong before he was even inside the mansion's front door.

"You have everything you need," Mr. O had told him during one of his phone calls. "You have the cell phone I gave you. Use only that phone when you call me. I gave you a laptop and a case. You have the code to get inside the security gate. I've informed Mrs. Ortega that you'll pick up my package Wednesday morning. Your ticket from Miami to Los Angeles is reserved. Go to the ticket counter for your boarding pass. I can't afford any delays. Do you understand that, Sammy?"

Like I'm deaf and dumb.

Sammy figured out who the real fuckup was when he got to the ritzy house in that ritzy neighborhood called Pelican Cove and discovered Mrs. O wasn't home. Then the safe combination Mr. O gave him didn't work. He was fiddling with the numbers for the fourth time when he heard a door close somewhere in the house.

Mrs. O walked into the bedroom in a white terry-cloth robe, her hair wrapped in a blue towel. Sammy nearly had a heart attack on the spot.

"What the hell are you doing in my bedroom?" she screamed.

Sammy gasped. She stood on the other side of the bed, too far away to grab. His heart pounded as he sputtered, trying to come up with a good answer. "I rang the doorbell and you didn't answer."

Mrs. O dashed to the bedside table and yanked the drawer open. The next thing Sammy knew, she had a Luger pointed at his head.

"Put that old thing down before it goes off!"

"Benny told you how to get in, didn't he? That son of a bitch."

"Mrs. O, I'm supposed to pick up a package here. Mr. O said you were expecting me at ten o'clock." He glanced at his watch. "I was right on time."

Sammy wasn't the fastest thinker in the world, and he didn't always see the big picture when he made his plans, but he did notice details. The manual safety was still engaged on the Luger, and he could tell Mrs. O didn't have any idea what he was talking about. He put his hand out and took a step in her direction.

She tried to fire as soon as he moved, glanced at the safety, released it, and raised the gun again.

Charging around the bed with amazing speed for his size, Sammy bulldozed into the woman and knocked her off her feet. The Luger flew out of her hand and skidded under the bed as he took her down.

Sammy landed on top of her hard enough to break her ribs. He lay there and tried to catch his breath, squashing the life from Mrs. O's body while she beat at his sides and made gurgling noises that irritated the hell out of him. He bounced his bulk against her chest to shut her up. Her eyes rolled back in her head and her jaw sagged. He felt for a pulse in her throat. Nothing.

His right knee hurt like hell and the smell of Mrs. O's soap was strong enough to jam up his sinuses. He shifted to one side and rolled off her body.

Stupid broad. I told her to put the gun down.

After struggling to his feet, he pulled up his pant leg and dabbed at his scraped knee with his handkerchief. That made it sting worse. He half-heartedly nudged her head with his foot. The sight of her, sprawled like a rag doll, her eyelids wide open with nothing showing but the white parts, freaked him out. The towel had fallen to the floor, and her wet hair stuck out on all sides, making her look like that broad with the snakes on her head. He shivered and turned his back. *The bitch should have answered the door.* She had screwed up his job and maybe his life. She had no one to blame but herself.

He returned to the wall safe and tried three more times, studying the numbers on the slip of paper before he spun the dial. No luck. He sat on the edge of the bed to think. After a few minutes, he pulled the laptop case to his side, retrieved the cell phone, and made another call.

"Mr. O, I got a problem."

Sammy heard his boss draw in a deep breath before asking in his heavy Cuban accent, "What's wrong now, Sammy?"

"It's this combination you gave me. It don't work. Are you sure you gave me the right numbers?"

"Shit. Maria probably changed it and didn't tell me. Look on her desk. She keeps a copy of the combination taped to the inside back cover of her day calendar."

A minute later, Sammy picked up the phone he'd placed on the desk. "Got it, Mr. O." He carried the phone to the safe and held it to his ear while he tried the combination with his free hand. "Okay. It's okay. I got it open."

"Is there an envelope inside?"

"Yeah, one of those flat brown ones, and other stuff. There's a big pile of cash, too."

"Open the envelope and tell me what's inside."

"Uh, looks like some checks."

"That's what I need. Take the envelope and leave everything else where it is. Don't forget to shut the safe and spin the dial." Mr. O paused, but before Sammy could say anything else, he added, "You better get out of there before she comes home. She'll go nuts if she finds out I told you how to get inside."

Sammy didn't know what to say. Should he tell Mr. O what he'd done? Wait until he got to L.A.? Never mention it? He was pretty sure Mr. O would shit coconuts when he found out his wife was dead.

"Is something wrong, Sammy?"

"Look, Mr. O, I'm sorry. What happened isn't my fault—"

"What do you mean? That she didn't show up? Don't worry about it."

"No. It's—"

"Tell me about it when you get to L.A.," Mr. Ortega said. "Go to the airport. Take the envelope and guard it with your life. Make sure you have the phone with you. When you get here, come straight to the hotel and call me. I'll be waiting."

"I'll—"

"Sammy. Don't mess with the envelope. Put it in your briefcase and don't let anyone else see it. Don't even look at it again. Understood?"

"Yeah, understood."

"I mean it. Don't open the envelope again."

"Got it. I got it." Sammy said, ending the call.

Damn, the checks must be a real big deal.

He should have taken a better look when he had the chance.

As he transferred the brown envelope to his laptop case, he noticed a slim box and peered at the pieces of jewelry inside. Red stones, looking expensive against the red velvet lining. If he took them, Mr. O would figure it out.

He thumbed through the huge stack of cash and decided Mr. O couldn't possibly know exactly how much was there. The handful of hundreds pulled from the middle, just in case Mr. O marked the top and bottom, fit nicely into one of the inside pockets of the case. Afraid he'd lose the cell phone if he carried it in his pocket, Sammy stuffed it in the case as well.

He checked his watch after he closed and locked the safe. Plenty of time. All the stuff he had snatched rested safely in the case he was to deliver to Mr. Ortega. He'd move the cash to his own pocket before he landed. No doubt Mr. O had a good reason for not taking the goods with him when he left home. Probably had his wife steal something while he did business out of town so he couldn't be blamed.

Mr. O was a crook and a mean son of a bitch. A big-time, rich-as-sin, vicious slimeball. Sammy didn't understand why his boss had never been caught, had never served even one night of jail time as far as Sammy knew.

He pushed Mrs. O's body aside and braced himself against the bed as he knelt to look for the Luger. It lay within easy reach. He pulled it out. Older than he'd thought, like a World War II souvenir. Probably worth something. The gun would be safe stashed in the trunk of his car at the Miami airport until he returned from L.A. He'd figure out what to do with it later.

CHAPTER 3

Glades, Florida
Wednesday, January 22

Lynnette checked her watch. Eleven-thirty. Carl's appointment was scheduled for one o'clock. She wondered if he planned to come back to the house before his appointment, then decided to wait until noon before she made her move.

She returned to the kitchen and opened the bottle of red wine she'd bought for their one-week anniversary dinner. Carl's lunch sat on the table, untouched. She dumped the food, plate and all, into the trash. *What the hell's the difference? I won't be here.*

Using a short water glass, she poured a small amount of wine. It tasted good, but she needed a clear head. She corked the bottle and left it on the counter. She carried a can of diet root beer and a glass to the patio and thought about the last two months, trying to figure out the exact moment she'd lost her common sense.

She had left her Indianapolis home and her friends behind and flown to Miami only a few weeks before, thinking she had a job in advertising sales with *The Miami Herald*. But the job no longer existed by the time she arrived. Budget cuts. The only job she found right away was in an oceanfront bar in Fort Lauderdale. The need to defend herself from intoxicated jerks while she took orders and served drinks led her to a self-defense class in nearby Glades, and to Carl.

Never in a million years would she have suspected him of being the kind of person who'd hit women. He'd been her instructor at the class. No one would expect a stealth attack from the very person who teaches you how to defend yourself!

She hadn't been in Florida long enough to make new friends. The women in her self-defense class seemed nice enough, but she only knew their first names. It was hard to bond while they visualized each other as attackers to be fended off using elbow thrusts, thumbs to the eyeballs, and toe stomps.

The waitresses and bartenders where she worked came and went as fast as the weather changed. None of them had been around long enough to become more than a passing acquaintance.

Carl was a cop. That had seemed like a good thing. Now she remembered things she'd learned in her former job as a reporter for *The Indy Reporter*. She had covered two stories in different Indiana towns where a cop regularly beat the crap out of his wife.

If she called the cops on Carl, would it bring even more trouble into her life? Wouldn't they all stick together?

Her new mother-in-law, a lawyer in West Palm Beach, wouldn't help. Carl's mother thought he could do no wrong.

Domestic abuse hotline? Shelter for battered women? Those organizations took care of victims. She refused to think of herself as a victim.

What then? She could try the old light-a-fire-in-his-bed alternative, of course. Or a bit of rat poison in his salad dressing. She chuffed at her inappropriate thoughts. She could imagine the prosecuting attorney's question: "Why didn't you just leave, Mrs. Foster?"

Her answer: "Because I was pissed off!"

Nah, that won't fly.

It would have been nice if she'd come from a larger family.

Her only living relative, if she didn't count her soon-to-be ex-husband, was her stepmother. Ramona had moved back to her condo in a Southern California retirement community after Lynnette's father died. They hadn't been in touch since just before Lynnette and Carl tied the knot.

She glanced at her watch. A little after noon. She carried the can and her glass inside, shoving the patio door closed with her foot. Before packing her carry-on bag and her laptop, she changed into black jeans, a sweater and running shoes. Called a cab. Wrote a note and tossed it on the kitchen table.

Carl, I'm not coming back. I'll get my finances in order and file for divorce as soon as I'm settled. I don't want to talk to you. L.

While she waited for her cab, Lynnette went through the motions, doing the things she'd do on an ordinary day before leaving the house. She closed the blinds and pulled the drapes across the patio door, unplugged the coffee pot, dumped the grounds and rinsed the decanter.

A car horn honked. Before she got to the door, the cab driver honked again. As she placed her purse strap over her shoulder, she automatically checked the thermostat. The house would be hot and stuffy when Carl returned if she didn't adjust the temperature. She didn't give a rat's ass. She shut off the air conditioner and fan, grabbed her bags, set the lock, and pulled the door shut.

Hollywood, California
Wednesday, January 22

Albert Getz studied the reference books in *To Die or Not to Die*, the newly opened mystery bookstore in Hollywood. All the new releases on forensics, police procedure, weapons, and poisons were there. He pulled down a copy of an older, well-known reference, *Murder and Mayhem* by D. P. Lyle, M.D., and opened it to the Table of Contents.

"Can I help you find anything?"

Albert looked over his shoulder, saw the man who earlier had manned the cash register at the front of the now empty store and answered, "I think I found it."

"Just got that in yesterday. You a mystery writer?"

"No, but I wrote a book mystery writers use for research. I'm a retired professor. Used to teach criminal justice classes in the sociology department at Central CU." Albert took off his reading glasses and tucked them in the breast pocket of his tweed jacket. He held the book next to his chest with his left hand and, with his right, fumbled in his pocket for his pipe. He pulled it out, stuck the stem into one corner of his mouth, and sucked in the sweet taste of cherry tobacco.

The shop owner raised his eyebrows.

"It's not lit," Albert said between his clenched teeth. "It's never lit." He took the pipe out of his mouth. "I quit smoking five years ago." He tapped on the book he'd selected and added, "I'm going to do a website and a blog to help market my book. Need to see how this guy does it."

"You're going to buy that one?"

"Yes." Albert's cell phone rang. He stuck the pipe stem in his mouth and grabbed the phone out of his pocket. "Yes?"

Ortega the Cuban again. God, he hated that man. Getz turned his back on the bookstore employee and walked away.

"I have a job for you, Getz. You know Sammy Grick from Miami?"

"Fat Ass Sammy Grick? Sure. Doesn't he work for you?"

"He does, but just for a few more hours. I need him killed."

"When?"

"He's on his way to L.A. with a package for me. I'd like you to be here, waiting for him. Where are you now?"

"Hollywood."

"Call me when you get to Century City and I'll give you the

26

hotel name and room number."

"Payment today?"

"As soon as the job's done."

After replacing the phone and pipe in his pocket, Albert strode to the front of the store, paid for the book, and headed toward the parking garage where he'd left his car.

Miami, Florida
Wednesday, January 22

It took nearly two hours for Lynnette's cab to get to the departure ramp at Miami International. After she drew the daily limit of cash from one of the airport ATMs, she worked her way through the maze toward the Overland Airlines ticket counter.

Scooting her laptop bag along the floor and rolling her carry-on forward, Lynnette finally neared the front of the line. As she reached for her case, she brushed against the prominent rear end of the short, fat man in front of her. He turned and glared, studying her face with no change of expression.

"Sorry," she said.

The fat man turned away. The line shuffled forward. He waddled to the counter, leaving his own case to block Lynnette's path. She maneuvered around the obstacle. He gathered his driver's license and boarding pass and turned, nearly bowling Lynnette over as he lunged for his case and hurried away.

"Butthead," she whispered as she stepped to the counter. The ticket agent stared at Lynnette's face, trying to compare it to the photo on her driver's license. "Ma'am, would you remove your sunglasses?"

She did. "Car accident," she said. "Sitting too close to the air bag. Won't do that again."

The agent nodded, regarded her face a little longer, then placed the license next to his keyboard.

"What's the next flight out of Miami?" she asked.

"Where to?"

"Oh. LAX." He had already begun to type when she added, "Or Burbank. John Wayne."

The agent stared at Lynnette, then turned to his monitor as his fingers moved across the keyboard. "We'll start with Los Angeles." He tapped on the keys for a few seconds, then studied his screen. "I can get you on the 5:30 flight, but the only seats left are first class."

"Direct flight?"

He shook his head. "One stop. Denver. Same plane takes you on to L.A."

"How long is the layover?"

"Ummm. Looks like an hour."

Lynnette said okay without asking the price. She booked the ticket with her Indiana driver's license and her own credit card, both in her maiden name. The clerk barely raised an eyebrow, and the exorbitant charge slipped through the system without question. Too bad she and Carl hadn't received the new joint credit cards they'd ordered. Her ticket would have been a small price for Carl to pay for her bloody nose and black eye. He shouldn't get off this easy.

It took her almost thirty minutes to get through security. The short bank of seats for travelers to put on their shoes and reorganize their possessions was almost full. Lynnette set her case on one seat while she replaced her laptop and zipped it closed. Before she had a chance to move it, the fat man charged forward, grabbed her case and set it on the floor, put his own case and shoes next to it, and dropped into the seat with a grunt.

Lynnette shifted to one side when she felt the guy's meaty thigh rub against her leg.

Taking the extra seconds to replace her identification in her billfold and zip her boarding pass into the outside compartment of her purse, she was still tying her shoes when the fat man left. When she arrived at the gate area, she saw him disappear into the men's room. She shuddered and said a silent prayer he wouldn't be on her plane.

With more than two hours to wait until her flight boarded, she needed something to do. At the newsstand she bought a paper and a bottle of water and settled down to read.

As soon as she could, she followed the line into first class, found her seat, stowed her carry-on in the overhead compartment and put her computer and purse under the seat in front of her.

The fat man she'd seen at the ticket counter and again at security entered the cabin. Without apology, he bumped the arms and shoulders of seated passengers with his case and bulky body. He stopped at Lynnette's row, which caused her a moment of panic. She relaxed when he dropped his belongings into the seat across the aisle and struggled to remove his jacket. He threw it into the window seat, then leaned over and raised the armrest. With a grunt, he heaved his case to the floor and shoved it out of sight with his foot. From where Lynnette sat, it appeared the fat man's butt spread into the window seat, even though he clearly intended to sit on the aisle.

Within minutes, the plane began its slow exit from the gate.

Lynnette didn't have a solid plan yet, but she'd been working on it. She'd arrive in L.A. about midnight, so she'd find a motel room and get a little sleep before moving on. From Los Angeles, she could take a shuttle south to Ramona's place. Carl might look for her in L.A., but he'd have a hard time tracing her movements if she didn't rent a car. He didn't know exactly where her stepmother lived, either. The complex was a gated facility covering hundreds of acres. Manned security gates guarded each entrance. Maybe by the time Carl showed up,

Lynnette would have moved on. Or maybe Ramona would ask her to stay for a while. She sure as hell wouldn't allow Carl in the door.

Ramona might say "I told you so." Lynnette could live with that.

CHAPTER 4

Miami, Florida
Wednesday, January 22
Sammy slid toward the aisle so the little rise where the two airplane seats came together didn't push against his tailbone when he leaned back. *At least that bastard I work for booked me two seats in first class.* He was known all over South Florida as Fat Ass Sammy Grick for a reason. He needed that extra space. If there'd been only one seat or if he'd been back with the el-cheapo flyers, Sammy swore he'd have taken Mr. Ortega's loot and headed for parts unknown.

Nah, that was stupid. If he did something like that, Mr. O would send a couple of goons to track him down and cut him into little pieces.

He looked at the small space between his knees and the seat in front of him. "Like being in a submarine," he said.

The laptop case he'd stuffed under the seat kept him from stretching out his legs. He used his feet to pull it forward, shove it toward the window seat, and push it back underneath. With one flick of his thumb and forefinger, he unfastened the button at the waist of his pants, then pulled a handkerchief from his pocket and mopped his forehead and neck.

He needed a drink. The attendant call button was overhead, but Sammy couldn't reach it. With enough force to send a jolt of pain up his arm, he banged his fist on the armrest, just once. He didn't want to piss anybody off, get restrained with plastic

31

handcuffs and dragged off the plane. That would be a disaster, in more ways than one. The appointment Sammy had in Los Angeles was too important. And considering what he had done just a few hours before, he needed to get his ass out of Miami as fast as he could.

Cooped up in this damn airplane and waiting for one of those broads to bring him a drink ranked right up there with all the rest of the things he hated. He belched, sour acid rising into his throat. God, he hated flying.

CHAPTER 5

In the air
Wednesday, January 22

Lynnette celebrated her escape from Miami in the air, somewhere northwest of Orlando. Her second martini arrived with five olives, just as she'd ordered, accompanied by a sympathetic smile from the flight attendant who looked everywhere except at Lynnette's battered face.

As she sipped her drink, Lynnette thought about Carl, thought about him coming home and finding her note. Would he be angry? Hell, yes. Throw something? Punch a hole in the wall with his fist? Probably. She held her icy glass against her cheek, as close to her nose as she dared. How had he kept his rage hidden all those weeks they'd talked and dated, planned the wedding, enjoyed the weekend honeymoon on Duck Key? He was so sweet, so sexy.

Would Carl's mother believe her son capable of hitting his wife in the face? What about Carl's friends?

She pulled her purse into her lap and dug for aspirin, swallowing two tablets with the rest of her drink. She reclined her seat and closed her eyes.

By the time the plane crossed the Florida state line, Sammy was nursing his third skimpy dose of Jack Daniel's. During boarding, he'd glared at each new passenger who walked past, mentally cursing the foreigners as he labeled them frogs, ragheads, wet-

backs, or whatever.

Only when the young girl with the ponytail and the hiking boots walked past did Sammy weaken for a moment. He had a soft spot for kids. Not in a weird way. He liked kids. He felt sorry for them, too. It was tough being at the mercy of bullies, teachers, and cops who treat kids like crap.

Sammy averted his eyes when the girl looked him up and down. No doubt checking out his fat belly and the way his ass overflowed onto the empty seat by the window. Some kids had no manners.

Now, with the plane in the air and Sammy not even close to feeling drunk, he leaned into the aisle and hollered, "Hey."

The flight attendant peered around the corner of the galley, saw Sammy wave his glass in the air, and ducked inside. Before Sammy had a chance to yell any louder, the attendant re-appeared with another J.D. and a cup of ice.

He handed over his credit card and took the tiny bottle from her hand. "Just one? It ain't even a swallow."

She tried to hand him the cup of ice, but he pushed it away. "We're out," she said.

"What? Out of booze? No way."

"No, out of Jack Daniel's." She trotted back to her little hideout before he could think of something else to order.

Out of Jack Daniel's. *Shit a goddamn brick.* He banged his head against the headrest and closed his eyes. He'd been drink-ing since third grade. He sure as hell didn't intend to quit today.

"Hey," he hollered again. He tilted his head to the side so he could see all the way to the cockpit door, his eyes open but squinted in what he considered his dangerous look—the one that said, *Don't mess with me.* What could she do about a dirty look? Throw him to the floor and handcuff him? Spray mace in his face? What?

Instead, she whipped out of the galley opening and down the

aisle with four bottles in her hand. All J.D. "Found some more. I'll need your credit card again." She walked away before Sammy had a chance to say, "Thanks." Not that he would have bothered.

With all four bottles emptied into his plastic cup, it almost looked like a real drink. He lowered the seat tray on the window side but kept his fingers gripped around the cup after he set it down. He leaned back and considered how to keep Mr. O from finding out what he had done to Mrs. O. There had to be a way to deliver the goods, get his money, and be long gone before anyone found out.

Once he escaped Mr. O's reach . . . well, that was the problem. He would never be out of Mr. O's reach, if he didn't get something on Mr. O, something big. When he got to L.A., before he caught a cab to the hotel, he'd find a private place where he could look inside that brown envelope. It might be the only way to save his ass.

CHAPTER 6

Glades, Florida
Wednesday, January 22

Carl got home at seven o'clock in the evening. He left the car in the driveway, thinking he might go out again later. He fumbled with his key, his ability impaired by the half-dozen beers he'd knocked off since leaving the meeting with IAD.

A blast of hot air stifled him as he entered the house. He stumbled inside, slammed the door shut, turned on the hall light, and checked the thermostat. Ninety-five degrees. He flipped the switch to Cool and moved the dial to sixty-five, cursing Lynnette's lack of consideration.

In the kitchen, a piece of paper on the table caught his attention. He picked up the note and read it three times.

Carl felt his face turn red. He dropped the note and began to rhythmically clench and unclench his hands as though working the feeling into numb fingers.

It was bad enough he had to go through all these interviews with IAD. Six weeks or more of counseling with a psychologist. Anger management classes. Now this? He balled up his fist and slammed it on the table.

"Hey, man. You got a problem?"

Carl jumped at the sound and looked toward the kitchen door. A street kid leaned against the doorjamb. A Puerto Rican. Maybe fourteen, fifteen years old. Red bandanna wrapped around his head. Small tat of a snake on his neck. Straggly beginnings of a moustache and goatee. Not someone Carl would expect to see in his own house, on his street. He faced the kid, his hands empty and in the open. "What are you doing here? How did you get in?"

"You left that big door unlocked, man."

"What do you want? You want to take stuff? Take it. I don't give a shit." He reached for his billfold.

"Nah. Don' do that. I don' want your stuff."

Lynnette would have been home if they hadn't fought. He wondered why she'd turned off the air conditioner, why she'd left the patio door unlocked. "Then how come you're here?"

"Look at me. You know me?" the kid said.

"Should I?"

The kid raised his right arm and motioned into the darkened living room behind him. Two more punks stepped into the hallway and strolled into the kitchen with insolent purpose. Carl sucked his breath in alarm. The boys smirked. With all the force his arms possessed, Carl tried to upend the kitchen table and hurl it toward the doorway, but he didn't move fast enough. They caught the front side of the table and shoved, pinning him against the counter.

There were knives in the kitchen. He had a loaded gun in the bedroom. But he was trapped. He had to wait, bide his time, try to look fearless.

Carl unbuttoned and rolled up his sleeves, then sighed. "Okay. What do you want?"

"You sayin' you don' remember me?" the first boy said.

Carl looked him over, shook his head. "No."

"Think 'bout last night. Think 'bout when you and your buddy beat my li'l brother."

Carl felt the weight of his heart on top of his stomach, pressing down. How had they found him? Followed him home? "You don't have to do this," he said, his voice shaky.

The first kid raised his arms as if he had no idea what Carl was talking about. "Do what?"

"Anything. To me. I've already been suspended from the force. My partner, too. They're doing an investigation. I've got to take classes so I don't lose my temper."

"That sounds good," the first kid said. "But, see, we done our investigatin' before we even come here. That's like takin' the law into our own hands. Right? Kinda like you did when you kicked my brother in the face instead of taking him to juvie. He's gonna be blind in one eye now. You know about that?"

Carl tried to look sympathetic. But then he made eye contact with the first kid and realized from the dead gaze that the kid didn't care what Carl felt or said. Sweat beads pooled in the hollow at the base of his throat and trickled down his chest. He glanced toward the door to the garage, willing himself to shove the table hard, then run into the garage and out the side door to his car.

The first kid looked at the door, looked at Carl, and chuckled. "You ain't got the guts, man." He wandered into the hall and disappeared from Carl's view.

The other boys pulled the table back so Carl was no longer wedged in place, but one stepped between him and the door to the garage. The other stood in the hall just outside the kitchen and watched him with a menacing stare.

Sweat trickled down Carl's sides from his armpits. He tried to take a deep breath but couldn't. He knew what they were thinking. He knew what they were going to do. Paralysis seized his brain. His body took over.

With a sudden lunge, he rushed around the table toward the boy in the hall and knocked him off his feet. Carl ran toward the bedroom where he kept the loaded gun in his bedside table. He didn't slam the door, but jumped on the bed and scrambled toward the other side.

One of the boys grabbed his right ankle and pulled. Carl couldn't reach the table. A hand grabbed his left ankle from the other side. Carl grabbed for the lamp cord, but failed. The punks jerked him backward so hard his knees popped. They tried to cross his legs, but Carl lunged for the headboard and fought to remain face down. He didn't want to see them. Didn't want to see what they were going to do.

One of the boys wrenched Carl's hand from the headboard. With a heave, they rolled him onto his back.

The first boy sauntered from the doorway to the bed. He waved a paring knife back and forth. The boys released Carl's ankles. He struggled to sit up. Something pricked at the left side of his throat. He closed his eyes. He smelled jalapeño and old sweat. He felt the wetness grow chill as it spread down his pant legs.

Carl wished he and his partner had left the Puerto Ricans alone. He wished he could stop crying and begging them not to kill him. And he wished he'd die quickly, that it wouldn't hurt.

None of Carl's wishes came true.

CHAPTER 7

In the air
Wednesday, January 22

"Miss, please bring your seat back forward and stow your purse. Miss. Wake up, please."

Lynnette heard the voice, felt the hand shaking her shoulder, but the voice and hand seemed far away, on the other side of a dense fog. She couldn't fathom what they had to do with her. Her persistent attempts to ignore them, however, were sabotaged when her seatback abruptly snapped straight up. She opened her eyes and found the flight attendant trying to stuff Lynnette's purse under the seat.

The airplane hit turbulence. The flight attendant lost her balance, toppling across the empty aisle seat and elbowing Lynnette hard in the ribs.

"Sorry," she said as she struggled to her feet. "Sorry I had to wake you, but we're having trouble. We need all the seats—"

"Trouble? What kind of trouble?"

"Something mechanical. I don't know." The flight attendant brushed off her skirt with her hand and smiled. "It'll be fine." But she didn't look Lynnette in the eye, and Lynnette felt another surge of anxiety. She thought she smelled burning rubber. The flight attendant started down the aisle, wobbled again when another pocket of turbulence sent the plane into a series of bumps and bounces.

Lynnette clasped her hands in her lap. *God, please don't let this plane crash. I swear I'll do everything right this time if you please, please, please don't let this plane go down. Amen.*

"Miss."

The hand pressed her shoulder again. Lynnette sat up straight and opened her eyes. Had she spoken her frantic prayer aloud?

"Miss, this child is traveling alone. She's frightened. The adults sitting in her row don't speak English." The flight attendant waved her arm around the first-class cabin. "You're the only woman up here. I'm putting her next to you. Would you talk to her? Put her at ease?"

The girl who stood in the aisle looked about ten, maybe eleven. Ordinary-looking kid. Straight brown hair pulled into a ponytail. Jeans, hiking boots, a pink and purple striped shirt. The girl's eyes were wide, her face pale, her bottom lip trembling.

"Sure. Have a seat," Lynnette said.

The girl accepted the flight attendant's help with her seatbelt without acknowledging Lynnette's presence. Once buckled in, however, and given a granola bar—apparently the flight attendant's idea of comfort food—the girl turned to Lynnette and stared. Lynnette returned the girl's gaze, making no attempt to hide her bruised face.

"How'd you get the black eyes?"

Taken aback, Lynnette didn't answer.

"Probably ran into a door, right?"

"No. Car accident."

"Oh, sure. My mom has those too. Doors and cars. Also fell down the stairs and broke her arm once. That ever happen to you?"

"What?"

"Maybe you're accident-prone. That's what Mom says she is. Seems like it came on sudden, though. About the time she got her new boyfriend."

"Hey, this is more than I want to know. Can we talk about something else?"

The kid blew a little puff of air and sat back. "Whatever."

The plane bucked and did an air skid to the left. The girl gripped her armrests and braced herself by jamming her feet against the seat in front of her.

Lynnette closed her eyes and clasped her hands and repeated her prayer. This time she didn't bother with "please" or "amen."

She felt a small hand on hers. Heard the girl say, "It's okay."

Lynnette opened her eyes, felt ashamed . . . and embarrassed. "I was just resting my eyes," she muttered.

"Yeah."

"Let's cool it with the sarcasm, okay?"

The kid rolled her eyes. "You sound like my mother."

"No kidding. Your mother must be a saint."

"Nah. She's a slut."

"Hey, watch your mouth. That's your mother you're talking about."

"That's what my Aunt Maxie says."

"Your Aunt Maxie has a way with words. Let's not go there, okay?" Lynnette paused, then asked, "What's your name?"

"Delilah."

"Delilah? Nobody names their daughter Delilah."

"Yeah, I know. I just said that for fun. What do think my name is?"

Lynnette looked the girl over from her ponytail to her boots, which were still firmly braced against the seat in front of her. "Emma. You look like an Emma."

Delilah was quiet for a moment, then muttered, "Emma. Em. Like Auntie Em in *The Wizard of Oz*." She paused a moment longer. Then she said, "That totally sucks. It's an old woman's name."

"Auntie Em's name was Emily. And your language sucks, kid."

"Yeah, tell me about it."

"Can I call you Dee?"

"No. I hate that. Call me kid, like you did before. That's what my dad calls me."

"Okay, kid. Why aren't you in school?"

"What's it to you?"

Before she could think of anything to say, the plane rocked and slid right. Lynnette grabbed the girl's hand. "My name's Lynnette." Her voice sounded high-pitched and breathless.

"You totally look like a Lynnette," the kid said. Her voice sounded calm and confident.

Lynnette looked at her, wondering what she meant, wondering what a "Lynnette" was supposed to look like. "What does your mother call you?"

The kid pulled her hand away and rubbed her neck. "Smart mouth. Brat. Whatever."

"I totally get that."

"Call me Grace," the kid added as though Lynnette hadn't spoken. "I like Grace."

"Fine. Grace. That's a lovely name."

Lynnette swallowed her next question as the plane rocked them back and forth, performing a series of jolts and lunges that rattled her teeth. This time Grace grabbed for Lynnette's hand and held on tight.

The captain announced they would be circling the Denver airport for a while. He apologized for the bumpy ride but blamed high winds in the Denver area, and, oh, by the way, they needed to use up fuel before they could attempt a landing, just in case.

Minutes later, the retching sounds began. Flight attendants

staggered along the aisle with a supply of barf bags. The next thirty minutes made Lynnette swear off air travel for the rest of her life.

CHAPTER 8

Denver, Colorado
Wednesday, January 22

No one applauded the safe but late landing in Denver at 9:00 p.m. By then, Lynnette doubted if the passengers cared whether they lived or died. The only thing worse than nausea was nausea in the presence of someone else's vomit. When even the flight attendants couldn't hold it in, Lynnette began to wonder about the pilot and co-pilot. Were they up there in the cockpit, puking up their guts?

She couldn't continue on to Los Angeles until she felt less queasy. It didn't matter. She could do what she damned well pleased.

The crew gave those passengers disembarking in Denver permission to gather their things and leave the plane, with instructions to check with an airline employee regarding connections. Lynnette was more than ready to go. She pulled her computer and purse from under the seat, stepped across the kid's legs, and opened the overhead bin.

"Where are you going?" Grace asked.

"Sorry, Grace. I have to split. You take care of yourself." Lynnette turned and glared at the grossly fat man who now studied Grace's face with interest. He looked away, fumbled with his seatbelt, then pulled a rumpled handkerchief from his shirt pocket and mopped his brow.

The flight attendant hurried toward Lynnette from the

cockpit, raising her hand as though to stop her from retrieving her luggage. "Wait, dear. You need an escort to go with you."

"You must be kidding!"

The attendant laughed. "No, I mean this young lady."

Lynnette glanced at Grace and saw she had pulled her backpack from under the seat and stood as though she'd planned to follow Lynnette into the airport. Grace plopped into the seat and stared toward the window.

A shout came from the back of the plane. "Someone here needs help!"

"Hey, don't forget about this kid," Lynnette said. She pointedly looked at the fat man and then raised her eyebrows as she looked at the flight attendant. She gestured too late. The attendant had turned toward the shout and rushed toward the rear of the plane, forcing passengers back into their seat rows as she went.

Lynnette took her carry-on, her laptop case, and her purse and walked off the plane.

Twenty minutes later, armed with a map that showed the bus station, the 16th Street Mall, the Amtrak station and all points of interest in between, she boarded a bus. Her first stop at the bus station was the restroom. When she finally wrestled her bags out of the stall and turned toward the sinks, she saw a kid in a pink and purple shirt, washing her hands. A kid in a ponytail and hiking boots, a mini-backpack strapped across her shoulders.

"Hi," Grace said. She looked away, seemed to search for the towel dispenser, finally spied it by the door.

"What are you doing here?"

"I don't want to fly the rest of the way sitting across the aisle from that creepy fat guy. Anyway, you left. I figured you had a good reason."

"Yeah, but kid, I'm a grownup. I don't need a good reason to change my mind. I can do crazy stuff. Did you tell anyone where you were going?"

"Uh, duh! Like they would have let me leave?"

"How'd you get off the plane? Didn't anyone try to stop you?"

"Some old guy in the back had a heart attack. Even the pilot went to help. I think he wanted to try out those zapper things. He seemed pretty excited."

Lynnette looked around the restroom. "Don't you have luggage?"

"Just my pack."

"What did your mom say?"

"Nothing."

Lynnette watched Grace as the girl continued to face the towel dispenser, drying her hands over and over. "You didn't call your mom, did you?"

Grace shrugged. "I can't."

"What? No phone? You can use mine."

"No . . . I mean I'm not supposed to."

Lynnette walked over to Grace, placed her hand on the girl's shoulder and turned her far enough to see her face. "Explain."

"After she took me to the gate at the airport, Mom went to Daytona with her boyfriend. She said not to call her until I wanted to come home. She said if I wanted to live with Dad so bad, then I obviously didn't need her."

"So you're going to Los Angeles to live with your dad."

"Yeah."

"So you called him instead of your mother."

Grace didn't answer.

"Grace, you called your dad, right?"

"Not exactly."

"What do you mean, not exactly? You got off the plane and you didn't tell anyone? You didn't call your parents?" Lynnette grabbed Grace's hand and pulled her toward the restroom door. "I saw a cop in the waiting room."

Grace jerked her hand away. "No way. Don't turn me over to a cop. You know what they do with kids like me? They stick us in foster care."

"Don't be ridiculous. They'll call your dad and help you get to L.A."

"That's not how it works. They won't be able to reach my dad and they'll call Social Services to take care of me, and they'll assume my folks don't want me and I'm a runaway, and I'll be stuck in some home with a pervert and a lousy cook and half a dozen other foster kids who wet the bed and skip school—"

"Where did you hear stuff like that? Never mind. Tell me how to get hold of your dad. We'll call him now."

"I can't."

Lynnette gritted her teeth, counted to ten, and took a deep breath. "Why not?"

"He's in Kandahar."

"Kandahar. You mean—"

"In Afghanistan? Yeah."

"Why is he in Afghanistan if he knows you're on your way to California to live with him?"

Grace took a deep breath and blew the long puff of air out through her pursed lips.

"He doesn't know you're coming?" Lynnette heard her voice grow higher and thinner as she spoke. "Your mom didn't let him know you were coming? What was she thinking? Didn't he tell her he'd be out of the country?"

"They don't talk. I told her he said okay."

Lynnette shook her head. She had to turn the kid in. She couldn't leave her alone in Denver, especially not at night.

She glanced at her watch. It was already after nine. She had

48

no intention of dragging Grace around the country with her. *Hell, as soon as I cross a state line with the kid in tow, I could face kidnapping charges.*

When the airline realized they'd lost a child, they would notify the police. There would be cops all over the city looking for Grace. They'd have her description, would be looking for that pink and purple shirt.

"What's your dad doing in Kandahar? How long will he be gone?"

"He works for the government. He said he'd be back in a week."

"How long has he been there?"

"Three days."

"What were you going to do in L.A. by yourself for the next four days?"

Grace took a sudden interest in her backpack, unzipping the top and feeling around inside. "Stay at his place," she mumbled.

"By yourself?"

"I took care of myself most of the time in Miami. What's the big deal?"

"Your mom left you by yourself while she went out with her boyfriend?"

"Yeah. But Mom works. She's a waitress."

Lynnette frowned. How could she possibly drag this kid around for four days?

"If you even look like you're going to tell a cop, I'll run away," Grace said. "Think about it. I'll be out on the streets in downtown Denver. At night. Perverts and white slave traders everywhere. I'll probably disappear and never be seen again. I'll be sold into prostitution. Me, a little kid. That will be on your conscience, Lynnette. You'll never forgive yourself."

"You watch too much TV, kiddo." Lynnette slung her purse strap over her shoulder and reached for her bags. "Come on.

Let's get out here. We'll talk."

"I need to change my shirt first."

"Smart. Is this the first time you've run away?"

Grace grinned. "I do watch a lot of TV." She pulled a light blue shirt and a dark blue padded vest from her pack and changed out of the top she'd worn on the airplane. "If I go out there with you, you promise you won't tell the cop?"

"We'll talk. For now, we'll just talk."

"Okay. But I'll run at the first sign—"

"Fine, I got it."

Lynnette glanced around the station waiting room, checking to see if the building had wireless access. No signs. She'd have to pull out her laptop and try. She knew how to find the train station, knew she could hike it without any trouble, but it would be a pointless exercise if the schedule showed no westbound train until the next day.

First she had to deal with the kid. If she turned Grace over to a cop, what would happen? They probably *would* put Grace in the custody of Social Services in Colorado until they contacted one of the two parents. And then what? Would one or both parents be charged with neglect? Would Grace be removed from her home? From both homes?

"Look, Lynnette, you were flying to L.A. You're still going there, right?"

"Yeah, but I don't feel like flying now. I might take the train."

"Can't I tag along? I won't bother you. I won't even talk. Just let me stay close enough so weirdo creeps think you're my mom."

"You think I look old enough to be your mother?"

"Or my sister. My aunt. Whatever."

Lynnette studied Grace's face, tried to figure out how much of what she'd said was a lie and how much the truth. "You have to call your dad."

"I told you. He's in Kandahar."

"Doesn't he have an answering machine? Or voice mail on his cell phone?"

"Sure. Both."

"Then call and leave a message in both places. Do you have a cell phone, or do you need to use mine?"

"I have one."

"Then call. Now."

Grace unzipped a pocket in her backpack and pulled out her phone. She turned it on and waited for a signal. Then she stood up.

"No," Lynnette said. "Stay here. I want to watch you make the calls. I want to hear the messages you leave."

"You don't trust me?"

"That's correct."

"Bummer."

"Just do it."

Grace made the calls. Left the messages. Gave her dad Lynnette's first name. Told her dad about the bumpy flight, that she was safe and might travel on to California by train. Said she'd call again when she found out for sure. Said she'd call every day 'til he got back. Told him again about the nice woman who promised to watch out for her. When Lynnette motioned for Grace to give her the phone, she handed it over.

Lynnette left her full name and cell phone number on the dad's answering machine.

Almost satisfied, she insisted on one more thing from Grace— her dad's name and contact information, just in case. She wrote down the name, Bob McCoy, and the numbers Grace gave her. Then, to cover her ass a bit further, she asked for a number where Grace's mother could be reached. Reluctantly, Grace finally gave Lynnette her home number in Miami. She said she didn't dare give out her mom's cell phone number or she'd be killed.

Lynnette shifted her glance to the teenage girl sitting behind Grace in the next row of bus station seats.

The girl, who had turned her head and clearly eavesdropped on their conversation, stared at Lynnette's right eye. "Quite a shiner you got there," the girl said. "Run into somebody's fist?"

CHAPTER 9

Denver, Colorado
Wednesday, January 22

Sammy desperately needed to take a leak but he refused to do that on the plane. The thought of wedging his body into one of those fucking upright coffins filled him with anxiety. He had to wait until he was inside the airport where he'd make a beeline to the nearest restroom. With one foot stuck into the aisle to hold his place, he wrestled his briefcase from under the seat and pulled it onto his lap.

After struggling to his feet and into the aisle, Sammy moved toward the exit, ignoring the frantic activity going on at the rear of the plane. He'd barely made it into the airport before two blue-uniformed guys carrying satchels and an oxygen tank shoved him aside. Another one followed, pushing a stretcher on wheels.

He rushed into the handicapped stall of the first men's room he found, dropped his pants to the floor, and sat down. His chin propped on one fist and his elbow digging into the top of his thigh, Sammy stared at the floor. His gaze shifted to his briefcase.

Something wasn't right. "Son of a bitch!" he screamed.

Total silence descended throughout the restroom.

Sammy began to sweat. He pulled his case closer to his feet and examined it from all sides. It had outside pockets with zippers. His case had outside pockets but they snapped. This one had two zippered compartments. Sammy's case had only one. He opened both sections and examined the contents, hoping he suffered from some kind of short-lived memory lapse and that he'd find Mr. O's stuff inside. Instead, he found a laptop computer, a cell phone, wires and computer crap, file folders . . . but nothing that belonged to Benny Ortega, or to Sammy.

He closed his eyes and leaned forward, his head cradled in his hands. He tried to think. Every step of the way, he'd kept his hand on the briefcase, just like Mr. O said. Hadn't he? Even in the car on the way to the airport, he'd placed his case on the passenger seat, right next to him. It had never left his sight.

As he'd passed through security, he'd kept one eye on the case and waited until the path through the security sensor cleared before he even pushed the bag forward on the belt to be X-rayed. He passed through the sensor and waited for the case on the other side. No one had touched it.

Wait. When he stopped to put on his shoes, he set the case on the floor while he tied his laces. *I only have two hands, for God's sake.*

He took a deep breath. The woman with the beat-up face. It had to be her. She had gotten off the plane before he had time to get his case out from under the seat. He glanced at his watch, then used a handful of toilet paper to swipe at the sweat dripping from his nose. Hopeless. Too much time had passed. She'd be long gone.

Sammy left the men's room and headed for the nearest bar. He placed the case on the table in front of him and glared at it as though it would feel threatened and give up its secrets. A waitress took his order for a burger and fries and a double J.D. While he waited, he removed the folders and studied the papers inside.

★ ★ ★ ★ ★

Lynnette figured the teenage girl hanging out at the bus station was a runaway. Probably a druggie. She looked about fifteen. Black jeans, black ankle-high boots, black leather jacket, black hair, black lipstick. Pierced body parts—nose, ears, lip. Radical girl hitting up folks for money.

"Or did he take a baseball bat to your face?" the girl said.

Annoyed by the teen's curiosity, Lynnette still didn't answer.

"She *says* she wrecked her car." Grace glanced at Lynnette before continuing. "But my mom says stuff like that when her boyfriend beats her up. I think Lynnette's boyfriend hit her."

"Husband," Lynnette said. "My husband hit me. Now let's drop it. Do not bring this up again. Ever."

"Your husband?" The teen raised her eyebrows. "Did you off him?"

"Yeah, I offed him all right. What do *you* think?"

"Honest? You killed him?"

"Don't be ridiculous."

"Can you spare a few bucks?" The girl held out her hand as though she expected Lynnette to oblige her without question.

"No." Lynnette ignored the girl's outstretched palm, which seemed to hover in the air. Out of the corner of her eye, she saw Grace hand over a couple of one-dollar bills.

"Thanks, kid," the girl said. "What's your name?"

"Delilah."

"Wow. Delilah, huh? You don't—"

"Oh, for Pete's sake, we're not going through this again," said Lynnette. "Her name is Grace."

"Hey, Grace. I'm Brittany."

Lynnette exchanged a glance with Grace, but neither said a word. Grace smirked.

The teen took her hand away, still clutching Grace's dollar bills, and walked toward the end of the bench. A few seconds later she stood in front of Grace. "I'm just jerking you around. If my name was Brittany, I'd kill myself. My friends call me Blue."

"Why?"

"Because I am." Blue tilted her head and looked sad.

"Blue. I like it," Grace said. "Names are important. They should mean something. Like mine. Grace. Graceful, like a ballerina." She hopped up and performed a pirouette, made clumsy by her hiking boots.

Blue laughed. "Yeah, like me. Always singing the blues." She sang the words off-key and laughed again.

Lynnette thought Blue's laugh sounded a bit forced. She was trying too hard to buddy up to Grace. Blue already had some of Grace's cash. What next? Her cell phone?

"Listen, I need to talk to Grace," Lynnette said.

"Sure," Blue said. "Don't mind me."

"I mean in private."

"Okay. Fine. But I heard you talking earlier. About the train. I can tell you the California Zephyr leaves at eight in the morning, if it's on time, which it never is. Goes to Emeryville up north, almost to San Francisco. Then you have to take a different train to get to Los Angeles. You need a place to stay overnight?"

Lynnette shook her head. She didn't want to imagine the kind of flea-ridden dive this girl might suggest.

"There's a real nice hotel just up the street. Swanky."

"I don't think so."

"Money trouble? No problem. I'm flush." Blue pulled a wad of bills out of her pocket and waved her hand in front of Lynnette's face. "You can pay me back someday. And it would be cool staying overnight down here. I planned to take a bus north, but maybe I'll stick with you two and ride the train. Haven't done that in a while."

"Wait a minute," said Grace. "You kept my two dollars."

"Hell, yes."

"I want my two bucks back."

"Don't be silly, kid."

"I'll call that cop over here."

"I bet you won't."

Lynnette patted Grace on the knee. "Stop it. Grace, forget the money. Beat it, Blue. We don't need your help."

"Fine," Blue said, but didn't walk away. "Look, if you guys are in trouble, maybe I can help."

Grace gawked at Blue as though she'd said her toes were webbed. "You?"

"Sure. I have resources."

Lynnette laughed. "You hang out at the bus station looking like you do and take money from kids. What kind of resources do you have besides that roll of cash?"

"What's wrong with the way I look?"

"Well, for starters," Grace said, "you dress like a Goth. The ring in your nose freaks me out. And you take money from kids."

"That doesn't have anything to do with the way I look."

"Yeah, it does. It makes you look like a beggar and a liar."

"Oh, crap. Here's your two bucks."

"Thanks." Grace stuffed the two bills in her pocket and smiled at Lynnette. "What do we do now? Go to that hotel?"

"Yes." Lynnette stood up and maneuvered her purse and bags into position so she could take Grace's hand.

Grace, however, balked. "I want Blue to come with us."

"Are you crazy?"

"She needs us."

"There is something else you could do instead of spending the night here," Blue said.

"What?" Grace asked.

"Take the bus north. Goes to Fort Collins. I live there. You'd get out of Denver tonight, just in case your husband's looking for you."

"What time does the bus leave?" Lynnette asked.

"Quarter to twelve."

"What about me, Lynnette?" Grace said. "I don't want to go to Fort Collins. That's the wrong direction. Anyway, she probably sleeps under a bridge and dumpster-dives for food."

Blue laughed.

"Might be safer in a smaller town, though." Lynnette glanced at her watch. From the looks of the crowded bus station, she wondered if they could even get tickets.

Grace made a point of looking at the rest of the people in the bus station, then motioned toward Blue's attire. "I don't know if it would be safer or not. Just look at her."

"Don't be fooled by my appearance, little girl," Blue said. "I'm a college student and I live in a house with three other girls."

"Oh, right. People who look like you aren't students. They drop out before they graduate from high school."

"Did you ever hear about not judging a book by its cover?"

"They why do you dress like that?"

"It's a long story. I'll tell you later."

"Come on," Lynnette said, giving Grace a little push toward the ticket counter. "Let's do it. We're better off on the bus than hanging around in downtown Denver at night. When we get to Fort Collins, we'll get a motel room. I'll bring you back to Denver tomorrow."

After buying the tickets, Lynnette, with Grace in tow, walked to the snack bar and sat at a table. Blue joined them a few minutes later. "Get the tickets?" she said.

Grace nodded. "I still don't want to go. Can't you come up with a better idea, Blue?"

"I don't think so. And after that smart-aleck remark about me dumpster-diving, I'm having second thoughts about helping you."

"See?" Grace said, poking Lynnette on the arm.

Lynnette pulled away. "Stop it, Grace. I can't think with you two sniping at each other. Blue, if you're a college student, you need to act your age."

"What kind of college student are you?" Grace asked. "What do you want to be when you grow up?"

Blue crossed her arms over her chest and leaned back. "I have two majors. I'm studying a lot of different things."

"Like what?" Grace said.

"You're one nosy kid, aren't you?"

Grace looked at the table and made a face that clearly said, "Whatever."

CHAPTER 10

Denver, Colorado
Wednesday, January 22

By the time Lynnette and Grace finished eating, they had less than an hour to wait. Lynnette still had to figure out the best way to get herself and Grace to Los Angeles. Grace expected her father to return from Afghanistan on Sunday, or so she said. They could continue to leave messages on his cell phone and answering machine, but Lynnette had a feeling they would reach Grace's mom first. What if the woman called the police? Or worse, what if she threatened to call the police if Lynnette didn't escort Grace to Florida at Lynnette's expense?

Lynnette stared at the tickets she'd laid on the table. "I wonder if this is a good idea."

"I don't think it's a good idea at all," said Grace. "How do you get anywhere from Fort Collins, Colorado?"

"That's not it," Blue said. "She's still trying to ditch her old man. She's afraid he'll find her easier if she goes to a small town."

"Look it up on the Internet," Grace said. "Maybe there's a way to connect up with the train from there. That's how I figured out the best way to get to Los Angeles. Amtrak's on there. And Greyhound. All the airlines."

Lynnette studied Grace's expression with concern. "You figured it out? Grace, did you buy your own ticket or did your mom do it?"

60

Grace laughed. "My mom doesn't know how to use the Internet except for email. The only other thing she does on the computer is play Minesweeper."

"Your mother does not know where you are, does she?"

"Yes, she does. She watched me while I made the reservation and she filled in the credit card number herself."

"She took you to the airport gate and watched you get on the plane?"

"Yes."

"But she never talked to your dad to confirm he planned to meet you at the airport."

"I told you. They don't talk."

"This is so farfetched," Lynnette said.

Grace widened her eyes and let her jaw drop as though she couldn't believe Lynnette would doubt her word. Blue laughed out loud.

"When is your mom supposed to get back?" Lynnette asked.

"Monday."

"And by then your dad would be home."

"Honest, Lynnette, she's not going to check on me."

"And what if she did? What if she decided to call your dad and make sure you arrived safely?"

Grace didn't answer.

Blue looked on, intensely interested in the exchange, but said nothing.

The kid was beginning to get on Lynnette's nerves. When Grace had told her earlier that she lived on her own a lot, Lynnette had not believed her. Now she wondered. She could be in a whole lot of trouble if anyone stopped Grace and questioned her. "The facts, Grace."

"Everything I told you is true."

"Did you leave a message for your mom on your home phone?"

61

"Yes. I did. Honest."

"You have to call her cell phone, too. Even if she gets mad. You have to tell her."

"But I can't. I told you. She'll kill me." Grace looked Lynnette in the eye. "And she'll call the cops. Report me missing. She'll tell them I've been kidnapped because she won't want to tell them she put me on a plane and didn't make sure my dad would be there at the other end and that I got there okay. They'll put out an Amber Alert and show my picture on TV. And Mom will go running home so the reporters can find her and she can do one of those Mommy interviews where she sobs for the camera and begs for the kidnappers to return her baby girl. And if they find me, Lynnette, they're going to think you stole me."

"But you'll tell them otherwise, won't you, Grace?"

Grace stood defiantly with her jaw set and her arms folded across her chest.

"I don't think it's a problem," Blue said.

"Oh, it's a problem," said Lynnette.

"No, if Grace leaves messages on her mom's phone every day, and also calls her dad every day, they'll be sure she's safe. And if anyone wants to blame you, I'll testify that you tried to protect Grace because she threatened to run away if you told. It's not safe for little kids to be on their own anywhere, but especially a big city like Denver."

Lynnette shook her head. "This is a stupid move."

Grace said, "But you'll let me stay with you, right? Can we look up the train schedules on the Internet now?" She glanced at Blue. "Just to make sure Blue told us the right thing."

Lynnette glanced around, looking for a wireless access sign. She seemed to be the only person in the bus station with a laptop computer. Now that she considered the other passengers more carefully, she realized few of them had real luggage. Some carried backpacks, some had suitcases, but many were surrounded by cardboard boxes and black trash bags, presumably full of their possessions.

Lynnette, Grace and Blue still sat at the table just outside the snack bar. Lynnette's purse sat firmly wedged between her feet, her carry-on bag rested on the floor between her and Blue, and her computer case leaned against the table leg, propped against her foot. She leaned over and reached for the handles, found one, pulled the case out and started to unzip the side that held her laptop. She froze, her hand trying to make sense of the one-zippered case when hers had two zippered compartments. She grabbed the handgrips and lifted, staring at the case for a moment. Finally, she set it in her lap.

"What's wrong?" Grace asked.

"It's not mine. How in God's green earth did I get the wrong computer case? My cell phone is in that case, my flash drives, CDs. Files, financial stuff." She set the case on the floor by Grace's feet and took a deep breath, surprised she could breathe at all. Her chest felt as though she'd swallowed marshmallows. Her stomach, too.

When had she put the bag down long enough for someone else to pick it up? She thought back to the cab, paying the cabbie, going inside the airport, her stop at the restroom, the ticket counter, Security . . . Security. The fat man who sat next to her to put on his shoes. The shithead who copped the attitude because her case took up the only available seat.

Oh, no. The fat man has my laptop case!

What if he was on his way to Los Angeles? How would she ever find him? There had to be something inside the case that identified the owner. She unzipped it and methodically checked its contents. A small Toshiba laptop. A brown envelope, fastened only by its clasp. A bundle of one-hundred-dollar bills. A cell phone. Lynnette turned on the phone.

★ ★ ★ ★ ★

It can't get much better than this, Sammy thought, as he perused Lynnette Hudson's brokerage statement. Her account totaled $475,722.37 as of December 31. And the woman had penciled some words labeled "User ID" and "Password" at the top of the page, right next to her account number. *Ditzy broad.* He had to play this right. He had to get his own bag for Mr. O, and he had to clean out this woman's account before she figured out what he'd done. He held the opportunity of a lifetime in his hand—access to her account and her laptop. One mighty big obstacle lay in his path: he only had about fifteen thou in his bank account. If he suddenly transferred big bucks in, the Feds would be onto him in a flash. He couldn't get to this broad's dough without help, and whoever helped him would want a piece. And getting Mr. O's stuff had to come first. Sammy sighed and shook his head.

He pulled out a pen and lifted a page off the legal pad in Hudson's bag. From her account statement, he copied her full name, account number, user ID, password, date and balance, as well as the name and address of the broker. He thought for a moment, then made a list of her individual investments as well.

He hadn't even looked through the second zippered compartment where the laptop was stored. He pulled the top open and felt inside the pockets. In addition to cords and wires, Sammy found Hudson's cell phone. He could work with that. Thank goodness she didn't have one of those newfangled contraptions with all their little codes and apps, whatever apps were. He turned on the phone and waited for a signal. Then he called his own cell's number. The call went to voice mail. Two minutes later, he tried again. Voice mail.

He set the phone on the table in front of him and stared at its nasty little face as he suppressed the urge to slam it across the room. He had to keep his temper under control. He needed that phone. And he didn't need airport security hauling his ass out of this bar, especially while he possessed the broad's property and was only a few steps away from transferring her money into his own bank account.

He gulped his drink and signaled the waitress for another by raising his glass in the air and waving it. He pressed redial on the cell phone. Voice mail. The waitress slopped his drink as she set it down, tossed a couple of extra napkins on the table, and hurried away. A muttered stream of obscenities rolled off Sammy's tongue as he grabbed the napkins and wiped the bottom of his glass. He shoved the wet napkins onto the puddle of watered-down whiskey and stared into space, afraid to let the waitress see how pissed off he was.

He hit redial again. Voice mail. He slammed the phone on the table hard enough to crack the back cover. The bartender glanced his way and moved to the other end of the bar.

The airline announcement blasted from the speaker over his head, and Sammy took the news as though thrown a life jacket. His flight to LAX had been cancelled. The voice instructed passengers to report to the counter at the departure gate to book a new flight. He now had a reason to be in Denver long enough to retrieve his case.

Sammy lumbered to his feet, threw enough money on the table to cover his bar bill, picked up the phone, and hit redial.

CHAPTER 11

Denver, Colorado
Wednesday, January 22
Seconds after Lynnette had turned on the cell phone, it found a signal. Before she could access its contact list, the phone rang. She answered.

She listened for a few seconds before trying to interrupt the man's diatribe.

Blue jiggled Lynnette's arm and shook her head.

The man on the other end of the phone continued to speak as though he had little interest in anything she had to say. "Your name is Lynnette Hudson, and I know everything about you. If you don't stay exactly where you are, and protect my case and its contents with your life, I will slice your throat from ear to ear. There is no way you can escape—nowhere to go. I will find you." His threats became even more graphic until finally Lynnette, pale and breathless, ended the call and turned off the phone.

Everything she had in her case identified her by her maiden name, Lynnette Hudson. He had her financial records and all the information in her cell phone and laptop. This was identity theft waiting to happen—if it hadn't happened already.

She held the man's cell up and examined the keys. Looked like a new phone. Even had a photo feature. "I suppose this has one of those GPS trackers," she said. She looked at Blue. "Do you know anything about this stuff? Does the GPS work when the phone is turned off?"

Blue nodded. "It might. Depends on the phone and how the owner set it up."

"If I throw it away here, whoever tracks the signal will know I took the bus."

Blue shook her head. "He wouldn't know for sure where you went from here unless he knows how to use mapping software and you still have the phone. Why don't you throw it in the trash? Or give it to one of these people?" She waved her hand toward the collection of passengers now lined up at two of the boarding doors.

Lynnette turned her back on Grace and leaned closer to Blue. "He threatened me. He said if I touched anything in the case, he'd kill me. He said if I gave the case or anything in it to anyone else, he'd still kill me and then he'd kill whoever I gave it to. He said he might kill me anyway, just for stealing his case."

Blue held out her hand.

Lynnette started to give her the phone, but changed her mind. "What are you going to do? I don't want to put anyone else in danger."

"I won't give it to anyone. I'll destroy it."

"No. That's not a good idea. I need to put it back in the case. He said to protect all the contents of the case with my life."

Grace tapped Lynnette on the shoulder. "What happened, Lynnette? Who called?"

"Just a guy. The guy who wants his stuff."

Oh, God, thought Lynnette. She had to take charge. She didn't dare get rid of the fat man's case, but she couldn't risk putting the teen and the kid in danger. She'd have to ditch them. Her skin felt very cold, her shoulders heavy, her eyes watery. The phone felt warm and sweaty in her hand. She laid it on the table.

Damn you, Carl. This is all your fault.

Blue leaned forward and spoke in a low voice. "This guy you stole the case from—did he say if he's still in Denver?"

"I think so. Maybe he's at the airport. He can't be in the air because he used the phone. And I didn't steal his case, Blue. Mine looks almost the same as his. He grabbed the wrong one when he left Security."

"He thinks you stole it, but here's the deal. If he's in Denver and he knows you were on your way to L.A., then he knows you're either still at the airport or you took a bus or a shuttle or a cab. What if you took the case back to the airport and left it with baggage claim? You could call him . . . oh, nuts, how would you get your own bag unless you waited there and did the exchange?"

"How could she go to the airport?" said Grace. "Our bus leaves in a little bit."

"Never mind," Lynnette said. She turned to Blue. "Why not do the exchange here? I could have the security guard hold this one, and ask him to exchange the bags because this guy scares me and I don't want to see him again. My cell phone is in my case. If he keeps it with him and turns the phone on, I can call my own number from his."

"Check it out, see if he answers."

Lynnette picked up the phone, then laid it back down. "I still wouldn't be able to get on this bus. And you two can't be here."

"I'll take Grace to Fort Collins with me. You catch up with us as soon as you can." Blue pulled a ballpoint pen from her backpack and wrote two phone numbers on a clean napkin. She pushed the napkin toward Lynnette and said, "The top one is my cell phone. The other one is the landline at the house. We'll be fine if we wait there."

Lynnette had second thoughts about dumping Blue and losing the benefit of her many talents. On the other hand, she had plenty of reservations about turning Grace over to Blue's care. She left the phone on the table, but moved the fat man's laptop case to the floor between her chair and Grace's.

"Who are you, Blue? Are you really a student? Why should I trust you to watch out for Grace?"

Blue reached into her backpack again and pulled out a woman's wallet. She lined up her driver's license, voter's registration card, two credit cards, and a photo identification card from Colorado State University. All were in the name of Teresa Young.

Grace pulled the driver's license closer and peered at it. "You're twenty-three years old?" She stared at Blue. "Are these fake?"

Lynnette took the driver's license and examined it carefully. She set the license on the table and looked at Blue. "Well? Are they fake? I figured you were about sixteen."

"No. They're real."

"Then why all this?" Lynnette waved her hand up and down to indicate Blue's makeup, tattoos, piercings, and clothes.

"You don't look like you're twenty-three," Grace added. "And you don't look like you ever went to college, either."

"It's a long story."

"You better start telling it," Lynnette said with a quick glance at her watch. "I'm not letting you take Grace anywhere unless I'm sure she'll be safe."

"Okay. I'm a grad student at CSU. Sociology. I'm working on a thesis about crowd behavior, so I go places where crowds hang out. I go to concerts and political rallies and—"

"Looking like that?" Lynnette said.

Blue sighed, reached up to grip her black hair at the crown, and pulled off her wig. Her short reddish-brown hair clumped close to her head. She dropped the wig on the table and ran her fingers through her hair to fluff it up. Then she stuck her index finger in her mouth, wet it, and rubbed the tattoo of a heart on her forearm. The color faded and disappeared.

"Wow," Grace said. "Aren't any of them real? They look real. Can I get one like that little dragon on my leg?"

"I need more," said Lynnette, ignoring Grace's excited chatter. "Do your parents live in Fort Collins? Who are they? Do you live at home? Do they know you're wandering around the country like this?"

"Yeah, I'm officially living at my home. That's the address on my I.D. My dad lives just outside Fort Collins. He knows what I'm doing, but he's not super happy about it. I check in with him about five times a day so he doesn't worry so much."

"Your mom?"

"They're divorced. She lives in San Francisco. I spent summers out there until I got my bachelor's degree. When I started on my master's, I decided to take summer classes, too. Working on the thesis gives me a little more freedom to go around, do research, you know?"

Lynnette glanced at her watch. Time was running out. She looked at Blue's collection of cards again before pushing them across the table along with the napkin. "You can put the cards away. Write down your address, just in case."

She turned to Grace. "Will you feel safe with Blue?"

"Sure."

"Will you do everything she says?"

"Sure, unless it's something bad."

"I won't tell you to do anything bad," Blue said. "You'll be fine."

Lynnette turned on the fat man's phone. When she had a signal, she dialed her own number. The guy answered on the first ring. He sounded furious. Lynnette imagined him, flushed with rage, a gun in his shoulder holster and a knife at his waist. That was ridiculous. He couldn't have carried a gun and knife onto the plane. She had to stop with the crazy thoughts.

"You turned off my phone, you bitch. I been trying to call you." The guy's voice increased in volume until he yelled, "If you touch anything in that case, I will not only kill you, but I will cut you up in little pieces first! I'll find everyone whose name and address is on your phone or in your email and I'll kill them all!"

Lynnette had the passing thought that she would be a lot better off if the first person on her email list, Carl, died. Then she thought of the people she loved who wouldn't see this guy coming and would never understand what they had done to deserve a horrible death. And it would be her fault.

"Look, buddy, just listen a minute. I want to return your case and everything in it. I'm sorry about the phone. I panicked and turned it off. I won't touch anything. But I don't want to meet you. You scare me. I'm in downtown Denver at the bus station. I'm going to turn your case over to a security guard and explain the mix-up. You need to come here and find the guard. You show your I.D. and make the exchange. I'll come back later to pick up mine."

The creep's next words were drowned out by an announcement for the northbound bus to Fort Collins.

Lynnette asked the man on the phone to repeat what he'd just told her, listened to the guy's response, and ended the call. She left the phone on, thinking she might call the police, thinking this guy would kill her if he found her, thinking Grace would be safer with the cops in Denver than she might be with Blue.

"Look at this," said Grace.

Lynnette set the phone on the table before turning to see what Grace wanted. "What are you doing?"

Grace had the guy's case on her lap and was thumbing through the stack of hundred-dollar bills.

"Put that back inside," Lynnette said. She glanced around

the waiting room to see who might have noticed. "You want me to get mugged or something? Hurry up. Your bus is going to board in a minute. You have to get in line."

"Wait." Blue reached for the money.

Lynnette grabbed the cash out of Grace's hand and stuffed the wad inside the case. She started to close the zipper, but then peered at the brown envelope. She pulled it out, opened the clasp, and looked inside. Checks. Maybe a half-dozen large checks drawn on different companies and different banks. Two of the checks totaled more than a million dollars.

"What is it?" Grace asked.

"Just papers. It's nothing." Lynnette refastened the clasp and slid the envelope back into place. With one swift zip, she closed the case, set it on the floor, and placed it between her feet.

"Papers?" Blue said. "If it's only papers, why are your hands trembling?" She shoved her chair back and looked under the table, eyeing the case with renewed interest.

"Is it something bad?" Grace asked. "Maybe you should call the Feds."

Blue and Lynnette looked at Grace and then at each other. Grace had proposed something far more profound than what her childish experience would normally suggest.

Lynnette placed her hand on Grace's shoulder. "What do you know about the Feds?"

"Lots. My dad—"

"Damn it all to hell, Grace. What does your dad do with the government?"

"FBI."

Lynnette's first emotion was joy. Grace's dad could help. Her second was despair. It would be four days before he returned from Afghanistan. Her third was fear. What would happen to her if she didn't return this case to the fat man and get her own case? If she went straight to the police, what would happen to Grace?

"You guys have got to get out of here." Lynnette read the address, phone numbers, and email address written on Blue's napkin, then stuffed it in her purse. "Go on, take your packs and get in line." She sat at the table, watching, until they boarded the bus and the bus pulled away. As she gathered up her things, she discovered Blue's wig lying on the floor next to her carry-on. She stuffed it into the outside compartment of her bag. She turned off the fat man's phone and put it in her purse.

The plan, as she had outlined it to the girls and to the fat man, was to leave his case with a security guard, let the guard make the trade, and then she would board a bus to Fort Collins to meet up with Grace and Blue.

Now she wasn't so sure. One glimpse at the checks had set her reporter's curiosity on high alert. She had covered a check theft case a few years ago. The thief had never been caught, but a bank had been held liable for cashing the check. Lynnette wanted to know a lot more about the contents of the fat man's case before she turned it over to anyone. She might need to take Grace's advice and contact the Feds.

Sammy took the broad at her word and headed for the cab stand at baggage claim level. He walked forever, waited for the train, rode to the main terminal, struggled with the escalator, then walked another mile. She'd gone to the fucking bus station. How in the hell would he explain a trip to the bus station to Mr. O? He thought about what he would say, then realized he couldn't get in touch with his boss until he got his case. Mr. O had programmed his number into Sammy's phone, and Sammy never bothered to memorize it. The only other way he could find Mr. O involved calling every hotel in L.A. And even that wouldn't work if Mr. O used a different name. Sammy gripped Lynnette's case a little tighter and lumbered out the door to find a cab.

CHAPTER 12

Denver, Colorado
Wednesday, January 22

Lynnette strode across the waiting room and entered the women's restroom with the case and her purse, pulling her carry-on. The restroom was empty and reeked of lemon and bleach.

With her carry-on propped against her leg and her purse strap over her shoulder, she set the fat man's laptop case on the counter and methodically went through all of the pockets, pouches and dividers. She pulled out the wad of cash and thumbed through the one-hundred-dollar bills, trying to estimate the total amount. Somewhere around $25,000, she guessed. She tucked the cash securely under the mouse.

Next she pulled the brown envelope out of the case, removed the checks and studied them one by one. They had to be stolen or counterfeit; she had no doubt about that. None of them looked computer-generated. All appeared to be hand-typed, a couple even had erasures as though correcting typos. What had she stumbled into? A two- or three-million-dollar heist?

She took a deep breath and slid the checks inside the envelope, fastened the clasp, and put it away. She zipped up the case and set it on the floor.

The fat guy could get here anytime. If he took a cab, he might be out there already, looking for his bag. He'd find the only security guard on the floor, check with him, get nothing, and be furious.

Even so, how could she justify letting a big-time thief get away just to save herself and reclaim her hopefully replaceable possessions? If she called her brokerage firm first thing in the morning, she'd get the password changed and a fraud alert placed on the account so nothing could happen to her savings. As for the friends and relatives listed on her phone and laptop, she'd contact them all and warn them to be careful. Lynnette shook her head. How in hell could all this happen in one day? *I'm tired, I'm scared, and I'm not thinking straight. I need to take a deep breath and—*

A woman and two kids entered the restroom. The woman, who appeared to lay her makeup on with a trowel, looked at Lynnette curiously but didn't say anything.

Lynnette no longer had any intention of going through with the trade. She wondered how she could get past the guy without him seeing her or his bag? She had the phone. Should she call the Feds as Grace had suggested? How would she do that? Dial information and ask for the FBI? In the middle of the night?

But if she did get the FBI, they'd confiscate the case. Not to mention hold her for God knew how long to ask endless questions. What would Blue do with Grace in the meantime? Blue might end up in trouble because of Grace. Whatever happened would be Lynnette's fault, no matter what her intentions had been.

And if the FBI took the case, all the checks, and the cash, she'd never get her own stuff and her chance at a great story would vanish. If there even was a story. The fat man might be nothing more than a courier, delivering checks to avoid the delays of the postal system. Guarding them with his life.

Her old boss at *The Indy Reporter,* Dave Buchanan, would love the opportunity to find out. If they managed to stop a major crime before it happened, it would be an incredible scoop.

On the other hand, if they held onto goods that rightfully belonged in the fat man's possession, she and Dave could be the ones charged with a crime.

Lynnette shook her head in confusion. She wondered if the fat man played a role in a bigger conspiracy. Maybe he'd actually stolen the checks. She thought about him lumbering around various big companies, trying to remain anonymous while he snatched important documents from the hands of loyal employees. It was more likely he'd ripped off someone's laptop case. Maybe he'd pulled a switch with someone else too. Maybe he didn't even have her bag anymore!

She relaxed and let out a slow breath. He had to have her bag. She'd dialed her own phone number earlier, and he'd answered.

Thursday, January 23

Even with light traffic, it still took almost thirty minutes for Sammy's cab to travel from DIA to the bus station. By the time the cab pulled up in front of the building, it was after midnight. Sammy would happily have beaten the cabbie senseless if he had so much as smirked at the puny tip Sammy included with his fare. As he struggled out of the cab with the woman's laptop case, he almost tripped over the curb. He tried to recover his balance by grabbing the inside door handle. It didn't work. He lurched against the cab and caught his hand in the door as it slammed shut.

The cabbie jumped out to open Sammy's door. When he took Sammy's elbow as though to help him onto the sidewalk, Sammy jerked his arm away and turned toward the driver, ready to punch him in the nose. The cabbie took one look at Sammy's face and left Sammy at the curb.

"Fucking foreigner," Sammy muttered. He pulled his handkerchief out of his pocket and wiped the sweat off his face and neck. Then he turned up his collar against the cold. His hand hurt. He couldn't bend his fingers. He tried to examine the back and palm, but the lights outside the bus station threw off a weak, diffused glow.

Lynnette reached for her carry-on, retrieved Blue's wig, and laid it on the counter. She combed her hair away from her face with her fingers, tucking stray ends behind her ears.

Focus. How could she get away with the laptop case and its contents and get the whole package to someone who could figure it all out?

She'd call Dave at the *Reporter* and see if he had any great ideas. Maybe flying to Indianapolis from Denver made sense. She had Blue's phone numbers. She could let her know. That way, Lynnette could turn the checks over in person, then leave. She and Dave could even meet with the FBI—right after they photo-copied the evidence.

But that didn't solve the problem of Grace. She couldn't put the responsibility for that on Blue.

Lynnette pulled on the wig and pushed her own hair inside. She arranged the wig until it looked natural around her face. Her face. Pathetic. There was no way to hide the still-puffed-up right eye and bruises. Nothing in her purse or suitcase would disguise her face.

Still carrying Lynnette's case, Sammy entered the station and sat on the nearest bench. His hand throbbed now, even though it didn't look too bad. One strip of skin across his knuckles seeped a little blood. He made a fist. The fingers closed without too much pain.

A quick glance around the station told him there were only two employees in the room—a counter clerk and a security guard. A few passengers waited, lined up in front of one of the doors. A few more walked about, and two men slept on benches. He didn't see the broad from the plane.

The security guard watched him as though he thought Sammy might have escaped from the zoo. It pissed Sammy off, but his body didn't seem to care much. He could hardly keep his eyes open. A nap on one of those benches wouldn't be too bad. But business had to come first. He grunted as he struggled to his feet and approached the fake cop in his khaki uniform. The cop watched as Sammy lumbered in his direction. Sammy glowered to keep the cop on his toes, but tried not to go overboard. *Gotta keep my cool.*

As soon as he drew close enough for the guard to hear, Sammy told his story—the mix-up at the airport and the phone call between him and the broad. He skipped the part about the threats he'd made that had spooked the woman so bad she wouldn't meet him face-to-face.

The guard shook his head as soon as Sammy told him about the plan to exchange the laptop cases. Sweat broke out on Sammy's forehead again. He launched into a description of Lynnette. The guard kept shaking his head.

Sammy's voice grew louder. Beads of perspiration dribbled down the back of his neck. His injured hand began to tremble. He took a step back as he felt a wave of nausea.

"Hey, are you sick?" the guard said.

"No, I'm okay. I just gotta sit." Sammy moved to the closest bench. Now he couldn't take a deep breath. He set the case on the floor beside his feet. Another fucking anxiety attack, he thought. The third one in the last six weeks. Just one more sign he needed to see one of those damned knife jockeys. *Fuck!*

"You want me to call an ambulance?" the guard said.

"No . . . don't call an ambulance . . . I'll be fine . . . I'll sit here a minute . . . I'm just upset . . ." Sammy stopped and sucked in air. There. He could breathe again. He pulled his damp handkerchief out of his pocket and tried to wipe the sweat off his face, but his hand throbbed. His knuckles were more discolored now. Purple in places.

Holy shit. What have I done to deserve this?

"Maybe you ought to have a doctor look at that hand."

Jesus. Would this guard never stop? Sammy took a couple of deep breaths and wiped his hand across his brow. "I told you, I'm fine. If you want to help, get someone to look in the restroom, see if there's a broad . . . a woman in there with a case sort of like this one. You can't miss her. Her boyfriend beat the crap out of her and messed up her face."

"You sure you're going to be okay?"

"Yes, dammit! Just do what I asked so I can get out of here."

The guard ambled toward the ticket counter. Sammy clenched his uninjured hand into a fist and pressed it against his chin.

CHAPTER 13

Denver, Colorado
Thursday, January 23

The mom came out of the restroom stall with her kids, did a double-take when she saw Lynnette's new look, but did not comment. They left the restroom, but in less than a minute the mom came back, alone. "There's a guy out there looking for you. He said something about a woman with bruises and that she carried a laptop case. Are you in trouble?"

"Yeah." *Oh, God, trapped in the restroom.* Lynnette stared at the floor, at her carry-on, the laptop, and remembered the time she'd attended a meeting and toted her entire computer case inside her suitcase so she'd have the convenience of wheels.

"Can I do anything to help?" the mom asked.

"Maybe." Lynnette looked at the woman's face, crossed her fingers and hoped she carried all that makeup in her purse. "My bruises. Do you have anything that will cover them?"

"Oh, sure." The woman opened her bag, dug around until she'd produced liquid foundation, eye shadow and mascara.

A female janitor with ROSA embroidered on her pocket strolled in and unlocked a supply closet near the exit. An oversized black trash bag tumbled out. She dragged it toward the door and propped it against the wall. Rosa pulled a bottle of spray liquid cleaner from the closet, took a handful of paper towels, and wiped down the sinks. When she glanced at the two women in the mirror and saw the image of Lynnette's face, she set her cleaner and towels on the counter and stared. "Oh, baby, that's a man that deserves some serious punishment. I hope you runnin' away."

"Yeah. He's out there now," Lynnette said. "He thinks I'm in the station, but he doesn't know for sure. I don't know what to do." *Why did I lie?* Lynnette swallowed the temptation to spill the whole story. Time was running out. Any minute, the fat man might convince the cop to check out the restroom.

"Honey, the Lord must have sent us in here at this very minute just to get you out of trouble. You two hurry up and get that mess on her face covered up."

It only took a few minutes, but by the time they were finished, Lynnette looked like a different person. Except for the puffy eye. She didn't know what she could do about that. Wearing her sunglasses inside would be way too obvious. The bags were a different matter. She explained her idea to the two women as she placed her carry-on and the laptop case on the counter.

Within seconds, she'd transferred most of her clothes and toiletries into her laundry bag and handed it to Rosa. Lynnette stowed the fat man's case inside the carry-on and zipped it closed, fastening the locks with garbage bag ties as she usually did. She realized at the last moment that red yarn marked the handles of her black luggage. He might have noticed. Lynnette picked at the knots until the yarn came free, set the carry-on on the floor, and stuffed the yarn in the trash can. Rosa put the laundry bag on the floor under the towel dispenser.

Lynnette dug around inside the bag until she found her bottle of Tums. She shook four into her hand and chewed them all at once. After tossing the bottle back inside, she entered one of the stalls and sat on the toilet with her head in her hands, leaving the other two women to watch her things. She had to admit, she didn't have the slightest idea how to get away from the fat guy.

She retrieved a pair of jeans, another shirt and sweater, a red-hooded sweatshirt, and her brown Reeboks from the laundry bag. Extra underwear and socks went into her purse. She changed as fast as she could, adding layers to plump up her lean body, knowing she had to get out of there in a hurry.

The image in the mirror frightened her. Her swollen eye stood out like a neon sign flashing, "Look, look," even with her hood covering her head. If she pulled it too far over her face, she'd call even more attention to herself, especially with all the makeup.

"I have an idea," Rosa said. "I got that whole big bag of mops that I already took off the handles, and now they need toting outdoors to the curb for the laundry truck. Hold that bag up so's the man can't see your face, walk out the door, and then take off like your pants was on fire.

"Look at you," she continued. "Don't you have a coat? That little sweatshirt ain't gonna keep you warm enough once the sun goes down."

"I know. I don't have a coat. I thought I was going to California, not Colorado." What she said sounded stupid, as though she'd jumped on the wrong plane, or jumped off a bus in the wrong city. She sighed. "It would take too long to explain."

Rosa returned to her supply closet and took a purple ski jacket with dirty cuffs from the wall hook. "I got this one. It ain't fancy, but it'll keep you warm. There's gloves in the pocket too. You take it."

"I can't do that. You'll need your coat."

"Nah, this is my old one. I'll call my old man and tell him to bring my new one when he picks me up." She pushed the old jacket at Lynnette. "I mean it now. You put this on and then git that bag out to the curb."

"What about my carry-on?"

"I'll take it," the mom said. "I'll walk across the station to the other side and go on out the door." She pointed toward the direction she'd take, then she pointed the other direction, toward the side of the station where the buses parked, and moved her arm in an arc to show Lynnette where to go. "When you get outside, you trot around the corner, grab your suitcase, and head downtown."

"Your kids—"

"They're okay. They're with my sister. And look, I have plenty more makeup at home. You better keep this stuff." She shoved a bottle of liquid makeup and a plastic case with four shades of eye shadow into Lynnette's hands.

Rosa's plan seemed too simple to Lynnette. Surely the fat man wouldn't be fooled, but what else could she do? She thanked Rosa and the mom, and stashed the makeup in a zippered section of her bag. Grabbing Rosa's hand, Lynnette pulled the hood up, hooked her purse strap over her head and across her shoulder, and put on the jacket. With her hands in the gloves and the mop bag propped on her left shoulder, her right arm across her face, she left the restroom, adding her own final touch to her disguise. She limped across the station with the stiff gait of someone with one bum knee. She didn't look for the fat guy until she was on the sidewalk.

By the time she reached the front of the station, the mom was waiting. Lynnette peered around the corner to make sure the fat man hadn't spotted her. She dropped the bag of mops at the curb, put her arm around the mom's shoulders and gave her a hug. "What's your name?" she asked. "I can't let you go without knowing your name."

"Ann. Yours?"

"Lynnette."

"Good luck, Lynnette. Now go."

Lynnette took the handle of her carry-on and headed toward the 16th Street Mall. She figured it wouldn't be a good place to hang out for long, not in the middle of the night. But she also couldn't go to the nearest hotel. Even if they'd take her, looking the way she did—like a tramp who should be sleeping at a shelter. A shelter! She'd bet her bottom dollar she'd find a shelter for the homeless in downtown Denver. Would she find one that wasn't already full? Maybe she'd get lucky. She walked a little faster.

While Sammy waited for the guard to send someone into the restroom to look for Lynnette Hudson, he turned and checked out each person in the waiting room. Satisfied, he watched the door of the women's restroom, sure he would recognize her if she came out, even more positive he'd recognize his laptop case.

A woman and two kids had gone in earlier. They came out, but the woman left her kids with someone else and returned to the bathroom. Then a janitor went in. Someone with a limp came out with a big trash bag. Then that woman who'd been with the kids earlier came strutting out wheeling a carry-on bag and walked out the front door.

What the hell? Sammy turned to check out the kids. They stood in line by the boarding door. He glanced toward the front door, frowned, then watched the ticket counter clerk stroll across the waiting area and enter the restroom. Within a few seconds, the clerk returned with the janitor and joined the security guard, who now leaned against the ticket counter.

Twisting around the other way so he could see better, Sammy watched the three as they talked. The guard turned once and pointed toward Sammy, and they all stared at him for a minute. The janitor shook her head and returned to the restroom. Sammy faced the front doors just as the woman who'd been with the kids walked back into the station. She no longer pulled the carry-on suitcase behind her.

"Son of a bitch!" Sammy yelled as he jumped up. "You," he

screamed at the woman as she walked past, "I need to talk to you."

From the corner of his eye, he saw the guard run in his direction. He noticed the shocked expression on the woman's face. He felt cold. His hand throbbed. When he glanced down, he saw his fingernails were blue. An odd sensation like a huge rubber band snapping across his upper back took his breath away and melted his legs. He tried to grab for the bench as he went down, but his hand went numb. The last thing he saw was Hudson's laptop case, which rested a couple of inches from his nose.

CHAPTER 14

Denver, Colorado
Thursday, January 23

A strange assortment of people congregated in the darkness outside the front doors of the women's shelter, most sucking on cigarettes, most underdressed for the chill that had crept into the air at sundown. A little old lady in a sassy red beret, stained sweatpants and sweatshirt, and battered tennis shoes chatted with a younger woman whose layered dress, slacks, shirts, and sweaters made her body look rotund even though her face and neck were scrawny. The younger one leaned against her grocery cart full of trash bags and shook her finger at the red beret. The little old lady backed away and disappeared through the shelter doors.

Lynnette stepped away from the shadow of a nearby building where she'd lingered to see if the fat man had followed her. He had not. She guessed he'd check the downtown hotels first. Limping again, she crossed the street toward the shelter, her purse strap over her neck and shoulder and gripped tightly by her left hand. She pulled her carry-on behind her. Once inside the shelter, she'd stay out of sight in case he showed up later. With her wig and makeup, he'd be less likely to spot her, especially if she kept her purse and suitcase out of sight.

The shelter looked nothing like she had imagined. Two desks sat by the entrance, one at either side of the door. One large room lay beyond the desks. Cots filled three-quarters of the room, most less than six inches apart. Lynnette guessed thirty or forty of them. A woman with a pillow and a blanket occupied each cot.

Carts and baskets on wheels filled much of the remaining space, some parked next to the women who slept on the floor. A few rested on thick mats while others sat on benches set against the walls. Others waited in lines at what appeared to be restrooms. It was quiet considering the number of people in the room.

This is unbelievable. She had expected maybe a dozen or so homeless in a shelter. She glanced around. There had to be more than fifty women in that room. A female security guard strolled through the area, her hands clasped behind her back.

Lynnette didn't have to say anything as she approached a lady who sat at one of the front desks and shook her head. "No beds. We're full." She waved toward the packed facility to indicate the truth behind her words.

Lynnette pointed toward the area where women slept on the floor "What about there?"

"We're out of mats. You'd have to sleep on the floor." She looked Lynnette over, her gaze lingering for a moment on the wig, glanced at her purse and her carry-on, then finally studied Lynnette's face. "Shouldn't you be at the safehouse? They'll come get you if I give them a call."

"No, no. It's nothing like that. I just need to get out of the cold for a few hours, 'til my bus leaves in the morning. If I can use the restroom, rest over there on the floor, I'll be out of here in no time."

"No smoking inside," the lady said. "No talking or loud noises. Watch your stuff or it'll be gone. There's water and coffee in the back. If you're still here at five, we pass out muffins and bagels."

Lynnette nodded. "There aren't any kids here."

"Family shelters are separate." The lady didn't volunteer any additional information.

Lynnette got in one of the restroom lines. She received a few curious looks from others as she passed, still towing her carry-on, but no one spoke to her. By the time she came out, very little space remained. With her arm around her carry-on and her purse stuffed between her suitcase and her stomach, Lynnette rested on her side as far toward the rear of the room as she could get. With a couple of grocery carts blocking her view of the doors, she felt hidden and unlikely to attract attention. She was restless, worried about whether Grace was safe with Blue. When she closed her eyes, the smell reminded her of a women's locker room after a losing game. Soft weeping, unwashed body odor, an air of defeat and humiliation. Lynnette fell asleep within minutes, in spite of her tears.

Los Angeles, California
Thursday, January 23

Benny Ortega woke with a start and checked his watch. He'd dozed off in the hotel room's easy chair while waiting to hear from Fat Ass Sammy Grick. *Grick the Prick. Where was he?* He should have shown up more than an hour ago. Benny checked his phone to see if he'd had any messages, wondering if he'd slept through a phone call. Nothing. A call to Sammy went straight to voice mail.

Something's wrong. Benny called his techie guru in Miami.

"Yeah?"

"It's me," Benny said. "I need to know where my guy is."

"Uh, what time is it?"

"What difference does it make? This is urgent."

"Okay. I got it. Hang on. I need to bring up the tracking program."

Benny paced the room as he waited. Three minutes passed.

Four. "What the hell are you doing?" he yelled.

"Okay, okay. I got it. He's in Denver."

"What? Are you sure?"

"Yeah. Hang on, maybe I can get a fix on his exact location." Again Benny waited.

"Here it comes," the tracker said. "He's moving along 16th Street in downtown Denver. The log says he was at the bus station before that."

"Stay on it. I want to know every step that son of a bitch takes. I'll get back to you."

Benny hung up and dialed the phone again. "Getz, where are you? Didn't I tell you to be here before Sammy Grick shows up?"

"I am here, Mr. Ortega. I'm in the lobby. Do you want me to come up?"

"Damn it, doesn't anybody listen to me? Didn't I tell you I wanted you to be here when Sammy arrived?"

"Yes, sir. I thought you meant here in the building. Surely you don't want me to handle this in your room."

Benny took a deep breath. "You're right. But something has changed. I'm sending you to Denver. Come to my room and I'll explain."

Forty-five minutes later, Benny completed an online transaction that fattened Albert Getz's offshore account by $250,000. He confirmed by phone that Getz would be the only passenger flying to Denver on Benny's private plane. With luck, Albert Getz would be hot on Sammy's trail before sunrise.

CHAPTER 15

Glades, Florida
Thursday, January 23

Glades police officer Maggie Gutierrez and her partner, Officer Dan Franklin, arrived at Carl Foster's house a little after three o'clock on Thursday morning. Two calls had come in, the first from Foster's partner, Sam Jacobs, and the second from one of Foster's neighbors. As luck would have it, Maggie's beat included Foster's neighborhood.

All the information she had so far was station gossip and the dispatcher's call relaying the duty officer's report. Foster and his partner had been suspended from duty as of two o'clock Wednesday afternoon. They were on the hot seat for beating up a Puerto Rican kid whose worst offense involved hanging around his no-good brother and his brother's drugged-up pals.

According to Jacobs, the two men had hit the bars around two-thirty in the afternoon and stayed out until nearly seven. Jacobs said he finally got tired of listening to Foster bitch and moan that he'd be better off dead than jailed on assault charges, so Jacobs decided to go home. Foster had said he planned to go home too, but the last Jacobs saw of Foster, his car was weaving down the street.

After dinner and a couple of beers, Jacobs began to wonder if Foster had made it home okay. He began phoning Foster. When he couldn't reach him, Jacobs checked with the police and the local hospital. After that, he thought about Foster's tendency toward rage, and called in a report. Once duly recorded in the log, the call went to Maggie, who sat with Dan in a coffee shop, trying to relieve the fatigue that sets in during a quiet shift.

Before they'd received their carryout refills and returned to their car, a second call came in. One of Carl Foster's neighbors reported that his dog had started barking around seven. The neighbor brought his dog inside, but it remained agitated all evening, growling and pacing the hall near the front door. The neighbor decided the cops should come take a look in case someone or something prowled around outside the house. The neighbor lived next door to Foster.

Maggie and Dan sat in their squad car a couple of houses from Foster's place, observing the neighborhood, discussing what to do first. Maggie tapped her fingers on the steering wheel as she peered through the windshield. Foster's house was dark. The lights were on in the house to the east. She sighed and looked at Dan.

"What? You got the fidgets?" he asked.

"Yeah. I don't like this. I've heard the stories. Foster's a walking time bomb."

Dan shrugged and opened his door. "Doesn't matter. We got a job to do. Want to talk to the guy next door?"

Maggie nodded.

The man opened his front door and stepped outside as they approached. They listened to his story about his dog, and then walked toward Foster's house.

Mindful of Foster's troubles and his reputation for losing his temper, Maggie stood to the side of the door instead of directly in front. She used her flashlight to knock. No answer. She rang the doorbell. "Carl Foster, this is Officer Maggie Gutierrez. My partner and I are here on a prowler call and need to check your backyard."

The dog next door started barking. Maggie knocked a little

harder the second time. She pressed the doorbell twice, each time hearing four chimes ring inside the house.

"Check around the side," she told Dan. "See if his car's in the garage. Look over the fence but don't go in the yard until I get there."

As Dan left the porch, he put his flashlight in his left hand and held it out to his side. He unsnapped his holster and placed his right hand on the pistol grip.

Maggie stepped back and ran her own light over the front windows. The blinds were securely closed. She flashed the light across the front yard, noting one car in the driveway, then shone the light into the shrubs at either side of the front steps.

Dan rounded the corner of the house and joined Maggie near the front door. "One car in the garage. No one out back. All the blinds are closed. There's one window on this side with a few slats bent the wrong way. All I can see is a man's feet with his shoes on. The shoes are hanging off the edge of the bed like maybe Foster's sprawled across it, sleeping off a drunk. There's a screened-in patio with a sliding glass door. The drapes are pulled."

"Okay, let's try this again." Maggie pounded on the front door and pushed the doorbell several times. "Carl Foster, Mrs. Foster, is anyone here?"

No sound came from inside the house.

"Call it in, Dan. I don't want to go inside without authorization. Tell the dispatcher we have reasonable suspicion of an occupant in jeopardy and we need to clear it with the super."

The response came over the radio in less than two minutes. "We can check the backyard while we wait for backup," she said.

They headed for the gate. Maggie stood by the fence and watched Dan while he checked the bushes and the shed inside the yard. He turned and watched while Maggie shone her light into the patio room, then on the sliding glass door. A twelve-inch wide space gapped between the door and the doorjamb. *Nobody leaves a door unlocked and cracked open in South Florida, especially at night.*

Slipping on a sterile glove, Maggie tried the screen door into the patio room and found it unlocked.

Taking three slow steps backwards, she ended up with her back pressed against the wall just to the side of the tiny patio. Dan joined her. She explained about the doors and told him to continue checking the perimeter of the yard. When he finished, Maggie sent him to the front of the house to wait.

In a few minutes, Maggie saw the beam from a flashlight bobbing through the gate. One of the two officers from the backup cars accompanied Dan. Maggie instructed the officers to take a position at the front door.

"It's quiet," she said. "We're going in based on the barking dog, the unlocked door, and Foster's statement to his partner that he might as well be dead. Get dispatch to call Foster. If he's sleeping, maybe the phone will wake him up."

She then opened the screen door, crossed the patio, and waited beside the sliding glass door for Dan to catch up. He maneuvered his elbow into the space between the door and the doorjamb. With the force of his upper arm, he slid the door all the way open without touching any part of the door with his hands.

The drapes, which had been pulled closed, were the only obstacle between them and the inside of Foster's house. Dan reached out with his flashlight and caught the edge of the fabric, slowly pulling it to the left as he shone his light around the room.

"Carl Foster? This is Glades P.D. Are you okay?" Maggie waited a minute. There was no response. "We're coming inside now. Your partner called and said he was worried about you.

You in here?"

Maggie slipped through the opening as Dan continued to hold the drape aside and light the way. When she saw the floor lamp a few steps from the door, she stepped further into the room and turned it on.

The hum of the refrigerator and the faint ticking of a clock on top of a bookcase were the only sounds she heard.

"It's freezing in here," she said.

"Yeah, weird. Hey, Foster's married, right?" Dan said.

"Yeah. Got married last Saturday. That waitress from the bar you got kicked out of last month."

"That wasn't my fault."

Maggie raised her eyebrow. "Getting wasted and smarting off to a homicide detective wasn't your fault?"

"He started it." Dan took a step into the living room and called out, "Hello? Anybody home?" He paused, waited, then spoke again. "Carl Foster, you here? Glades P.D. Got a call you might be in trouble." Dan looked at Maggie. "Newlyweds, huh? You don't suppose they're down there going at it?" He indicated the hallway with the tilt of his head.

"You yelled loud enough. They would've heard." She opened the front door. One officer stepped inside and one stayed outside. "We think he's in the bedroom," Maggie told them. "His partner said he was in bad shape, talking how he'd be better off dead than in jail. He might have tried something, or he might be waiting to blow our heads off. You guys stay alert." She glanced at the officer standing inside. "Stay here and watch that patio door. Cover me, Dan." She checked behind the couch and entered the hall, standing aside for him to pass.

When he reached the kitchen, Maggie watched him inspect two large cupboards, a pantry, and the door into the garage.

"Hey," he said, pointing out the car keys hanging on pegs over the counter and the bottle of wine and the glass sitting next to the sink. "Guy's probably just wasted."

From the doorway Maggie saw a large wooden knife block on the counter. One knife was missing, probably a paring knife judging by the position and size of the empty slot.

It crossed her mind that Foster might have taken the knife to the bedroom and slit his wrists.

"Dan, check out that piece of paper on the table."

He read the note and frowned, then walked to Maggie's side, leaned closer so his lips were near her ear and whispered, "His new wife? Looks like she took a hike."

"Probably didn't like the idea of being married to someone who beats up kids."

Maggie edged along the hall toward the remaining rooms. All the doors were closed. She turned the door handle on the first room. A bathroom. She led the way to the next door, and hesitated when she caught a whiff of foul air. Sharp, worse than rotten eggs. The smell of someone who shits his pants and then pukes all over the mess. She made eye contact with Dan, then sniffed the air and grimaced.

He nodded.

She opened the door, saw the man sprawled across the bedspread, the blood, and walked to the other side of the bed.

No pulse.

"Call it in," she said. "I think this is Carl Foster. He's dead. Tell the guys out front."

After Dan had left, she studied the room and its contents. Blood had splattered on the walls and carpet and pooled around the body. Foster lay on his back, a gaping wound running across his throat. A paring knife, also covered with blood, had been stabbed into his hand.

Whoever did this was one angry man. Maggie remembered the note on the table. *Or one angry woman.*

★ ★ ★ ★ ★

Two police cars showed up first—Maggie's sergeant and the shift lieutenant. Crime scene investigators. Medical examiner. The place turned into a madhouse within twenty minutes. Thirty minutes later, Maggie watched Detective Mark Prince climb out of his unmarked car and survey the scene. He frowned as he spotted Dan, then strolled over to Maggie as though Dan didn't exist.

"It was a homicide," she said.

"Crime scene crew says yes. You first on the scene?"

"Yes, sir."

"Tell me."

Maggie began with their arrival and gave Prince every detail she could remember.

He maintained eye contact as she spoke, then said, "Good job."

She liked that.

"Come with me," Prince said as he turned toward the house.

"Sure." *Holy cow.*

She followed the homicide detective. He strode past Dan without even a glance. Maggie ventured a quick look, saw Dan's face, decided she'd best keep her grin to herself, and simply nodded at her partner as she passed.

CHAPTER 16

Denver, Colorado
Thursday, January 23

Lynnette woke to the sound of a food cart's squeaky wheels and the smell of coffee. She lay on her side and had used her lumpy purse as a pillow. She stretched one arm across the carry-on and tucked her fingers through its handle.

"On your feet, ladies. Time to rise and shine. Coffee's ready. Food's in the back. Don't forget to wash your hands."

An unappealing odor of urine and vomit drifted through the shelter. Lynnette sat up and looked around. Women pulled their possessions together and shuffled toward the restrooms. Most stared briefly at Lynnette, their gazes lingering on her hair, before moving on without comment. She reached up to check her wig and realized it sat askew. She tugged it into place.

"You're on the run, ain't you?"

The voice came from behind her. Lynnette turned. A young woman sat on a folded blanket and leaned against the wall. Lynnette shrugged and looked away.

"Me, too," the girl said. "My pimp caught me skimming the take."

"Oh." Lynnette didn't know what else to say.

The girl was stick-thin and wore jeans and a dirty T-shirt. Stringy brown hair hung around her face in a tangled mess. Lynnette glanced around the room and saw half a dozen women she figured must be prostitutes from their low-cut blouses, extra-short skirts and high heels. This one didn't seem the type.

"How long you been on the street?" Lynnette asked.

"A long while," the girl said. "Long enough to know those that belong and those that don't. What are you doing here?"

Lynnette got to her feet and straightened her clothing. "I need coffee."

"We don't want you here if the cops are looking for you."

"Don't worry. No cops. I got stranded downtown when I missed my bus."

The girl looked her over, checking out Lynnette's luggage and purse. "Looks like you could've gone to a hotel. Why didn't you?"

"Nice talking to you," Lynnette said. "But I need some of that coffee."

"Why you takin' your bag with you?" the girl called out as Lynnette walked away. "Afraid I'll steal something?"

Pretending she didn't hear, Lynnette went straight to the restroom and got in line. A few minutes later she stepped inside. While she was there, she applied a fresh coat of makeup to her bruises and scrubbed her hands. With the strap of her purse again across her neck and shoulders, leaving one hand free, she went straight for the food cart, filled a Styrofoam cup with coffee, grabbed a bagel and tucked it in the outside pocket of her carry-on, and headed for the door.

The early morning sun hadn't burned through the frosty haze, so it looked as cold as it felt. She pulled the hood of her sweatshirt over her head and walked until she found a bench where she could eat her breakfast alone. The chill air kept her from lingering too long. As much as she feared going back to the bus station and running into the fat man, she didn't want to book another flight or rent a car and drive to California.

If she truly wanted to protect Blue and Grace, she needed to stay as far away from them as she could. The way she saw it, she had only two options. Either hurry to the Amtrak station and see if she could get a seat on the westbound train, or go to the bus station and head anywhere except Fort Collins.

She took the fat man's phone out of her purse and turned it on, then stuffed it in a pocket. If he called her, perhaps she could trick him into telling his location. She didn't want to return to the bus station until she knew for sure he'd moved on.

As she began to shiver, she stood and walked. Within a minute or two, the phone beeped. She pulled it out and looked at the display. Seventeen messages. The first three came from her cell phone number. She didn't recognize the others.

When she reached another bench, she sat down, pushed the hood off her head, and fiddled with the display menu until she retrieved the voice mail. Predictably, the fat guy used 1234 as his password.

As she expected, he was looking for her and he was furious.

Lynnette had only herself to worry about. Still, she couldn't get Grace off her mind. She considered calling Blue. She could even call Grace's parents and make certain Grace reported in.

Oh, hell. I don't know what to do. She glanced at her watch. Still too early to contact the FBI. She wondered if they had offices in downtown Denver.

She punched a couple of buttons to retrieve the next message, the one that didn't come from her cell phone.

"Sammy, you were supposed to be in L.A. by now. Where the hell are you? Call me."

A man's voice, a man with a Spanish accent. Cuban? Mexican? If the guy on the phone wanted to talk to Sammy, did he have something to do with the laptop case and its contents? Assuming this Sammy was the fat man, was he supposed to deliver the stuff to this guy who left the message? Lynnette listened to the next voice mail.

"Your Denver to L.A. flight was cancelled, you prick. I have to find out on my own that you didn't get on the next flight? What's going on? You trying something funny, Sammy?"

The phone rang. The number of the incoming call matched the ones from the man with the accent. Lynnette waited until the ringing stopped, then dialed her own cell phone number, wondering if the fat guy, Sammy, would answer. The phone went directly to voice mail.

"Some guy with an accent is looking for you. He sounds mad." She stopped, looked at the phone in her hand, and disconnected the call.

What the hell am I doing? Have I lost my mind?

After working her way through the phone's menu, Lynnette figured out how to set it to vibrate instead of ring when a call came in. Then she listened to more messages, three of them direct threats against Sammy's life. Too nervous to listen to more, she left the phone on and put it in her jacket pocket. The fat man hadn't called her since late the night before. He had turned off her phone. Anxious to get his case and in more trouble than Lynnette, he should be trying desperately to get in touch with her.

She pulled the phone out and checked the time of the last message left for Sammy. Nearly two o'clock in the morning. Nothing since. Very odd, considering the urgency of the other messages. She went over what she knew so far, then began to worry about the part she didn't know.

Sammy, the presumed owner of the phone and maybe the laptop, was supposed to deliver something to someone in L.A. and he didn't show up on schedule. This man in L.A. must be powerful—powerful enough to dispatch a couple of thugs to Denver to find Sammy. They could be in Denver already. They could have found Sammy early this morning and now have her stuff. Maybe that's why the calls stopped. The man in L.A.

might know she had the phone—and everything else in the case.

She looked over her shoulder. No thugs in sight. She tried to reassure herself. No one wanted to kill her. The fat guy had a nasty temper and a filthy mouth. If she returned his case, he would never bother her again. She took a deep breath. *No more craziness. No more paranoia.* She needed to think, get her priorities straight.

She glanced at her watch. Six o'clock. She needed to call her broker and the bank, but it was too early. They wouldn't be in their Florida offices for another hour. She pulled the phone out of her pocket and checked to see the balance of minutes remaining in the display. Plenty, thank goodness.

"Hey, aren't you cold?"

Lynnette jumped and thrust the phone in her pocket, pushed herself up from the bench, and grabbed the handle of her carry-on. "Yeah," she said. "I better get moving." She glanced at the woman in jeans and a heavy flannel jacket who had walked up behind her. Lynnette hadn't heard a thing. *If that had been the fat man, he could've killed me.*

"Come on in," the woman said, pointing to a tiny shop a few feet from where Lynnette stood. A sign on the door said *Caffeine on Tap.* "I'll give you a cup of coffee."

Inside the cozy shop, the woman pointed toward a table and chair in one corner. "You hungry? I have cinnamon rolls just out of the oven."

Lynnette turned down the rolls but accepted a huge cup of coffee.

The woman got busy behind the counter and ignored Lynnette for several minutes. An empty newspaper rack sat by the door. A small television occupied one end of the counter, its screen dark. Lynnette passed the time by reading the handwritten menu on the wall chalkboard.

The woman poured a cup of coffee for herself and leaned against the counter. "I don't want to be nosy," she said. Apparently she meant it, because she didn't say anything else, didn't ask any questions.

Lynnette chose not to answer at first, but then felt rude in the face of the stranger's kindness. "It's complicated."

"I figured that."

"I'd rather not talk about it."

"Okay. Suit yourself."

Lynnette sipped her coffee, feeling more and more uncomfortable as the coffee lady continued to watch her. "Listen, I appreciate the coffee, but I have to get to the bus station." She stood up at the same moment a door opened at the back of the shop and a man carrying two newspaper bundles strode toward the rack. She waited as he ordered a cup of coffee. After stacking the newspapers on the shelves, he handed a paper to Lynnette and laid one on the counter. With the cup of coffee in his hand, he shouted, "See ya!" and hurried out the door.

"Sure you don't want more coffee?" the woman asked.

"Thanks, no." Lynnette folded her newspaper and shoved it in the outside pocket of her carry-on.

"Whatever's going on, maybe I could help."

Lynnette shook her head. "I don't think so. Thanks, anyway."

"Why don't you sit and have something to eat?"

Too pushy. She acts as though she's trying to keep me here.

Had the fat man been here looking for her?

Without another word, Lynnette pulled the sweatshirt hood over her head and walked out the door. She crossed the street at the next intersection and walked away as fast as she could. She'd told the woman at the coffee shop she was headed to the bus station, so she couldn't go there. At the end of the block, she turned in the opposite direction.

At the next corner, Lynnette doubled back toward 16th

Street, where she stopped and peered around the corner toward the coffee shop. A police car sat in front, its lights flashing. An officer stood by the front door. The coffee lady pointed in the direction Lynnette had walked when she left the shop.

What the hell? Lynnette stepped out of sight and leaned against the building, rubbing her forehead as though to massage the frown away. It made no sense for that woman to call the cops. *What's going on?*

Hadn't she just told herself to pull it together, stop acting so paranoid? Now that she didn't have to worry about Grace, why didn't she return to the coffee shop to talk to the police? They could track the fat man and exchange the laptop cases. No muss, no fuss, no danger. *For Pete's sake, the cops probably stop there for coffee every day.*

Then why did the coffee lady point in the direction Lynnette had gone?

It had to be Carl. He had reported her missing or he had accused her of some kind of crime. He must have figured out she was in Denver by tracking the credit card purchase and charming some airline cutie into checking the passenger list for both legs of the flight. One call to Denver P.D. from one cop to another. That's all it would take. And here she was, wandering around downtown in the early morning, before most of the businesses were open. She'd stand out like a sore thumb with her carry-on bag. She had to ditch stuff right now so she didn't look like a stranded traveler.

Backtracking to an alley she'd passed only moments before, Lynnette hurried toward the nearest dumpsters and stepped between the first two. She pulled off the black wig and threw it away. She took off her jacket and turned it inside out so the gray, quilted lining showed. Next she removed the red sweatshirt and dropped it on the ground. Hoping the absence of red and purple would be enough to make her less obvious when seen from a distance, she slipped the jacket on inside out. Sammy's phone bumped against her hip. It would be harder to get to it, but she didn't think she'd have room in her purse for the phone. She threw the purple gloves on the ground with the sweatshirt.

The carry-on case came next. She took the newspaper from the outside pocket and stuffed it into her purse. After removing Sammy's laptop case, she stuffed the cash into her pants pocket. The brown manila envelope rolled easily and fit inside her purse. After peering around the dumpsters to make sure no one watched, she threw the bag away. She went through the rest of Sammy's laptop case and pulled out the things she would need. The laptop she'd carry under her arm. The phone charger and the computer's brick and cord went into her purse. Sammy had two flash drives in his case. She took them as well. When she had everything, she tossed the laptop case into the dumpster with the carry-on bag.

Her purse weighed a good ten pounds and felt way too full for comfort. She took a deep breath and let it out. *Comfort is not the primary issue here.* What could she discard? She took a quick inventory and removed her water bottle, a bag of cough drops, all of her keys, six ballpoint pens, and a half-empty notebook. She tore out a half dozen pages of the notebook and stuffed them back in her purse with a pen. After chugging most of the water, she tossed the bottle.

She couldn't do much about her purse and her brown Reeboks at this point. She listened for a moment and didn't hear anyone in the alley. Just as she stepped out from between the dumpsters, a bread delivery truck turned in from the street. She stepped aside to let it pass, then followed as it cruised almost to the end of the block before stopping. The back door into a business stood open. The aroma of bacon and coffee floated into the alley.

Lynnette ignored the bread man and thoughts of breakfast and walked around the truck to the end of the block. She needed a cyber café with no cop car parked outside the front door. Or anyplace with public computers, or wireless if she wanted to risk using Sammy's laptop. And she needed to be far away from downtown.

A college campus. Big cities had colleges, and college libraries often opened early to accommodate students. As she drew near one of the hotels, she saw a line of cabs in the circle drive. Lynnette walked across the street to the first driver and said, "Take me to the campus?"

"D.U.?"

"Yeah."

"What building?"

"The library."

CHAPTER 17

Denver, Colorado
Thursday, January 23

As soon as the taxi entered the ramp to I-25, Lynnette felt safer. By the time she watched the cabbie drive away from the library, she had shaken the anxiety she'd felt since hearing the first voice mail message from the man with the accent.

The cab driver barely looked at her. She'd done her best to avoid drawing his attention by staying quiet and giving him a good tip—not too big and not too small.

Lynnette entered the library and found the restrooms. Looking at herself in the mirror, she noted her bruises had turned a sickly yellow around the edges. She washed her hands and face and dabbed more foundation over the worst discoloration, blending it as best she could. She ran a comb through her hair and fluffed her bangs.

No one seemed to notice when she wandered into a large room filled with tables and ringed with low-walled study cubicles equipped with outlets. Signs placed throughout the room advertised free wireless, but Lynnette didn't want to use Sammy's computer unless she had to. Instead, she sat at one of the public-use computers and put her purse and Sammy's laptop on the floor between her feet. After slipping her jacket off and stuffing it behind her back, she logged on to her email account.

Nothing from Carl. Also, nothing from her bank or brokerage

firm alerting her to unusual activity on her accounts. She closed her eyes, trying to remember her bank passwords. Creating unique and secure passwords for each of her online accounts had a downside. While she struggled to remember, she reminded herself that Sammy the Creep had her statement, account number, login name, and password. *I'm an idiot.*

Besides the usual spam, her Inbox contained an email from Dave Buchanan at the *Reporter*.

That's odd. The two hadn't been in touch since she left Indianapolis.

She'd send an email to Blue first, then Dave. She'd have to go back to the investment account password later. Pulling her purse into her lap, she searched its contents for the napkin with Blue's information on it, then wrote a short email to let Blue and Grace know she was okay. If the two girls met the early bus from Denver, expecting Lynnette to be on it, they might think she'd taken off for good.

Then she opened the email from Dave Buchanan. It said: *Where are you? What's happened? Call now. Urgent.* She replied: *I have information that might be a story. Need to talk, but I lost phone list. Send work number stat.*

She heard a ping that signaled incoming mail. Blue wrote: *Where are you? I'll pick you up. Sixty minutes max.*

Lynnette frowned. Wouldn't it be better to avoid the girls? Why put them in danger? She would tell Blue not to come.

Her Inbox pinged again. She closed Blue's message and opened the response she'd received from Dave. He had listed three different phone numbers and added: *Call right now. Urgent.* Lynnette shivered as she jotted down the numbers and stuffed the paper in her pocket.

Another ping from the computer. Lynnette opened the new email from Blue. *You still there? Where are you?*

Lynnette hit Reply. *D.U. Library. Don't come. I have other plans.*

The answer came right back. *We're on our way. We went to campus and picked up my car. Watch for us. It's a black Kia Rio.*

Lynnette mentally kicked herself for mentioning her location. She hit Reply again and typed: *No, Blue. You and Grace are safe. You don't need to get involved. Too dangerous.*

She hit Send and waited. No response.

With a sigh, she hit Reply on Dave's email. *Dave, I can't call you yet. I need to get to a different phone. Will call in two or three hours and explain everything.*

She hit Send, logged out, and started to close the browser. Before she could do so, Sammy's cell phone vibrated against her hip.

She checked the display and confirmed the call did not come from her cell. The number didn't match the one used by the man she'd decided to call The Cuban, either. This new number came from a different area code, one she couldn't identify. She didn't answer it.

She listened to the remaining messages on Sammy's phone, hoping The Cuban had said something to give away his identity. If this guy wanted the goods Sammy had in his laptop case, and Lynnette now possessed them, The Cuban could be tracking her on his own.

Methodically, she went through the voice mail. The first two were from The Cuban. He threatened to kill Sammy if he didn't call. Then everything changed.

The last voice mail from The Cuban said, "If this message is received by Lynnette Hudson, also known as Lynnette Foster, you should know that Sammy Grick died early this morning in a Denver hospital. My representative picked up his personal effects. I know who you are, Mrs. Foster, and I have all of the information I need to track you down. Sammy had your laptop and personal papers. His case, which included items belonging to me, is missing. I understand why you don't want to be found, but I want the case and everything in it, and I want it now. My man has been dispatched to find you. He'll be in touch."

Holy shit! Who was this guy? Why would The Cuban in L.A. have a contact in Denver able to track the fat guy so fast? Or had he sent someone to Denver specifically to find Sammy Grick? She glanced around the room to see if anyone watched her. The hairs on her arms rose as though a cold breeze had blown through the room. Her heartbeat hopped once, then again. Her mouth felt dry. She set the phone down and reopened the browser. The Cuban had her name, her home address, and all the contacts in her computer email and on her cell phone. If he did an Internet search on her name, what would he find?

She brought up a search engine and typed in Lynnette Hudson. There were links to a couple of her old stories in *The Indy Reporter,* but little else. When she tried searching for Lynnette Foster, however, there was breaking news.

The first three entries were from the online version of the Thursday *Miami Herald*. The first entry's title read: *South Florida Woman Sought as Person of Interest.* Lynnette's hand trembled as she placed her cursor on the link and clicked. Seeing her photo prominently displayed at the top left corner of the article shocked her.

Carl. That bastard. What had he said? That she stole something and ran off? She started to read the article, then covered her mouth with her hand as she read the next sentence and discovered why the cops wanted to talk to her. She read it again, then leaned back in her chair and stared at the screen. Thinking to cool the flush of her cheeks, she put both hands to her face. She then thrust her ice-cold hands between her knees to warm them and hunched forward, trying not to cry.

The crawly feeling returned. She glanced over her shoulder and looked around the room. No one watched. She read the whole article. Someone had murdered Carl. The cops considered her a person of interest. They didn't know for sure, but thought she might be in Denver or Los Angeles. They reported she might be traveling under her maiden name, Hudson.

It must have been on television. That's why the coffee shop lady had called the police.

Did the cops think she murdered Carl? Why would they? The fact that she'd disappeared? The note she'd left on the kitchen table? She tried to remember exactly what she wrote.

Something else bothered her. She read the article again. *Ah, there it is.* There were no signs of forced entry at their house. Would Carl be foolish enough to leave the door unlocked? Or answer the door and let his killers walk inside? Not in a million years.

The patio door. I can't remember securing the sliding glass door. Lynnette felt sick to her stomach.

What else? She read on. Time of death. There might be a delay establishing time of death because the house was so cold when the cops found Carl's body. *That's my fault, too.* She had turned the air conditioner off when she left. By the time Carl came home, he probably had to crank up the air full blast to make the overheated, stuffy house bearable.

Had Blue or Grace seen the news? Were they picking her up only to turn her over to the police? Maybe the "we" Blue mentioned included Blue and her dad. Or Blue and the cops.

The email from Dave seemed suspicious as well. What had he said?

Where are you? What's happened? Call me. Urgent.

Would he alert the police that she'd be calling him soon? Lynnette heard whispers nearby. She closed the browser.

With a quick glance at her watch and another around the

room, she grabbed her purse and laptop and hurried to the restroom. She went straight to the handicapped stall at the back and locked herself in, sat on the toilet, and wept.

She had wished horrible things on Carl right after he hit her, but she never wanted anything like this to happen. Thoughts of what he might have gone through flooded her mind. She tried to push them away so she could decide what to do. A picture of the unlocked patio door intruded time and again. Was she to blame?

Dabbing her eyes with wads of toilet tissue, she took a couple of deep breaths and willed her feelings of guilt and self-pity to take a hike. She glanced at her watch. Another ten minutes before Blue might show up. Someone came in to use the restroom, then washed her hands and left. Lynnette went to the sink, applied cool wet paper towels to her eyes, then applied more makeup.

After peering closely at her reflection, she used her fingertips to brush at the edges of the flesh-colored liquid layered on her discolored face. She combed her hair again and fluffed it over her forehead. As she walked out of the restroom, she took her sunglasses out of her purse.

The sun had burned the haze away, leaving no sign of the early-morning frostiness. Even the mountains to the west appeared sharp and clear, the sky the soft blue of a baby's blanket. A park bench sat in the sun near the sidewalk. Lynnette sank onto the bench as though she'd completed a three-mile run.

Students with knit caps pulled over their ears, others with no caps at all, most with jackets and backpacks, rushed past. Older men and women, all carrying large briefcases, passed at a more sedate pace. *Professors?*

A man wearing an old-fashioned tweed jacket with suede elbow patches hurried along the sidewalk in her direction, surveying everyone he passed. He carried a black case in his right hand and held the bowl of a pipe in his left. As he approached Lynnette, he studied her as if trying to memorize her every feature. He took the pipe out of his mouth and tucked it in his jacket pocket. As he strode past, he continued to stare.

He wouldn't see much more than his own reflection in her sunglasses. Even so, Lynnette looked away to avoid his gaze. He paid too much attention to her. The case he carried in his right hand caught her eye. It looked exactly like the one she'd lost to Sammy Grick, but she couldn't remember a single identifying characteristic that would tell her for sure. *If I ever get it back, I'll carve my initials across both sides and tie yellow and pink yarn around the handles.*

Lynnette looked over her shoulder once and then again a few seconds later. When the man disappeared through the doors, she picked up her purse and the laptop. His behavior troubled her. He paid too much attention to the people around him. No one else did that.

Get lost in the crowd. Walk down the street. Keep pace with the students. Cross over. Walk back. Look like you know where you're going. Appear preoccupied, but pay attention.

Watch for Blue!

CHAPTER 18

Denver, Colorado
Thursday, January 23

Inside the DU Library, Albert found a quiet corner where he could make a phone call. When he reached Benny Ortega, he asked the obvious question. "How will I know her?"

"Can you get online?" Ortega asked.

"Yes. I'm at the library."

"There's a front-page article in the *Miami Herald*. It's been picked up by the wires. Search on her married name, Lynnette Foster, and you'll see it. There's a picture of her. Read the whole thing. Some guy at the ticket counter in Miami says she had a black eye and her face was all bruised, like she'd been in an accident."

"And she should have Sammy's briefcase," Albert said.

"He was supposed to be carrying a black laptop case. I'm guessing it looked like the bag she had, and that's how Sammy screwed things up. You have her case now?"

"I do. I have it with me."

"Good. Find her. The tracking device is in Sammy's cell phone so we shouldn't have any trouble as long as she keeps that phone."

"And you're sure she's still at this library?"

"My people will call me as soon as she starts moving. Right now, she should be inside the library, in the southwest quadrant. Floor unknown."

"May I ask a question?" Albert said.

"Shoot."

Albert chuckled at Ortega's choice of words. "Am I supposed to kill Foster?"

"That depends," Ortega said. "If everything happens the way I want it to, there will be no need."

"As long as she cannot identify you."

"Or you," Ortega said, and hung up.

Albert headed for the copy machines near the reference desk. It took ten minutes to copy Lynnette Foster's financial papers and the pages of her address book. When he finished, he placed the copies in his jacket pocket, found a computer, and brought up the *Miami Herald*'s website. After reading the article about the death of Glades police officer Carl Foster, he studied the photo of Foster's wife.

She was attractive, maybe late twenties or early thirties. He couldn't tell how tall she was, or the color of her hair, whether she might be wearing it in a ponytail or even have cut it short since the picture was taken. She looked like the dozens of young women he'd observed outside the library roughly thirty minutes earlier. *Like the one sitting on the bench by the sidewalk.*

He thought about her for a moment. Her hair was short, and she didn't carry a case for her laptop. Besides, Ortega had not said Foster was on the move. She should still be inside the library. Time to start looking. He planned to cover the southwest quadrant of the first floor, then the lower level, the first floor again, and then the two floors above. He'd need to recruit a female to check the restrooms. Not a problem. He could be very charming when he wanted to be.

CHAPTER 19

Denver, Colorado
Thursday, January 23

Lynnette walked around the block three times before she stopped at a coffee shop. She felt conspicuous as she traveled the same path over and over, especially when the between-class break ended and fewer students hurried from building to building.

With a large coffee and a cheese sandwich, she picked a small table in the corner near the front window, confident no one could see her while she could easily see everyone who passed or came inside. With her back to the other tables, no one except the inattentive barista was likely to notice the condition of her face. She slid her sunglasses up so they rested on the top of her head and unwrapped her sandwich.

She hadn't realized how hungry she was, but she took her time, savoring every bite. Patting her jacket pockets to see if she had room to carry an extra snack, she felt a moment of panic when her right side pocket felt emptier than it should have. She sucked in her breath and struggled to get inside the jacket, but she already knew. She had lost Sammy Grick's phone.

With a sigh of frustration, she slumped in her chair and bowed her head. Should she go back to the library and look for it? Should she let it go? Where the hell did she leave it? The restroom?

No. Before that. After she'd checked the calls, she had set the phone beside the computer and returned to search the Internet for her own name. She couldn't remember picking the phone up and putting it in her pocket.

She couldn't let it go. These people, whoever they were, could contact her only by phone, specifically that phone. And their location could be traced the same way, once she turned the checks and cash over to the authorities. Could there be something on Sammy's laptop as well?

She pulled the laptop closer and powered it on. There was no system password protection. A quick search of the word processing and spreadsheet software revealed no files. There were no photos, no calendars. She checked the recycle bin and found it empty.

What the hell did he use it for? Did the laptop belong to the fat man, or did it belong to The Cuban? Why would anyone worry about a stupid laptop he could easily replace?

She opened the two browsers whose icons were prominently displayed, and found they brought up the same home page, already signed in with the greeting, Hello, SG, at the top. When Lynnette clicked on Mail, the user ID and password were remembered, but there were no emails in the Inbox or Sent files. No names or addresses were listed in the Contact files. Even the Spam folder was empty. Either Sammy Grick or someone else had scrubbed this computer before beginning his trip, or it was brand new. Now she had no alternative. She had to retrieve the fat man's phone.

She looked at her watch. Blue could arrive at any moment. Lynnette took her trash to the waste bin, picked up her purse and the laptop, and went outside. She pulled her glasses in place, thankful the lenses were big enough to cover almost all of the bruises on her cheekbone and her discolored eye. The makeup on her nose did a decent job of masking the yellow marks.

Traffic was light, and there weren't many students around. She'd have no trouble spotting Blue. The trick would be convincing Blue to leave the car and go into the library to find the cell phone. There might be someone looking for Lynnette, but he wouldn't know Blue.

While she formulated her elaborate plan to drive around the block while Blue went inside, a little voice kept picking at her. "Wait," it said. "The whole idea of sending Blue and Grace to Fort Collins was to get them out of harm's way. Now you want to send Blue into the fray. Does this make sense to you?"

I need that phone.

The little voice had nothing more to say.

Lynnette strolled toward the bus stop at the corner. Before she turned to walk the other way, the Kia pulled to the curb across the street. Blue stuck her head out the window. "You need a ride?"

Lynnette ran across the street and opened the front door on the driver's side. "I left the fat man's phone in the library, but there might be a guy in there looking for me. Would you go ask at the desk?" She gave Blue the fat man's phone number, just in case.

The back window slid open. "I'll go!" yelled Grace. Before Lynnette or Blue could stop her, Grace jumped out and dashed toward the library.

"Oh, no," Lynnette said. "She doesn't even know what part of the library I was in."

"Get in," Blue ordered. "Hurry up. The kid's resourceful. She'll figure it out."

Lynnette climbed inside and slammed the door. Blue handed her a baseball cap. "Put this on."

"Where are you going?"

"Turn your back to the window and act like you're talking to me. I'll ease around the block to the parking meters. Grace will see us when she comes out."

Blue left the engine running while they waited. "What's going on?" she asked. "Who's inside looking for you? The fat guy?"

"No. He's dead. And I'm not sure this other guy is looking for me, but I think they somehow figured out where I am and followed—"

"Dead? How did he get dead?"

"It's a long story. I'll tell you when we get out of here. For now, take my word for it. I saw a man go inside the library. He carried a case that looked like mine. He kept staring at people, like he searched for someone in particular. There's him, and there's The Cuban on the phone, and the lady at the downtown coffee shop who called the cops because I'm a person of interest in my husband's murder."

She stopped when she realized Blue was staring at her in horror. "Oh, sorry, I shouldn't have blurted that out. It's okay, Blue. I didn't do anything wrong."

"You never mentioned anything about your husband being murdered."

"I didn't know. I just read about it online in the library. Somebody cut his throat, but it happened after I left."

"I don't get any of this." Blue looked at Lynnette's jacket, the bulging purse, and the laptop. "What did you do with the fat man's case? And your suitcase?"

"Later. I'll tell you everything later."

Lynnette stared out the window toward the front of the library, her nervousness increasing as the minutes ticked by. She twisted her watch and glanced at it repeatedly. "She's been gone ten minutes. Maybe I should—"

"No way. We'll wait five more, and then I'll go. Don't keep looking out the window. Look at me."

Lynnette turned her back on the library and studied Blue's

expression. "You look a lot different without the black eye makeup."

"Yeah? You look different too. Your nose is turning a very interesting shade of yellowish-greenish-purple. Ish. Your husband did that?"

"He did. One smack with his fist."

"And you cut his throat. Remind me never to make you mad."

"I didn't, Blue. Believe me. I didn't do it."

"Not even in self-defense?"

That's probably what the cops think.

Blue raised her eyebrows at Lynnette's silence. "The fat man's dead, too. You know, the more I think about it, driving here was stupid. Especially with Grace along."

"Honest, I didn't kill anybody, not even in self-defense." Lynnette looked at her watch. "It's time to get Grace."

"Come around here and sit behind the wheel." Blue got out of the car and held the door open for Lynnette. Then she jogged toward the building, ran up the steps, and disappeared inside.

The next few minutes passed so slowly, Lynnette thought her watch might have stopped. She tapped her fingers on the steering wheel, adjusted the heater fan, and compared the time on her watch to the clock on the dashboard. She was searching her purse for coins for the parking meter, preparing to leave the car parked while she looked for Blue and Grace, when she spotted them running down the library steps. Grace held Blue's left hand and seemed to struggle to keep up with the older girl's long stride. Blue held a cell phone in her right hand. She waved it at Lynnette as they raced across the lawn toward the car.

Lynnette threw the car door open and hopped out so Blue could drive. Grace and Lynnette scrambled in the passenger-side seats and slammed their doors. Blue jumped in the driver's seat. "Seatbelts!" she yelled, shifting into Drive.

"What happened?" Lynnette turned as far to the left as she

could and looked at Grace. "Are you okay?"

"Sure. Why?"

"You were gone a long time."

"I had to pee. The janitor put a closed sign in front of the first-floor restroom, so I had to go downstairs."

"This happened after you had the phone?"

"Yeah. That was easy. I saw a Lost and Found sign at the reference desk. I said my scatterbrained mom left her phone and did they have any turned in within the last hour or so. The lady still had this one sitting on the counter. We checked the number and it matched, so I took it. But then I had to go to the bathroom. I knew we had to ride all the way to Fort Collins, so—"

"Nothing bad happened? No one bothered you?"

"Not exactly. A guy had a case like yours, Lynnette, and he kept walking back and forth, looking around. When he saw me get the phone, he stopped and watched. Then he went to the big lobby and took out his phone. I went downstairs, and when I came out of the restroom, he was hanging around. He asked me who the cell phone belonged to, and I said it belonged to my dad and anyway I wasn't supposed to talk to strangers. I told him I'm supposed to start yelling if anybody bothers me, so he'd better get out of my way."

Blue laughed. "That's cool, Grace. You're something else, you know that?"

"That's what I'm supposed to do. And I'm supposed to run like the wind to get away from anyone I don't know."

Lynnette raised her eyebrows. "Then why did you follow me off the airplane and all the way to the bus station?"

"You weren't a stranger. The airplane lady introduced us, and you didn't even want to talk to me, so I knew you weren't weird or anything. Look, there's the guy." Grace ducked down and slid to the floor. "Is he looking this way?"

Lynnette kept her face turned away from the library, but Blue glanced toward the building as she crossed the intersection heading toward the interstate. "That guy with the case? Do you think that's yours, Lynnette? Should I go back around? You could jump out and grab it."

"And what if it's not mine? And even if it is, he'd have your license plate and he'd see you and probably see Grace. Not a chance. Keep going."

"Stop!" Grace screeched so loud that Lynnette slapped her hands over her ears.

Blue jerked the car toward the curb and slammed on the brakes. Grace opened the door. Blue reached out to grab her, but Grace jumped out and ran across the lawn.

Blue left the engine running and chased after Grace.

Without thinking, Lynnette opened her door and ran after them.

Grace caught up with the man first. She approached him from behind and grabbed for the handle of the case. She tried to yank it out of his hand, but he reacted too fast. He jerked the case toward his body, pulling Grace with it. With his free hand, he took hold of Grace's wrist and held on. A man riding past on a bicycle applied his brakes, spotted Blue coming to the rescue and pedaled away.

Blue hit the man from behind with her full weight, knocking him off his feet. Unable to stop her forward momentum, she fell on top of him. Grace, now free, took the laptop case and ran toward Lynnette. The man struggled to his feet. He had Blue hugged to his chest. He craned his neck to see which way Grace had run. Waving Grace toward the car, Lynnette continued her dash toward Blue, whose legs flailed wildly as she fought to get away.

Out of breath and acting on pure instinct, Lynnette ran straight for the man and kicked him hard on one knee. He lost his balance and fell with Blue on top of him. Lynnette kicked him again, this time connecting with his elbow. He yelled and released Blue. She scrambled to her feet and raced toward the car. The man rolled to a sitting position, cradling his injured elbow as he eyed Lynnette. She backed away. He looked past her, in the direction of the car.

Lynnette glanced over her shoulder, saw Grace climb into the back seat with the laptop case, and Blue round the front of the car as she headed for the driver's side. The man studied their faces. The thing Lynnette feared most—getting Blue and Grace involved in her troubles—was exactly what had happened.

"You can't get away, Lynnette Foster," the man called out as she inched backward. "We'll find you."

"Who are you? What do you want? The fat man's laptop? I'll get it now."

"That would help. But you could save us all a lot of trouble by giving me everything you stole from Sammy Grick. It belongs to my boss, and he wants it all back." The man scrambled to his feet and took a step toward her. "Get it. I'll wait here." He winced and seemed to hold his breath.

Lynnette ran to the car, grabbed the fat man's laptop, and pulled the power cord from her purse. She held them up for the man to see, placed them on the curb, then got back in the car. Blue maneuvered into the street and shouted, "Seatbelts!" as she drove away. Lynnette looked over her shoulder and watched as the man crossed the grass to retrieve the laptop. Blue turned the corner and sped away before Lynnette could see what he did next.

CHAPTER 20

Denver, Colorado
Thursday, January 23

Albert Getz knew his left elbow was dislocated, if not broken. He tried to keep his arm stiff. He held it close to his side to minimize the pain, but when he leaned over to pick up the laptop, he bumped his left hand. Sweat popped out on his forehead. He nearly cried out. There was no way to avoid it. He needed to go to the nearest emergency room and have his elbow X-rayed.

When he reached his car, he popped two of the prescription painkillers he always carried before jotting down the license number of the car in which Lynnette Foster and her young friends had escaped.

He put off the most important task until last. Retrieving his phone from his pocket, he dialed Benny Ortega's number.

"I retrieved Grick's laptop," Albert said.

"I don't give a fuck about the laptop. Where's Sammy's case?"

"As far as I know, the Foster woman still has it."

"How did you get the laptop?"

Albert told Ortega what had happened at the library. The silence from Ortega would have been frightening if Albert feared the man. However, all Albert could think about was his elbow.

"They saw you," Ortega said after the silence had lasted an uncomfortable thirty seconds.

"I'm afraid so."

"Does she still have the phone?"

"I'm figuring that phone is the one the kid picked up in the library. If she hadn't gone after it, we would have been screwed. I would have been looking for Foster inside the library while someone picked her up outside."

"But you'd still have her case, laptop and papers."

Albert acknowledged that with a silence of his own.

"You've lost our only bargaining tool."

"We can trade your belongings for her life," Albert said. He offered the idea to Ortega with the tone of a man who wouldn't hesitate to carry out the threat, but Albert only killed killers and men who hired killers. The innocent women and the feisty kid were in no danger whatsoever, at least not from him.

Ortega didn't say anything.

Albert waited a moment, then cleared his throat. "Mr. Ortega, what am I looking for? Papers? Drugs? How will I know if I have everything that belongs to you?"

This time Ortega answered right away. "We'll talk about that when you catch up to her. You said you had a license number. Give it to me. I'll contact my tracker and find out which way they're headed. I'll call as soon as I know."

"Fine. I'm heading for the emergency room to get my elbow checked."

"Keep your phone on."

Albert drew a deep breath as he ended the call. He'd been working for Ortega for five years, trying to find something that he could turn over to the Feds so Ortega would spend years in prison. He wanted him to suffer the same pain and humiliation Albert's brother had experienced when Ortega set him up in a drug deal gone bad. Albert's brother, the innocent owner of the body shop where the raid went down, died in prison. Albert walked out on his teaching job, adopted a new identity and went to work for Ortega. Being a hit man wasn't such a bad gig.

He got to kill plenty of slimeballs, and that didn't bother him one bit. And he made big bucks. He'd already earned enough to retire on, but he had one more important thing on his to-do list—take down Benito Ortega.

Albert made two more phone calls before he turned off his phone, the first to Sammy Grick's number. He left a message for Lynnette that he'd been ordered to collect all of Sammy Grick's possessions. He said he would be in touch very soon.

After a short chat with the Information operator, Albert started his car and drove to the nearest emergency room. He didn't tell the nurses about the painkillers he'd already taken before they removed his jacket and shirt for the X-ray. By the time a nurse hooked him up to an IV so the orthopedic surgeon could realign his elbow, Albert's pain had brought him to tears. He didn't care what they did to him or how long he slept afterward.

As Blue maneuvered her car out of the city onto I-25 and headed north, no one spoke. Lynnette was still shaken at how close Grace had come to getting caught by the man in the tweed jacket. Had he replaced Sammy Grick? If so, he sure seemed a different sort of thug than the fat man.

Or could he be a cop? Lynnette caught her breath. Oh, hell, what if he was a cop? She'd kicked him twice. Assault? On a police officer? What next?

The man had watched them leave, probably had their license number, certainly knew what they looked like. And he had called her by her name. She blew out a big breath of air and slumped in her seat. Whether he was a good guy or a bad guy, he knew her name.

"Blue, will your license number lead the guy in the library to your house on campus?"

"No. My dad transferred the car to me before I moved out. It has my dad's address on it." Blue reached over and patted Lynnette on the shoulder. "It'll be okay." She glanced in her rearview mirror and added, "At least, it'll be okay if we can keep that one under control. Hey, Grace, if you ever pull a stunt like that again, I'll personally skin you alive. From now on, you don't even wiggle unless Lynnette or I tell you to. Got it?"

"Got it."

Lynnette thought the girl sounded unusually subdued, but she couldn't see her because of the headrest. "You okay, Grace?"

"Yeah. I just wish my dad was here." Her voice shook.

"Me, too," Blue said. "He'd whip your butt for pulling a stunt like that. You know how lucky you are?"

"Yeah. Thanks, Blue." Grace's arms encircled Blue's neck in a hug before sliding out of Lynnette's view.

Blue patted Lynnette's shoulder again. "Guess I owe you one."

"And I owe you about ten. Where are we going?"

"First, we're going to stop and get gas while I call my dad and tell him we're in deep shit. Then, we're going to his house so we can all be in deep shit together."

"I'm sure he'll appreciate that."

"Yeah." Blue didn't flash Lynnette one of her sassy grins. She turned into the parking lot of a gas station connected to a convenience store and a fast-food restaurant and pulled up to one of the pumps. "I'm going to fill it up. Get me a burger, fries, and a small chocolate shake, will you? And better hurry. That creep might be right behind us."

CHAPTER 21

I-25 north of Denver
Thursday, January 23
Lynnette and Blue ate in silence, Blue waiting until traffic had thinned a bit north of Denver before she tackled driving and eating at the same time. Lynnette noted the girl was a good driver, alert and watchful. She glanced back once to check on Grace and saw she'd wadded her jacket under her head, leaned against the window, and was fast asleep.

The day had turned gray and the clouds hung low over the mountains to the west. They passed shopping malls and industrial complexes before leaving town. There was little to see after that except farmland, brown and barren until spring. She didn't intend to think about Carl, but when an image of her husband lying dead in their bed sprang into her mind, tears came unexpectedly. She sniffed, searched her jacket pocket for a tissue, and blew her nose.

"What's wrong?" asked Blue.

Lynnette took a deep breath and let it out. "I'll tell you later."

Blue leaned forward and peered through the windshield. "Lots of brake lights going on and off up ahead. Wonder if there's been a wreck."

Lynnette looked outside. *What next?*

They were a few miles north of Boulder when it began to snow and the wind picked up. Traffic slowed as the visibility dropped. Still, Blue seemed confident. Even though they saw a couple of vans that had slid off the road, Blue kept her car under control. Lynnette stayed awake and watchful. She welcomed the excuse to be alert and focused on traffic instead of dwelling on the horrible events that had altered her immediate plans. Her whole life, for that matter.

This time it was Lynnette who saw the brake lights come on in rapid succession in a line of cars ahead. "Look out!" she yelled. "Someone got rear-ended up there and cars are sliding all over the place."

Blue eased off the accelerator and moved further to the left in an effort to see up ahead. In minutes, traffic had come to a complete stop. Hazard lights flashed all around them.

Grace stirred in the back seat and sat up with a yawn. "Why are we stopping?"

"Looks like a wreck," said Blue.

"There must be an off-ramp ahead," Lynnette said. "You can see cars going off to the right."

"They're heading for the frontage road," Blue said. She edged to the right, trying to pull around the traffic, but the snow made it too difficult to see where the interstate stopped and the ditch began. A pickup truck ahead of her tried the same maneuver and successfully drove all the way to the exit. Blue followed in his tracks. At the top of the ramp, Blue turned left and stayed close behind the truck, all the way into the parking lot of a truck stop.

"I need to go inside and find out what the road conditions are like the rest of the way to Fort Collins," she said. "We might as well get coffee while we're here."

"And eat," said Grace. "I want a grilled cheese."

"Girl, you can't be hungry already," Blue said.

Lynnette said, "It's okay, Blue. We might get stuck here for a while, and Library Guy's probably too far behind to catch up, especially if the roads are getting this bad around Denver."

"You want something?"

"No, but let Grace have whatever she wants."

After learning which roads had been plowed and sanded, they piled into the car and continued north. Because of the icy packed snow, they made slow progress. A jack-knifed semi blocked their path at one point, forcing them to backtrack and take another route. It was well after midnight when Blue drove into Fort Collins.

Glades, Florida
Thursday, January 23

By evening, after Maggie Gutierrez had worked her butt off for seventeen straight hours, she couldn't wait to go home, take a hot bath, eat a peanut butter sandwich, and go to bed.

She had started the day with the grisly discovery of Carl Foster's body and reveled in the unexpected chance to help Detective Prince investigate a murder. Her partner had been ignored. She felt guilty about that, until she found herself acting as gofer instead of assistant to the homicide cop with an ego the size of the Hindenburg.

By afternoon, however, Prince had stopped barking orders. When Maggie threw out an insulting comment about his caffeine and sugar intake aggravating an already obnoxious personality, Prince acknowledged her presence. "You got balls," he said.

She drew herself up to her full height of five foot eleven inches. "Yes, I do. I also have brains and common sense. If you're not going to assign me to do any real work, I'd like to go home and get some sleep so I can work my normal shift tonight, during which my partner and I will fight crime."

"I can't assign you to do real work, Gutierrez. You're a patrol cop. You want to work Homicide, you need to pay your dues first, then pass the test. If you do that, you get to do 'real work.' "

"Like what?"

"Like tracking the wife's whereabouts."

"Lynnette Foster? You want me to find Lynnette Foster?"

"What did I just say? No. You're not Homicide. No, no, no. Do not touch this case."

He means yes, but he doesn't want anyone to know. Maggie looked at the clock on the wall. Seven o'clock. She walked away. She'd be lucky to get the job done by Friday noon. She sure as hell wouldn't accomplish anything in the next few hours, at night, with some departments closed and others manned by a skeleton crew, with no normal businesses open. And she couldn't even get a good start until she had gathered a little more information from the Foster home. If by some miracle she could turn up Lynnette Foster's Social Security number and credit card numbers, it would help.

Screw Prince and his no that meant yes. She needed a meal and a nap.

After the ten-minute drive home, over her peanut butter sandwich and a cup of coffee, she had second thoughts. Fifteen minutes later she parked in front of Foster's house and showed her badge to the officer assigned to keep the neighbors away from the crime scene.

Getting the information she needed was easy. There were three file folders in the drawer of a small desk in the bedroom, labeled Lynnette, Carl, and Joint. The Joint folder contained very little except the pages that had accompanied two new credit card applications.

Lynnette's folder held copies of her investment account statements, credit card invoices marked Paid on a card in the name of Lynnette Hudson, photocopies of her Social Security card and her Florida driver's license, and a printout of her email contacts with her own email address handwritten at the top of the page.

Maggie wrote down all the information she thought she'd need, lingering for a moment over the healthy balance in Lynnette's investment account. Then she tucked her notebook and pen into her pocket and went back to the station. When she returned to her desk in the squad room, she sent Lynnette Foster an email:

This is Maggie Gutierrez of the Glades Police Department. I need to speak with you on an urgent matter. Email me at this address, or call me.

Maggie added her telephone numbers and her police department signature. When she hit Send, she wondered whether Lynnette would answer.

With a cup of the vile black liquid the night shift called coffee in front of her, the list of credit card numbers, and the phone book open to the cab companies listed in the yellow pages, Maggie began making calls. Then she turned to the list of airlines. Occasionally, she reached for her mouse and refreshed her email Inbox.

"You been working all day?" Dan said as he approached her desk.

Maggie glanced up and grimaced. "In a manner of speaking. You can probably guess what I did for the first few hours—toted coffee and donuts to Homicide and ran errands."

He grinned, the little lift at the corner of his mouth telling her he enjoyed seeing her chopped down to size. With a tilt of his head, he indicated her computer monitor. "What now?"

"I'm making calls, catching up on paperwork."

"No more errands for Detective Prince?"

"Hell, no. He dumped me. I wanted to try and track the wife, but he said no."

Dan edged around Maggie's desk. "Don't mess with him or his case, Maggie. He'll kill your career."

She clicked the box to minimize the screen. "What if Lynnette Foster doesn't know her husband is dead? What if she's visiting friends, or went to a spa. Maybe she hasn't—"

Maggie grabbed the phone when it rang, then listened to a surly cab driver tell her about the bruises all over the face of the female passenger he'd picked up at the Foster residence the day before. She thanked him, then placed the phone in its cradle and rested her head in her hands. She was so tired.

"You need to get some sleep," Dan said. "Thirty, forty-five minutes, you'll feel better. I'll stay here and cover for you until it's time for me to clock in."

Maggie studied his face, wondered if she could trust him not to run to Detective Prince and report his suspicions, realized she had a serious problem if she couldn't trust her own partner and agreed. She slid into the back seat of her car, set her watch alarm for thirty minutes and dozed off.

CHAPTER 22

Fort Collins, Colorado
Friday, January 24
Friday morning. I should have been safe and sound at Ramona's by now. Instead, here they were in the wee hours of the morning, driving to the home of a man who probably had no desire to get pulled into her problems.

Lynnette looked at Blue. "I don't think we should involve your dad in this."

"What's the alternative?"

"You dump me at the bus station and I'll get out of your life."

"You're not very good at this hide-and-seek stuff, are you?"

"What do you mean?"

"The guy you kicked the shit out of saw the license number on my car. If he has any sources at all, he can get the name and address off the registration. My address is my dad's address. Dad's already involved, no matter where you go. And I've already called him."

"I'm sorry, Blue. I should never have let this happen."

"True. But this is the way it turned out. We need to pick up my dad and keep him safe."

Lynnette couldn't help but laugh. "With us?"

Blue glanced at her sharply, then realized what she'd said. "What are we going to do, Lynnette? How do we get rid of these men? Shouldn't we take our chances with the FBI?

They're not going to do anything bad to Grace if her father's an agent too."

Grace slapped her hands onto the top of Lynnette's headrest and said, "Stop."

Blue checked the rearview mirror and started to put her foot on the brake.

"No," Grace said. "I mean stop talking about all that stuff." She began to cry and talk at the same time, jumbling her words and sobs so Lynnette could barely understand her.

"Maybe you better find a place to pull off," Lynnette told Blue.

Lynnette put her hand on Grace's shoulder, but Grace pulled back and bent over her lap, her head cradled in her arms. She cried as though her heart would break.

Blue pulled into a supermarket lot and parked under a light. Lynnette opened her door and stepped out into the swirling snow. She got into the back seat with Grace and slid close to her, then began to gently stroke the child's back.

"What's wrong, Grace," she whispered. "What haven't you told us?"

Blue stretched her arm over the seat back and put her hand on Grace's head. "You're okay, kid," she said. "We'll be okay."

In an obvious effort to bring her tears under control, Grace sat up straight, rubbed her eyes, and took a deep, shuddering breath, then another.

Blue rummaged in the center console and produced a travel packet of tissues. She opened the package and handed it to Grace.

After wiping her eyes and blowing her nose, Grace leaned against the seat and clenched her hands in her lap.

"What's up, Grace?" Lynnette said.

Grace didn't turn her head to make eye contact with Lynnette. Instead, she looked at Blue and said, "I lied."

"Join the crowd. What did *you* lie about?" Blue said.

"My dad."

"You mean . . . he's not in the FBI?" Lynnette said.

"Not exactly."

Lynnette felt the skin prickle along her arms. The skin on her face felt hot. This was going to be something bad, real bad, she thought, almost afraid to ask. But she had to know. "What exactly does your dad do, and when is he coming back?"

As she watched Grace's face, she saw tears welling up again in the girl's eyes. Lynnette's heart seemed to sink toward her stomach.

"Oh, Grace," Blue said. "Your dad . . . he's—"

"Dead. He's dead. He's dead. I'm sorry. I'm so sorry I told you he was in the FBI and you thought he might be able to help us." Grace's words began to mix with her hiccups and sobs and her next words were almost unintelligible. "I'm sorry I went to get your case and the man saw our license and now Blue's dad might be in trouble, too." She wailed the next words, "It's all my fault."

Lynnette leaned against the door and stared at Grace, not knowing what to say or do. She had never completely trusted the girl's story about why she traveled alone, where she had come from and where she was going, but she had never doubted the existence of Grace's father who would be home from Afghanistan on Sunday. She shifted her gaze to Blue, who watched Grace with her eyebrows raised.

Blue made eye contact with Lynnette, shook her head and said, "Buckle up, ladies. We'll work this out after we get to my house."

It took another thirty minutes before Blue eased onto a steep road heading up the hill on the west side of Fort Collins. She crept upward, the snow crunching beneath the tires, until she took a sudden turn onto an even steeper driveway. Blue accelerated to fishtail through the snow, barely avoiding the trees that lined the path. When she braked and slid to a stop, the car rested sideways in front of a two-story brick home. Using the remote opener that rested in a cubbyhole below the radio, Blue raised the three-car garage door and pulled the car inside. A burgundy-colored sedan sat in the next bay, and beyond that, a large pickup truck with a snow blade attached to the front end. The garage door slid closed behind them.

Before she opened the driver's-side door, she looked over her shoulder at Lynnette and Grace. "Before we go in," she said, "I want to warn you not to lie to my father. He has a built-in bullshit detector. If you don't level with him, he'll call the cops and turn you over without a second thought.

"Also . . . Lynnette . . . before we picked you up, when Grace went to the bathroom at the house in town, I watched the headline news. I already knew about your problem." She glanced at Grace, who seemed to take a sudden interest in the conversation.

"What?" Grace asked. "What was on the news? What problem?"

"We'll talk about it inside," Blue said. She opened her door and got out.

"What?" Grace turned to Lynnette. "What's she talking about?"

"Something bad happened to my husband in Florida, Grace. I don't know very much about it yet."

"Is he dead?"

Lynnette nodded.

Blue opened the back door and motioned Lynnette out. Grace slid across the seat and stepped out behind her. As Lynnette followed Blue to the door that led inside the house, she felt Grace take her hand and hold on. Lynnette pulled the girl close to her side.

CHAPTER 23

Near Fort Collins, Colorado
Friday, January 24

Blue led them into the kitchen from the garage and stopped when she saw the man sitting at the kitchen table, a cup of steaming liquid cradled between his hands. "Daddy, what are you doing up?"

Lynnette glanced at her watch, then at the man she presumed to be Blue's father. He was fully dressed. A set of car keys lay on the table not far from his right hand.

He stood up to hug his daughter. "I stayed up late to watch an old movie on TV and decided to check my voice mail before turning in. I heard the weather reports and watched the ten o'clock news. Cars off the road, half a dozen accidents. After I got your message and realized you were out in this weather, I wanted to be ready in case I received a call from the police or a hospital."

"I'm sorry, Daddy," Blue stepped away from his embrace and touched Lynnette on the arm. "This is Lynnette Foster. The young 'un is Grace."

Blue's father shifted his gaze to Lynnette and sucked in his breath when he saw her discolored eye and cheek. "I'm Thomas Young," he said. "What happened to you?"

Lynnette took his hand, felt comforted by its warmth, sensed safety when he placed his left hand over hers.

"Teresa said you were in trouble and she had to save you.

What kind of trouble are we talking about?"

"It's a mess, Mr. Young. I'm afraid I've made the situation worse by coming here."

"Please. Call me Thomas." With a sweeping motion of his hand, he gestured toward the chairs around the table. "Sit down. Tell me what happened." He fetched the coffee pot and two more cups and brought them to the table. "Grace, would you like a cup of hot chocolate?"

"Yes, please."

He heated a cup of water in the microwave and stirred in a packet of cocoa mix as Lynnette related what had happened in Denver and why they might need to leave Fort Collins. When she reached the part where Grace had announced her father's death, they all turned to look at the girl.

"Is there anything you want to tell us, Grace?" Thomas asked.

She squirmed uncomfortably in her chair. "I guess."

He gave her a firm but sympathetic, fatherly look. "Just the truth, okay?"

"Okay," she whispered.

Lynnette glanced at her watch again. It was nearly three o'clock in the morning.

Grace looked at Lynnette first. "I'm sorry I lied, but if I'd told you the truth, you wouldn't have believed me. I know I should have stayed on the plane, but I felt sick and that creepy fat guy stared at me, and I thought the flight would get cancelled and I wouldn't get to Los Angeles in time . . ."

"In time for what?" Thomas asked.

Grace started to cry again, but she wiped her eyes with the back of her hand and coughed, then looked directly at Thomas. She cleared her throat. "In time for my father's body to arrive. If I'm not there, he won't have anyone."

By then, Lynnette was tearing up, but noticed Blue's eyes narrow. The older girl didn't seem touched by Grace's story.

Lynnette looked at Grace and watched her more closely.

Thomas said, "I'm so sorry, Grace. I realize this is hard, but we need to know the truth. If there's any way we can help, we will. You're telling us your father's body is being flown into Los Angeles on Sunday?"

Grace nodded.

"Was he in Afghanistan, like you said?"

"Yes."

"Was he really in the FBI?"

"Yes."

"Do you know what he was doing in Afghanistan?"

"No. It was secret."

"What about your mother? Where is she?"

"I don't have a mother."

Thomas looked at Lynnette and raised his eyebrows. She shrugged. "Grace told me her mom took her to the airport and then left for a vacation with her new boyfriend." Lynnette turned to Grace and stretched her arm across the table.

Grace took her hands out of her lap and clasped them on the table in front of her but did not touch Lynnette.

"If you don't have a mom," Lynnette said, "then how did you buy a ticket and get through Security and board that plane by yourself? It's not possible for a kid to do that these days."

Grace sighed. "I told you about my Aunt Maxie. She's real. She's my mom's sister. I live with her. None of the stuff I said about my mom is true except what Aunt Maxie says, that Mom is a slut. She left when I was a baby. I don't know where she is."

"So your Aunt Maxie took you to the airport and sent you to Los Angeles all alone to meet your dad's flight? Grace, that doesn't make sense," Thomas said. "Who was supposed to pick you up in L.A.?"

Grace took a deep breath, then blew it out. "A friend of hers."

"Does your aunt know where you are now?" he asked.

"Yes. I've been calling her. She's mad. I keep calling her and telling her I'm okay and she keeps yelling at me to tell her where I am and who I'm with and threatening to call the police."

Lynnette's stomach clenched at the thought of Grace's aunt calling the cops. "What about all those calls you left for your dad? The messages I left?"

Grace lowered her head to her hands. "I don't know. His number is still working, but I guess nobody answers it." She raised her head and glanced at Thomas, Blue, and then Lynnette. "I've only got two days left. I have to get to Los Angeles." Tears were once again streaming down her cheeks.

"You're sure not the same kid I met in the bus station in Denver," said Blue.

Grace raised her head and stared. "What?"

"The kid I met there was smart and tough and had everything under control. Now you're like a street kid. You change your story and your plan depending on the circumstances and who you think you can fool. When one plan fails, you come up with another one. What went wrong between Denver and here, Grace?"

"Teresa," Thomas said. "Don't."

Blue ignored her father. "Seriously, Grace, nobody changes this fast. First you're strong and now you're all weepy? Will the real Grace please stand up?"

Grace stood, her hands clenched at her side. "What do you know about it, Blue? You pretend to be someone you aren't all the time and act like it's all for school or something. It's still lies."

She turned to Lynnette. "You aren't what you pretend to be, either. If you were, you wouldn't be running away and you wouldn't have all these scary people after you." She looked at Thomas. "Did you see anything on the news about Lynnette?

141

Are the police looking for her? Do they think she killed her husband?"

Grace backed away from the table. "I don't care about any of you. I only want one thing. I want to get to Los Angeles by Sunday. How can I do that?"

"We're not finished here, Grace. Please sit down." Thomas turned to Lynnette. "Your turn. What's Grace talking about?"

Lynnette started with Carl's unexpected temper tantrum on Wednesday and briefly touched on all the events that followed. Blue seemed to sigh in relief when Lynnette explained that she didn't know of Carl's death until she got on the Internet at the library. Even Grace visibly relaxed as she heard Lynnette out. By the time Lynnette had answered all their questions, it was after five o'clock.

Thomas remained silent for a few minutes. Then he pushed his chair back and stood. "We're not going anywhere until this storm lets up. Last I checked, we were getting over an inch of snow an hour. The weather report said the winds should die by mid-afternoon and the snow change to light flurries. The security system is on, we have electricity and heat, and there's plenty of food. I suggest you all try to get a little sleep." He studied Lynnette's bruised face for a moment. "Did you take pictures?"

"No."

He picked up his phone and aimed it at her face from several angles. "You might need these later," he said. "Always take pictures." He put the phone in his pocket. "What else do I need to know?"

Lynnette pulled Sammy Grick's phone out of her pocket and showed it to him. "They're probably using this phone to find me," she said.

Thomas took the cell phone and looked it over. He turned it off and removed the battery. "It might be too late," he said, "but it's worth a try. If you need to make a call, put the battery in and turn it on." He handed it back.

"Are you sure that's the way it works?"

"Not one hundred percent. The technology changes too fast for me to keep up."

"What do we do if the guy from the library shows up here?"

Thomas pointed to a narrow, locked cabinet tucked between the refrigerator and the pantry door. "Do you know how to handle a shotgun?"

"Yes."

"Good. Sack out on the couch if you want. I'll let you know if I need you."

CHAPTER 24

Denver, Colorado
Friday, January 24

In the Denver hospital, Albert awoke to the clatter of rolling gurneys and supply carts. His elbow pain had been reduced to a deep, intense ache. Apparently he'd be released with only a sling because his left arm was bandaged with his elbow bent.

It was nearly five. He needed to get to his phone. By now Ortega had probably worked himself into a snit. Albert chuckled. Maybe he'd have a stroke and die.

Albert pushed himself to a sitting position with his right hand when he realized his IV had been removed while he slept. After dangling his feet from the side of the gurney for a couple of minutes, he slid off the bed and stood. Other than a bit of residual grogginess from the extra painkillers he'd taken, he felt steady enough. No dizziness. No disorientation. As a matter of fact, he felt as though he'd had the best night's sleep of his life. A cup of coffee and his pipe would make things much better.

A nurse poked her head through the curtain, then whisked it open. She pulled a package off the shelf of a metal cabinet, tore it open, and unfolded the fabric sling. Once she fastened it around his neck, the nurse patted his arm as though to admire her handiwork. "You're free to go, Mr. Getz, but you need to keep this on for the next couple of days. Don't drive for the next twenty-four hours. This packet contains four more Vicodin.

If the pain persists beyond two days, you'll need to see your own doctor."

Los Angeles, California
Friday, January 24

Earlier, after Benny spoke to his tracker and identified the location of the phone Foster hopefully still had in her possession, he left three messages for Getz. His phone rang five times before going to voice mail on the first two calls. On the third, the voice mail bimbo said, "The party is not available." Had Getz turned off his phone?

Benny had gone to bed, but he was so pissed off he couldn't sleep. All he could think about was how Fat Ass Sammy had screwed up his operation and croaked before Benny could dish out an appropriate punishment. Along with his other business ventures, Benny ran one of the biggest check-theft rings in the country. Losing over three million bucks as a result of one stupid mistake could not be tolerated. And to have those checks in the hands of this Foster broad, who might even snoop through them and figure out where they came from, was even more of a disaster. She might turn him in. She might try for a share of the take. She might fucking blackmail him for the rest of his life . . . at least until he got rid of her.

At four a.m., before he'd even had his first cup of coffee, Benny tried to call Getz again with no success. He wondered what the reading would be if he took his blood pressure.

After room service arrived, he took his coffee to the hotel room window and looked through the glass toward the ocean. The early-morning haze seemed lighter than it had been in years past, but Benny still couldn't see the water. He thought about Sammy again. Fat Ass Sammy Grick had been an outstanding screw-up all his life, but a useful screw-up. Benny usually hired him to do courier jobs, or to deliver a message.

People who owed Benny Ortega knew all about Fat Ass Sammy and his temper. Sammy scared people. Benny liked to scare people.

Why in hell, of all the people in the world, did his stuff end up in the hands of a woman being sought for the murder of her husband, a woman who would be caught in a matter of days? He had to find her before the cops did.

Time was running out. The only way to steal big checks was to establish a network of employees in critical jobs and strike fast. Take a check (preferably not a computer-generated document), alter it as needed, transport it out of state as fast as possible, deposit it in a new account under a fictitious name, buy a commodity such as gold coins with the funds, close the account, and move on. The checks he'd sent Sammy to pick up had been delivered to his home on Tuesday evening. They should have been in his hands before the banks opened on Thursday.

It was only a matter of time before the intended recipients questioned their customers about the missing payments. Customers might blame the post office for a day or so, but eventually they had to stop payment and issue a new check. At that point, the stolen checks would be worthless.

He had to get the checks back fast. To do that, he had to get them away from Foster. Getz had to find her. Before trying the assassin's phone again, Ortega called his tracker to find out where Foster and her little friends had gone after disabling Getz and driving away. He dialed Sammy's cell phone, hoping to confirm what the tracker reported, but no one answered.

Before he could dial again, the phone rang. "This is Ortega."

"This is Getz. Do you have a fix on Foster and the kids?"

"I've been calling you all night!" Ortega yelled. "I told you not to turn off your phone!"

Getz sighed. "I spent the night in the hospital, Mr. Ortega.

They must have turned off the phone after I conked out from the drugs."

"I don't care if you just got off the fucking Space Shuttle. If you can't follow orders, you don't work for me."

"Okay. I got it. Tell me where they are."

Ortega wasn't sure Getz's tone sounded sufficiently subservient, but that would have to wait. Right now, he needed the man to track down the envelope and do what Fat Ass Sammy had failed to accomplish.

"They're in Fort Collins," he said. "It's north on I-25, maybe an hour from the library where those little girls took you down. Here's the address."

CHAPTER 25

Denver, Colorado
Friday, January 24

Albert had no intention of heading north on I-25 to Fort Collins until he'd shaved, brushed his teeth, and had breakfast. He stopped at a McDonald's near the interstate and took his sweet time doing everything he felt needed to get done before setting out to do Benny Ortega's bidding. The same article about Lynnette Foster he'd skimmed on the Internet at the library the day before appeared on the second page of the newspaper he read while drinking his coffee. *A person of interest. Who would have guessed?* Maybe he was damned lucky he only got a dislocated elbow out of their brief encounter.

He wondered who the other woman and the kid were. The article didn't mention anyone traveling with Foster. He saved that section, then folded the rest of the paper and dropped it in the waste can with his trash. Sammy's phone number still went directly to voice mail. Albert left a message requesting that Lynnette call him back. He took the on-ramp to I-25 and drove into a heavy snowstorm at a quarter to six.

Halfway to Fort Collins, the storm intensified. The wind blew the heavy snow sideways, and Albert drove into a whiteout. The car tires slipped on the road. He eased his pressure on the accelerator. A bit further north, deep piles of snow lined the road. He scraped the passenger side of the car along the plowed banks that were barely distinguishable from the road before steering into the truck tracks he strained to see. An occasional abandoned car loomed before him, some trapped in snow banks. He slowed even more.

Brake lights flared a few feet ahead, tall lights that indicated he'd followed in the tire tracks of a truck, then a right turn signal flashed. Albert crept along behind the vehicle, down a curving ramp and onto a two-lane road that appeared to have been plowed at least once. Continuing to follow the truck, Albert saw the yellow hazy glare of parking area lights ahead. Then the running lights of at least thirty semis. And finally, a building lit inside and glowing through fogged-over windows. He maneuvered through the lot until he found a spot where he could nose his car up to a giant pile of snow. Seconds later he sat in front of a plate of scrambled eggs, bacon, a huge cinnamon roll dripping with melted icing and a mug of coffee. He wrapped his hands around the cup and lifted it to his lips.

Glades, Florida
Friday, January 24
"Gutierrez!" Detective Prince barked.

Maggie jumped and sat up straight. After grabbing the quick nap in her car, she had returned to her desk and concentrated on her calls. Focused so intently on her efforts to locate Lynnette Foster, Maggie hadn't heard the detective come in the door.

He stopped in front of her desk. "We got another one. I need someone to drive."

"Another body?"

"No, an alien invasion. Of course a body. You coming?"

"Hell, yes." She looked across the room at her partner who watched her without expression as he poured a cup of coffee. Maggie glanced at her computer monitor, refreshed the screen and confirmed she had no new emails. Grabbing her jacket off the back of her chair, she followed Prince out the door.

Near Fort Collins, Colorado
Friday, January 24

Lynnette checked on Grace and found her already asleep in Blue's room, her head cushioned by a pillow with a pink flannel cover. Grace clutched her phone in her hand, the charger plugged into a wall outlet. Lynnette checked the display to make sure the phone was fully charged, then unplugged it from the wall and laid the cord on the bed. She closed the door and went into the darkened living room. "I should check my email before I lie down," she said, mostly to herself. She spoke a little louder for Thomas and Blue to hear. "The guy I used to work for in Indianapolis tried to reach me. I should see what he wants."

Thomas said a few words to Blue, but Lynnette didn't hear. Blue walked over to the wall phone in the kitchen and punched in a number.

Lynnette leaned forward. "What's going on? Who are you calling?"

"She's calling CDOT," Thomas said. "The Colorado Department of Transportation updates weather and road conditions. Teresa, get I-25 south to Denver, I-70 west of Denver through Utah, and I-25 south to New Mexico. The Utah number is in the front of the phone book." He looked at Lynnette. "In case we have to get out of here in a hurry," he said.

"Maybe we should split up," said Lynnette. "You and Blue take Grace to L.A. by air. I take my stuff and split. It's obvious Grace would be safer with you."

"I thought the same thing at first. But after hearing your side of the story, I can't let you go off on your own. You could get killed before you even get to Denver. And if you make it back to

Florida, you'll need a lawyer. I didn't take the bar exam there, but I have friends who did. You're better off sticking with me. And since we need to keep you off the grid for a little longer, we can't buy you another airplane ticket until we're inside DIA."

"Will you be in a lot of trouble with the police for keeping me out of sight?"

"I will be if you're charged with a crime. This blizzard will serve as an excuse only so long."

"The article I read said I'm a person of interest."

"But it didn't say you were wanted for questioning or that you'd been charged. It merely said you had disappeared and the police hadn't located you. They won't necessarily issue a warrant for your arrest. We'll check the news again in a couple of hours and see if anything has changed. If so, I'll advise you of your next step. Until then, relax. Get some rest."

Los Angeles, California
Friday, January 24

"They're definitely staying put," Ortega told Getz. "Apparently the weather up there is bad. Get back on the interstate before they start closing roads. I'll call you if anything changes."

He snapped his phone shut and tossed it on the desk. If he ever got his hands on Albert Getz, he would kill him. What the hell was taking him so long to get to Fort Collins? What stupid excuse would Getz give if Ortega asked the question?

What about Foster? Ortega thought about her for a minute, then reached for his cell phone again. He dialed Sammy's number, this time waiting through the voice mail message for the beep. "Lynnette Foster, it is now seven forty-five on Friday morning in Colorado. I know you're in Fort Collins. I'm tracking you, and I have someone following you. When he catches you, he will retrieve the things you have in your possession that belong to me. Make it easy for him, Mrs. Foster, and you and your friends will survive the encounter. If you make it difficult, my man will do whatever is necessary."

Would she attempt to retrieve the messages? If she did, would she believe his guarantee of safety?

I-25 south of Fort Collins, Colorado
Friday, January 24

They're less than an hour ahead, Albert thought. *About the same amount of time I spent feeding my face.* He chuckled. Ortega must be going nuts. What could Foster have that Ortega wanted enough to send an assassin after her? What was in the case Sammy Grick had inadvertently switched with Foster's? Obviously, the laptop wasn't important. They'd already retrieved that.

Whatever Ortega wanted, Albert wanted even more. He couldn't imagine what it might be, but if Ortega would kill to retrieve the goods, they might be the means to nail the guy. Albert followed a semi onto the on-ramp of I-25, heading north toward Fort Collins. Alert from the double dose of caffeine and sugar, he guided his car into the wintry hell.

Near Fort Collins, Colorado
Friday, January 24

It was quiet throughout the house. Lynnette closed her eyes and tried to doze but couldn't make it happen. She stood up and walked to the window, pulled the curtains aside and raised the blinds. The windows were fogged up on the inside. She rubbed a spot clear, but could see nothing outside except piles of snow on sagging tree branches.

She sat down, pulled her purse into her lap, and unloaded the contents onto the couch. Then she emptied her pockets.

Thomas heard and walked in from the kitchen to see what she was doing. "Housecleaning?"

"I still have all this stuff I took from the fat guy's laptop case," she said. "Thought I'd look through it again, see what I can get rid of."

"What kind of stuff?"

"Phone, charger, cash—"

"How much cash?"

"Twenty or thirty thousand."

"Think he stole that too?"

"Maybe."

"Why didn't you give everything up to the guy at the library? Chances are that's all he wanted."

Lynnette thought of the checks but didn't say anything about them. "I know," she said. "It was stupid. I couldn't be sure, and with Blue and Grace along, I felt I should keep something for insurance."

She would need the phone charger as long as she carried the phone. She put it in her purse. Struggling to reach into the pocket of the jacket she'd thrown across the end of the couch, she took out Sammy Grick's phone, loaded the battery, and turned it on. It was still fully charged. She turned it off and removed the battery again. If there were any more calls from the bad guy with the Cuban accent, she didn't want to hear them.

Thomas returned to the kitchen. Lynnette lay on the couch and closed her eyes, once again hoping to sleep. She thought of Carl and how he might have been killed. Once she pushed that away, she thought of the phone calls from the fat man, then the even scarier calls from The Cuban. Mixed in were images of a flag-draped coffin coming off a plane and poor little Grace not there to see her father return. She felt overwhelmed.

The newspaper sections she'd saved and stuffed in her purse were still there. She took them out and began reading random articles from the business section.

CHAPTER 26

Miami, Florida
Friday, January 24

"What're we doing here?" Maggie asked. She checked out the fancy houses, mansions almost, in the expensive neighborhood Detective Prince directed her through as though he knew exactly where they were headed. "We're outside our jurisdiction."

"There's a reason, Gutierrez. Watch and listen."

Maggie looked out her side window and rolled her eyes. *There's a price to pay for the privilege of working with jerks.* "Okay, Detective. Whatever you say."

"That's a good girl. You stick with me and you'll make the grade a lot faster than that asshole you call your partner."

"So what're we doing here?" she asked again as Prince pulled up behind the three Miami Police Department squad cars that flanked the driveway of a mansion big enough to hold six apartments the size of the one Maggie rented.

Prince didn't answer. He opened his door and got out, then signaled Maggie to follow him inside. The cop at the door checked their badges and waved them through. "Upstairs," he said.

Death smelled one way in the first few moments, worse a few hours later. But as time passed, the odors changed and the stench intensified until it became so repulsive, few humans could tolerate it. Maggie had already learned that cops, especially homicide cops, pretended they didn't notice.

Stopped at the bedroom door by an MPD uniform, she and Prince waited. A woman's body lay sprawled beside a king-sized bed. Two men in plain clothes stood on the other side of the room, observing the crime scene crew comb the carpet, bag the dead woman's hands, and cover her hair with what appeared to be a surgical cap. One of the men skirted the edge of the room and approached the doorway. Prince said, "Long time no see, Detective. I understand you called to share some information. What's up?"

"Yeah. Here's the thing." The Miami detective held out a plastic bag containing a piece of paper with printing on it. "We found this on the floor, under the edge of the bed. On this side of the paper are scribbled instructions for getting through the security gate and into the house." The detective flipped the bag over. "On this side is a receipt from a car detailing company. Receipt's made out to a Sammy Grick."

Prince shook his head. "Don't recognize the name."

"I do," Maggie said. "Fat Ass Sammy Grick. Petty thief with a bad temper. He was on the hook for a couple of murders but somehow got off. Nobody cared because the guys he iced were worse shits than he was. But Grick's dead."

The Miami detective raised his eyebrows. "Who's this, Prince? Your replacement?"

Prince turned his back on Maggie. "So Grick probably got caught robbing the place and killed the lady of the house. How'd she die?"

"We're not sure. Massive bruises on her chest, maybe broken ribs. Looks like Sammy sat on her. But I'm not so sure he robbed the place. He works for the guy who owns this cottage. Heard of Benito Ortega?"

Maggie winced. "Is this his wife?"

"Yeah. The housekeeper discovered the body." He looked at Maggie. "You said Grick died. When did that happen?"

"Yesterday, I guess. We got a call from Denver asking if we could turn up any next of kin. Grick dropped dead in the bus station. Had a Glades address on his driver's license. They couldn't come up with a phone number, so they called us."

"Who's working the next of kin?" the detective asked.

"Me," Maggie replied. "I checked him out because it looked like he might have crossed paths with somebody Detective Prince is tracking. They were on the same flight to Denver and she was last seen on Denver's mall, only three or four blocks from the bus station."

"You called us because you found out Grick lived in Glades?" Prince said.

"Yeah." The detective held out the receipt so Prince could read it. "His car license number is on there, too. If the car's not at his house, maybe he left it at the airport when he flew to Denver."

Maggie looked at Prince. "Are we the ones who have to get the search warrant?"

Prince nodded. "We're on it, Detective. Let's go, Gutierrez. I have work to do."

One the way to the station, Prince gave Maggie the silent treatment until she had parked and turned off the engine. "Before you go," he said. "You made me feel stupid back there. I don't like feeling stupid."

Maggie looked at Prince in surprise. "What are you talking about?"

"Save the surprise reports for my ears only next time. I don't want to learn about something like Grick's death and his connection to the Foster case in front of Miami P.D. detectives."

"Okay, Detective."

"Do you have any more tidbits of information I should hear about?"

"Like what?"

"Like how you knew Lynnette Foster had been spotted on the Denver mall and I didn't. Or how you knew Foster and Grick had crossed paths before Grick died."

"That info came in through dispatch. It's all on the computer, filed under the Foster file number."

"I don't have time to sit in front of my computer, Gutierrez. People like you are supposed to do that and then report urgent updates to people like me."

"It didn't seem urgent at the time. Grick wasn't on our radar."

"You don't have radar. You have assignments. Don't go off half-cocked, trying to check things out on your own. You run any of this by your supervisor?"

"Not yet, sir, but I will do that as soon as I get inside."

He looked at her face as though trying to figure out whether she was properly respectful or whether she was being a smartass. Then he got out of the car.

Maggie hurried to catch up with him at the precinct's front door. "Wait. I forgot to mention one other thing."

Prince turned around.

"After I saw that report about Grick, I called Denver P.D. The cop I talked to said when the ambulance picked up Grick and took him to the hospital, they also picked up a computer case. An emergency room security guard took a look at it when they were hunting for contact numbers for Grick's family. He said the case contained a bunch of papers that didn't belong to Grick. He said the documents belonged to a woman, last name Hudson. The guard called the cops and they were supposed to pick up the case, but when the officers showed up, the case had disappeared."

"How is that relevant?"

"Lynnette Foster's maiden name is Hudson."

"So we're thinking Grick stole Foster's laptop case, and now someone else stole it from the emergency room?"

"We don't know."

Maggie didn't tell Detective Prince that she'd been trying to contact Lynnette Foster by email. With a Yahoo email address, even if she no longer had her laptop, Foster could still check her messages from anywhere in the country. It was a shaky attempt to find the woman and probably not a technique Prince would approve of, especially since he seemed eager to place the full blame for Carl Foster's murder on Lynnette. Maggie didn't think Carl's time of death would support Prince's theory, but they were still waiting for a time of death.

Maggie decided to keep the line of communication open to Lynnette, but to leave Prince out of the loop, at least for now. She sat at her desk and sent her target another email.

Near Fort Collins, Colorado
Friday, January 24

Lynnette woke with the newspaper clutched in her hands and her neck twisted at an uncomfortable angle. She heard voices. Thomas and Blue talking. Lynnette got up and walked into the kitchen. Thomas signaled Lynnette to join them. "I had an idea, but it didn't work out. I have a friend in Wyoming who's a retired pilot. He owns a six-passenger Cessna that he keeps at the Cheyenne airport. I called him to see if he could pick us up at the Fort Collins–Loveland airport and fly us out of here if we need him."

"He couldn't do it?" Lynnette asked.

"He would, but this storm still covers the southern half of Wyoming and part of Northern Colorado. It's moving toward the eastern plains, but very slowly. The jet stream, he said, was unstable. He might have to wait anywhere from six hours to a couple of days to take off. He could fly us into Burbank or Orange County, but he has no idea when."

"So there's no way you can deliver Grace safely to L.A. by Sunday?"

"I don't think so."

Lynnette felt terrible at the thought of telling Grace she couldn't meet her father's coffin. She was stuck here for the time being, still in the path of the dangerous men who wanted to find Lynnette.

"Will I get there in time?" Grace asked from the doorway. She rubbed her eyes and yawned.

"Grace, I'm so sorry," Lynnette replied. "Blue's dad did his best, but there's no way to get you to California on time."

Grace shifted her gaze to the weather outside the window. "Oh, well," she said. "It was worth a try."

Fort Collins, Colorado
Friday, January 24

Albert pulled the rental car GPS unit forward on its holder and turned it on, then called Ortega. "I'm less than five minutes from Fort Collins. The rental car has a GPS. I need the address where Foster's hiding out." As soon as he had the information, he dropped his phone on the seat and started tapping the GPS screen. When he felt the tires slip on the road, he grabbed the steering wheel with both hands and slowed down. The road looked dry ahead, so he tried to enter the address into the GPS again.

The car began a slow skid sideways. Albert returned his attention to the road and tried to steer into the slide. The front right fender of his car scraped against a concrete barrier and sent him careening across two lanes of traffic to the median. Spinning and bouncing like a bumper car, he watched several vehicles go off the road ahead of him. His car slid to a stop against a snow bank. Another car crunched into his driver's-side door. A third car rammed into his rear. Albert let out a long, slow breath and reached to unfasten his seatbelt.

Before he could do so, he heard the fast-approaching roar of a huge engine from behind, heard the grate of metal on metal. The airbag exploded into his upper body. He felt nothing, but for one brief instant, he hoped he had not been decapitated.

CHAPTER 27

Near Fort Collins, Colorado
Friday, January 24

Lynnette frowned at Grace while Thomas and Blue looked on with puzzled expressions on their faces. "Grace, what did you mean when you said it was worth a try?"

Grace plopped into one of the kitchen chairs. "When I said that about my dad being dead. He isn't. I'm sorry, Lynnette, but I want to be there when he comes home, before he gets a chance to talk to my mom and—"

"What? I thought your mom was dead," Thomas said.

"She's not dead. She's just . . . she doesn't want me to live with her anymore."

"What in the world ever possessed you to tell a story like that?" Thomas asked. "I believed you."

"I knew it," said Blue. "I knew you were lying. Do you have any idea how much time my dad spent trying to figure out a way to get you to California in time to meet your dad's coffin? Shame on you, Grace."

Lynnette could understand Grace's frustration with everything that had happened. From the rough flight and the weird fat guy on the plane to the confrontation with the guy in the tweed jacket at the Denver library, Grace had been involved in several uncomfortable if not terrifying situations. And on top of that, she might actually have a very un-motherly mother.

161

"I'm sorry," Grace said. "Really sorry. What will you do with me now?"

"I don't know," Thomas said. "We'll work something out."

"Not Social Services, okay?"

Thomas sighed. "We'll work something out. Don't worry. We can't do much right now, so we might as well take it easy, eat breakfast, check on the weather reports."

Later in the day, Lynnette, Thomas, Blue and Grace put dinner on the table while they listened to one of the cable news channels on the TV in the living room. Occasionally Blue leaned through the doorway and used the remote control to change the channel.

While they let the spaghetti sauce simmer, Lynnette pulled her laptop from its case, set it up on the counter that separated the kitchen from the dining area, and plugged it in. After it powered on, Blue signed Lynnette in to the wireless network.

Thomas set a pot of water to boil for the pasta and spread garlic butter on slices of French bread. After opening a can of peas, he dumped them in a small saucepan. "Not the fanciest fare, but it's the best we can do at the moment. And there's ice cream for dessert."

No one argued. The thought of going out in freezing winds and deep snow on slick streets to find a restaurant or grocery store hadn't appealed to anyone. They had napped instead.

For the first time since Grace had grabbed Lynnette's laptop case away from the man in the tweed jacket, Lynnette checked her email. Grace asked Blue if she could use the remote, then took it with her to one of the armchairs and began to flip through the channels. Blue sat beside Grace and stared at the television. Thomas continued to bustle about the kitchen. A couple of minutes later, he placed a glass of red wine on the counter in front of Lynnette.

"You could probably use this," he said.

"Definitely. Thanks."

Lynnette opened her Inbox to find two hundred and seventy unopened messages. She began by deleting the newsletters and advertisements. Even then, it appeared every email friend she ever had was trying to contact her. She counted over a dozen from her former boss at *The Indy Reporter.*

Her eyes focused on one address she didn't recognize. She scanned her Inbox and found one more recent email from the same sender. MGutierrez@cityofglades.gov. She moved her cursor to the first MGutierrez email and—

"Lynnette, you're on TV," Grace said, her voice scarcely louder than a whisper.

Lynnette looked over her shoulder. A news conference was in progress on one-half of a split screen, a photo of Lynnette on the other. As Grace turned up the volume, Lynnette slid off her chair and moved closer to hear the police spokesman.

"Originally, Lynnette Foster was considered missing and a possible victim of the same person or persons who killed her husband, Carl Foster," the police spokesman said. "At this time, however, we know Mrs. Foster left South Florida around the time of her husband's murder. We know she flew to Denver, traveling under her maiden name, Lynnette Hudson. We have since learned that during that flight, Mrs. Foster had contact with a known criminal, Sammy Grick. Authorities are investigating the possibility that Grick recently participated in the murder of a Miami woman. While Mrs. Foster and Grick were in Denver, Grick died of an apparent heart attack. When spotted on the 16th Street Mall, Mrs. Foster eluded the police. Her whereabouts are currently unknown.

"Under the circumstances, we have no choice but to consider Lynnette Foster a fugitive. Anyone who sees Mrs. Foster or knows where she is should contact Glades Crime Watch. The number and website is at the bottom of your screen. It is not known whether Mrs. Foster is armed, but she is considered dangerous."

Lynnette felt her cheeks flush as she stared at the screen. She glanced at Grace and found the girl watching her. "I'm not dangerous, Grace. I didn't kill anyone."

Instead of answering, Grace changed the channel. She tried to change it again, but Lynnette stopped her. A huge blue and white cloud on the weather map covered the southern half of Wyoming, the western part of Nebraska, and the upper half of Colorado from the continental divide to the eastern plains and on into Kansas. The numbers in the high mountains indicated a possible 26 to 34 inches of snow. Below 9,000 feet, the accumulation would be 12 to 15 inches with winds up to forty miles per hour creating treacherous driving conditions with zero visibility. Denver International Airport was shut down and would not reopen for at least six hours.

Los Angeles, California
Friday, January 24

Benny was still holding the phone to his ear when the bangs and screeches of metal impacting metal replaced Getz's voice. He yelled the hit man's name a couple of times, but realized he shouted into a dead connection. He redialed frequently in the next thirty minutes, but it was wasted effort. Getz's number had been declared Out of Service.

Benny's tracker enlightened him about the worsening weather conditions in Colorado. "I could triangulate if I detected a signal coming from Getz's phone," he told his boss. "But no signal, no trace."

"What would cause that?" Benny asked.

"These new phones should send a signal as long as they're operative and the battery is charged, even when they're turned off. If the phone is dead, your man either forgot to charge the phone or he completely destroyed it. Would he do that?"

"No. He wouldn't do that." Benny shook his head as he accepted the significance of the loud noises he'd heard at the end of his last conversation with Getz. "Something's happened. Maybe he had an accident. Make some calls. Denver and north. See what you can find out."

"I'm on it . . . wait a minute . . . hang on . . . something's going on in the front office. I'll be right back."

Annoyed, Benny paced the floor of his hotel room as he waited for the tracker to come to the phone. Ready to ream the man out for leaving him hanging, he bit his tongue when the next voice he heard on the telephone identified himself as a detective from the Miami Police Department.

"Mr. Ortega, I'm very sorry to tell you that your housekeeper found your wife's body in your home today. She was murdered."

Benny's knees felt wobbly. He grabbed the edge of the desk and lowered himself into the chair. "When did this happen? She was fine when I left for L.A. on Tuesday."

"You're in Los Angeles?"

"Yes, on business. What happened to my wife?"

"We're not sure. The medical examiner is trying to establish the cause and time of death but we don't have his report yet. Where are you staying?"

"What?"

"In L.A. Where are you staying?"

"Century City Plaza. Oh, my God. This is not possible. I'll come right back to Florida."

"That would be best. I'll have LAPD give you an escort to the airport."

"That won't be necessary, Detective. I'll be on my way in minutes."

"Let me know when you're scheduled to arrive. I'll have a car waiting for you."

"I have a car and a driver. I'm sure we can manage. I'll need to get off the phone—"

"I'm sorry, sir, but I need your cooperation here. I have a couple more questions. Your wife's body was found on the floor in a bedroom. Nothing seemed to be disturbed. Did you or your wife keep anything of value in that room?"

"Excuse me, Detective . . . I need to catch my breath." Benny held the phone away from his face, but did not put his hand over the receiver. He cleared his throat a couple of times, coughed, then put the phone to his ear. "We had cash, a few stock certificates and bonds my wife owned . . . not much. We kept it in a locked wall safe."

"We spotted the safe. It seems secure. Did you have any weapons? Passports?"

"My wife kept a gun in the bedside table. Our passports are in a safety deposit box."

"Any idea who would have given instructions to a known criminal on how to access your home?"

"A known criminal? No, of course not. What the hell happened?"

"We don't know too much yet, Mr. Ortega. We're waiting for word from the medical examiner."

"Wait a minute! Known criminal? You already know who broke into my house?"

"We need to talk to you as soon as you arrive," the detective said, ignoring Benny's question. "Do we need to send someone to help you with flight arrangements?"

"I have my own plane. I'll take care of it."

"My condolences, Mr. Ortega. I'll turn the phone over to your man here. Remember, call me as soon as you arrive in Miami. I can send a car for you."

Ortega ground his teeth as he waited for his tracker to return.

"Mr. O? They're gone. I'm so sorry about Mrs. Ortega. Is

there something you want me to do from here? Schedule your flight? Contact—"

"Just get the information I asked for. I need to know what happened to Albert Getz, and I need to know if there's an airport near Fort Collins, Colorado." Benny threw the cell phone on the bed. He began to pace from one side of his hotel room to the other while he considered his options. Finally, he turned on the television and clicked through the channels to find a weather report. He paused when he spotted the news conference and the picture of Foster.

As far as he knew, Foster still had the checks. Now she'd been declared a fugitive and appeared to be running from the police, so it was even more unlikely she would turn the envelope over to the FBI.

How in hell could this be happening? It should have been so easy.

But even when Sammy lost the case, whoever found it could have either turned it over to the cops or the FBI, assuming there existed even one person honest enough to do that. Or the finder could have stolen the money and tried to sell the checks to the highest bidder. Since nothing on the checks or the cash tied the items to Benny or his wife, and since the items were not in Sammy's possession at the time of his death, the cops couldn't connect Sammy to the crimes. Did they know Sammy Grick had entered his house? Is that what Sammy had tried to tell him, that he killed Maria?

His thoughts were interrupted as he heard Sammy's name on the TV. The police spokeswoman talked about a possible connection between Grick and Foster. Ortega's heart seemed to skip beats and then catch up, the sound pounding in his ears. Sweat broke out on his forehead. He set the television remote on the bed and rubbed his clammy hands on his shirt. *There's no way out of this,* he thought. *Unless I get to Foster and retrieve everything Sammy was bringing to L.A.*

CHAPTER 28

Near Fort Collins, Colorado
Friday, January 24

"Let me have it, Grace," Lynnette said. "I want to see what else they're saying."

She took the remote from Grace and flipped through the channels. One news channel was showing a commercial, but within seconds the television anchors returned with a "News Alert" banner flashing at the bottom of the screen. Even though the news conference had concluded, the anchors continued to talk about South Florida, this time discussing the murder of a wealthy woman in Miami.

"We have breaking news about the murdered woman. She has been identified as Maria Ortega, the wife of prominent Cuban businessman and financier, Benito Ortega, owner of Miami-based Ortega Enterprises."

Lynnette gasped and placed her hand over her mouth.

"What?" Grace whispered.

"Nothing. Shhh." Lynnette leaned closer to the television.

". . . and has been tied to fugitive Lynnette Foster, whose husband, a Glades police officer, was brutally murdered in his home about the same time Mrs. Foster disappeared. It has now been established that Mrs. Ortega was likely murdered between ten a.m. and two p.m. on Wednesday, January 22. Officer Foster's time of death has not been confirmed, but reports indicate he may have died as early as Wednesday morning. Mrs.

Foster's flight left Miami late Wednesday afternoon.

"It's not clear what the connection is between the murders of Maria Ortega and Carl Foster, but police say a suspect in the Ortega case, Sammy Grick, may have flown to Denver with Mrs. Foster and may have been in touch with her in that city."

They couldn't say Carl also might have died long after I left?

Grace tugged at Lynnette's sleeve. "What's going on? What does that mean?"

Lynnette didn't answer.

"Lynnette," Grace said, much louder than she'd spoken before. "What's going on?"

"Shhh."

Even louder this time, Grace said, "If you don't tell me—"

"Okay, okay."

"You might as well tell all of us," Thomas said.

He and Blue stood at the entrance to the kitchen, watching the TV. Then they sat in chairs across from Lynnette.

It took her almost an hour to bring everyone up to date. First she talked about the threatening cell phone messages from the man in the tweed jacket and The Cuban and then described the most recent news reports. She retrieved Sammy's cell phone from her jacket pocket and laid it on the desk. "There are more messages," she said, "but I haven't listened to them yet."

She pointed to the screen on her laptop. "I also have a bunch of emails, including two from someone at the City of Glades, probably the police department. There are a few from my stepmother, some from my friends. And the guy I used to work for at *The Indy Reporter* has sent at least a dozen."

"Lynnette, I don't know what to say." Thomas looked at her as if she had grown fangs. "You should never have dragged my daughter and Grace into this mess."

"We need to know everything," Blue said. "Especially what's on the voice mail. Do you want me to go through them?"

Thomas jerked his head to stare at his daughter. "I don't think that's a good idea."

Lynnette took a deep breath. "No, I'll do it. I'll do that first, before I read my email."

Los Angeles, California
Friday, January 24
By the time Benny's tracker called with the report of an earlier massive collision involving seven cars, a dump truck, and two semis on I-25 on the south side of Fort Collins, Benny was ready to fly into the northern Colorado blizzard, parachute over Fort Collins, and hike to Foster's location. He set his phone gently on the desk and turned toward the sliding glass door that opened onto a tiny balcony.

Benny's plane had returned from Denver after delivering Getz. Refueled, it now waited at LAX. The tracker had already pinpointed Foster's position in Fort Collins. Benny still had questions. How close could his pilot get to that city? How could they make the trip without filing a flight plan that would place him anywhere near Colorado? How could he travel through a snowstorm from wherever they landed to his target's location? He stared through the glass door and cringed at the nicotine-stained haze between his hotel and the ocean. Who could survive breathing air that color? He felt like throwing up.

He focused on his current situation. In spite of all the deals he'd made, all the projects he'd planned, he had never had so many things go wrong in such a short amount of time.

He picked up his cell phone and called Sammy's number.

Near Fort Collins, Colorado
Friday, January 24
Seconds after Lynnette turned on the phone, it rang. Startled, she dropped it on the desk and shook her fingers as though

they'd received a shock. Then she grabbed it again and listened to the call.

"You have things that belong to me, Mrs. Foster. Things Sammy Grick should have delivered two days ago. I know where you are. Stay there. Wait for me."

It was the man with the Cuban accent. She thought back, trying to remember the name on the news. Benito Ortega. "Yes, I know who you are, Mr. Ortega. I'm sorry to hear about your wife."

Why did I say that? Lynnette waited through the long silence that followed her words.

"Don't talk to the authorities about me, Mrs. Foster," he said, his words soft but more threatening than if he'd screamed at her. "Stay right where you are. I'll be there tomorrow. When I have taken possession of everything Sammy Grick was supposed to deliver to me, I'll help you get away. Do you understand?"

"Yes."

"Good. Leave the phone on."

"Wait! Where's the other guy? The one I gave the laptop to in Denver?"

After a long silence Ortega said, "Stay where you are and keep this phone turned on. I'll be in touch."

Lynnette laid the phone down and turned to face her three companions. "I think The Cuban is Benito Ortega and he hired Sammy Grick to kill his wife. Now he wants the stuff from the laptop case, stuff Grick probably stole after he knocked off Mrs. Ortega." She paused and thought for a moment.

"Oh, man," she continued. "The cops think there's a connection. They think I had something to do with this fat guy. Maybe they think I hired him to kill Carl." She stopped abruptly when she realized she was talking too fast.

"Did you?" asked Thomas.

"No, no, of course not." She held up the phone. "This Ortega guy said he was coming to get his stuff. He said he knows where I am. He said if I stayed here and gave him his things, he would help me get away. He talked like he thinks I'm on the run from the police and that I'm on my own. Maybe the guy at the library never told him about Blue and Grace."

"What stuff is he talking about? You gave up the laptop. So he's hot after the cash and the phone. That's all he wants?" Thomas frowned at Lynnette. "There has to be more. These guys wouldn't be threatening you unless you had something way more important."

Grace perked up at Thomas's question and said, "She's got that envelope with the papers in it. Don't you, Lynnette?"

CHAPTER 29

Los Angeles, California
Friday, January 24

Benny was packing his suitcase when his cell phone rang. His caller ID displayed a phone number he didn't recognize. He considered not answering, thinking at first it might be the police, then decided he had no choice.

"Mr. Ortega, it's Getz."

Benny dropped onto the edge of the bed, so startled he felt as though his knees had given way. He tightened his grip on his cell phone. "I thought you were dead."

"Yeah, well, it was close. There was a huge pileup on the interstate. When they finally pried me out of the car, they forced me into an ambulance. I'm still in the emergency room. Have a broken nose and two cracked—"

"I don't care about your injuries. Are you able to continue?"

"Yeah, okay. I am. But the car . . . I need to get another car. And my cell phone got crushed between the console and—"

"Damn it, Getz. I don't care! Find a way to get to that house in Fort Collins. Foster's there for now, but I don't trust her to stay put. Steal a car, steal a phone. I don't give a fuck how you do it, but no more talking. When you find her, call me."

Benny crossed the room to the bathroom door, pulled his fist back, and slammed it into the door. Then he punched the door again and again until the rough edges of the hole scratched his knuckles and drew blood.

Fort Collins, Colorado
Friday, January 24

Albert stood at the emergency room reception desk, the dial tone buzzing in his ear. He gently replaced the receiver in its cradle and pushed the twenty-dollar bill across the counter toward the receptionist. "Thanks," he said, "this should cover it."

The receptionist slipped the twenty into the center drawer of the cubicle's desk.

"Am I okay to leave now?" he asked.

"Yeah. But the weather's bad out there."

He limped toward the sliding glass doors that led to the parking lot. He'd shoved his left arm back in the sling, and beneath the tape strips his nose felt like a baseball. He tried to take a deep breath but the tape pulled against his chest and the dull ache in his ribs grew sharper. He gasped. Now that he'd begun to move around, every muscle in his body hurt. It was hard to walk. He wondered if he'd be able to move at all in a few hours.

The only coat he had was his tweed jacket. He couldn't get it all the way on. He struggled to push his right arm into the sleeve, leaned over to work the jacket over his left shoulder, and then used his right hand to clutch the jacket closed in the front.

If he planned to do anything Ortega had ordered him to do, it would have to be now. He wished he could walk away, but he found it difficult to give up. He wanted the money Ortega owed him, even if he didn't need it, and he wanted to get close enough to Ortega to take him out of the game. To accomplish both those goals, he had to find the Foster woman and retrieve Ortega's possessions.

As the first set of doors slid open, cold air seeped through from outside. When the second set of doors opened, a blast of icy wind threw a flurry of snowflakes into his face and down his neck.

This isn't going to work. I can't steal a car. I can't even drive a car.

He returned to the warmth of the emergency room lobby, his eyes tearing from the cold and wind. He didn't bother to wipe the tears away. "It's much colder than I expected," he said to the receptionist. "Could you call me a cab?"

He had to give her credit. Even though she looked at him as though he'd lost his mind, she made the call then told him the cab company had pulled all their drivers in until the streets were plowed. "The plows are only working the interstates for now," she said.

Albert sighed and shuffled toward the waiting room. He looked at each of the four people scattered about, sprawled in the hardback chairs. A woman bundled in layers of sweaters and worn sweatpants bent forward, hacking hard enough to cough up her lungs. The three unshaven men wore soiled jeans and jackets and knitted caps pulled over their ears. One had blood on his hands. Albert cringed and took a seat on the other side of the room.

A television sat high on the wall. When he heard the words Miami, Grick, and Foster, he jerked his whole body so he could see the screen. The sudden movement sent pain like a machete slice through his body. He groaned and clasped his right arm to his ribs as though to hold his chest together. Tears flooded his eyes, blurring the newscaster who described the joint Glades and Miami police news conference that had just ended.

"You okay, man?" one of the waiting room occupants yelled.

"Fine," Albert replied. "I'm fine."

"Didn't sound fine," the man said.

Albert ignored him and focused on the news report. He

couldn't believe it. The woman who had Ortega's stuff was not only a person of interest, she was a killer. He had thought he sought a ditzy female who managed to escape because she had a run of luck, but maybe she was a clever and ruthless thief who knew exactly what she was doing. Maybe she knew the fat man, even worked with him. Maybe she had planned to steal Ortega's stuff from Grick all along. Albert wished he knew exactly what she had.

From what Ortega had told him, it looked as though there were four people in the Fort Collins house. The big question? Did they have weapons?

Who the hell are these people?

Albert tried to lean forward to put his head in his hands. He couldn't. His elbow ached, his chest hurt so bad he couldn't take a deep breath, and his face had begun to throb. He eased out of the chair and returned to the reception desk. "I need something for the pain," he said.

"Didn't they give you a prescription?"

Albert raised his eyebrows, looked toward the door, then at the receptionist. "Are you fucking serious?"

The receptionist drew in her breath and pushed back from the counter on squeaky wheels. Her crepe-soled shoes sucked at the tile as she rushed toward the treatment bays. In less than a minute, she returned with a doctor who looked about twenty and a security guard with fullback shoulders and no neck.

Albert leaned on the counter and tried to look apologetic. "I'm sorry I said what I did. I can't stand the pain." He turned to the doctor and held out the written prescription for Vicodin. "I can't get out of here to fill this, and I'm hurting. It's killing me to move my fingers and toes." The doctor and the guard stared at his mouth. They frowned as though they hadn't understood a word he said. Albert realized he was trying to talk without moving his lips. "Hurts," he said, trying to enunciate clearly. "Hurts bad."

The doctor left, then returned with two tablets and a glass of water. The guard escorted Albert to the waiting room. As he leaned his head against the wall and shut his eyes, waiting for the painkillers to kick in, he heard the Miami/Grick/Foster story all over again.

No one mentioned the little kid or the teenager traveling with Foster.

CHAPTER 30

Near Fort Collins, Colorado
Friday, January 24

Thomas turned to Lynnette. "What envelope? What's inside?" He held out his hand.

"I don't think you want to know."

"Let me see the envelope. Right now. Otherwise, I take Blue and Grace and go to the police."

Lynnette felt her inner reporter kick in. More than anything else at that moment, she wanted to protect her story. She wanted to contact Dave at *The Indy Reporter* and tell him she had probably stumbled into a huge crime involving theft and maybe bank fraud, and she had the evidence to go with it.

But there was nowhere to go until the storm ended and the roads were cleared. Stuck with the possibility Benny Ortega would show up as soon as the roads were plowed, Lynnette decided to play along. She pulled the brown envelope out of her purse, opened the clasp, and pulled out the checks. Thomas, Blue and Grace looked over her shoulder.

For only the second time since she had come into possession of the envelope, Lynnette went through the checks one by one.

Grace went back to her seat in front of the television.

Blue cleared her throat. "They're checks. I thought you had photographs."

Thomas didn't say anything. Lynnette glanced at his face.

His cheek moved as though he clenched and unclenched his jaw.

"Wait. Show Dad that big check," Blue said. "The one for five-hundred thousand."

Lynnette found the one Blue wanted to see.

"That company's corporate headquarters are in Pompano Beach. One of my roommates works there during the summer," Blue said. "Looks like they're paying for a few truckloads of office supplies."

Lynnette held up another check. "This company is based in Fort Lauderdale. It's a vendor for the bar I worked in. The check is made out to a company in Indianapolis that manufactures restaurant supplies—napkins, cups, paper towels."

"Why would the fat man be carrying an envelope full of checks?" Blue asked.

"Checks that Benny Ortega says are his," Lynnette added. "I think the checks were stolen and that Sammy Grick was supposed to deliver them to Ortega. I don't know for sure, but it's possible Ortega has a way to cash these things before the people who were supposed to receive them even know they're gone. That would explain why he's so desperate to get them back."

"We need to get these checks to the FBI," Thomas said.

"Wow," Blue said. "You think so?"

"If they're stolen, they've been transported across state lines, probably with the intention of using a bank where this Ortega guy has inside help. Those are federal crimes."

"I can't go to the FBI yet," Lynnette said. "Neither can you, not if you want to stay out of trouble. Think about it. You'd have to explain about me, you'd have to explain about Grace, and then you'd have to explain why you let us stay with you in Fort Collins when you already knew Grace had run away and the police were looking for me. That's too much risk for you and Blue, and at some point, I have to go back to Florida and try to straighten out my own problems. I can turn in the checks—"

"No!" Grace screamed. "I can't go to Florida." She threw the TV remote on the floor and ran to Lynnette. "If you try to take me back, I'll run away."

Lynnette reached out, but Grace backed away, her face red and her fists clenched. "I mean it," she said. "I'm going to California, whether you take me or not."

"Whoa, whoa," Thomas said. "Nobody's going to do anything that will hurt you, Grace. I'm sure Lynnette doesn't intend to take you to Florida or turn you in to the police."

Lynnette tossed the checks on the desk and leaned back, hands folded in her lap, her gaze on the child. Something wasn't right.

"Grace," Lynnette said. "Let's talk."

Blue said, "You've lied again, haven't you? I bet you don't have a dad who lives in L.A. I'll bet you don't even have an Aunt Maxie."

Grace backed away from Lynnette and Blue and sat on the edge of the couch. "You don't understand," she whispered.

Blue's jaw dropped open. "Am I right?" She reached out and grabbed Grace's arm. "You little creep. Do you ever tell the truth?"

Thomas put his hand on Blue's arm. "Don't be too harsh. You don't know the circumstances."

"Bullshit, Dad. If she's been lying to us all along . . . damn. Why didn't I see it?"

Grace jerked her arm free and folded her arms across her chest. She glared at the floor.

Blue put her hands on her hips and stood in front of Grace. "Kid, I've talked to plenty of runaways while I've been working on my thesis. You are so typical. I can't believe I didn't catch on sooner."

Grace continued to stare at the floor.

"See what?" Lynnette asked. She studied Grace's expression and body language, thought about the stories Grace had told so far, and considered Grace's threat to run away. "I've believed every story she told me for the last two days."

"Didn't you notice the way she watched you while she talked? Street kids do that. They know body language. They can spot a pushover a mile away. And remember all that stuff she said about Social Services and being in the system like she knew exactly what she was talking about? Twenty to one this kid is a runaway from a foster home."

Blue put her hand on the top of Grace's head. "And twenty to one, her foster family hasn't bothered to report her missing." She put her finger under Grace's chin and nudged the girl's head up. "What about it, Gracie? Am I right?"

CHAPTER 31

Fort Collins, Colorado
Saturday, January 25

Albert woke up when two men entered through the sliding glass doors into the trauma center, stomping and wiping their feet on the mat. They stopped and chatted with the girl at the reception desk, then strolled into the waiting room, stripping off coats, hats, and gloves on the way.

"Phew, it's cold out there," said the older man.

"No shit," said the other, who looked barely out of his teens.

"Think we can finish before five?"

"We can get this end done by four, if the wind don't start up again."

Albert struggled to his feet and approached the men. "You're plowing now? Is the storm over?" He looked at his watch. It was ten after one. He'd slept a couple of hours.

"Weatherman said it's moving east," the older man said. "We're getting an early start. We got twenty-five lots to clear."

"Do you have any jobs near Horsetooth Reservoir?"

"Nope. That's clear over on the west side of town. It won't get plowed until the snow stops and it's daylight. The roads up to the dams are steep and the visibility is next to zero. Too easy for a plow to slide off the road," said the younger man.

"I need to get up there. How would I do that?"

"I'm not sure it's possible." He looked Albert up and down. "You're all banged up. Do you even have winter gear with you?

Parka, hood, gloves?"

"No. Wiped out my car in a pileup on I-25. I've been stuck here ever since."

"Aw, man, that sucks. You must be miserable." He turned toward the older man and waved him toward the door. "Why don't you give him that coat we got in the truck for stranded drivers?"

"Yeah, we can do that. Sorry we can't help you get up the hill, though. The only thing I can think of is renting a snowmobile. There's a dealer about a mile from here." He glanced at his watch. "Doubt he stayed open during the night, but with the storm winding down and the possibility of picking up a few new customers, he'll probably open up early this morning. The business is called Clyde's Ski-Ride. He's in the phone book."

Albert sighed. "Thanks. Any chance you could drop me over there? I'd be happy to pay."

"Nah, not necessary," the younger one said. "Just call it good old Colorado hospitality. But you have to wait—"

"I've got a better idea," said the older driver. "We gotta do Clyde's anyway and it's the only one we have on the north side. When we get ready to head up there, we'll take you with us."

Albert could not believe his good fortune. Due to the kindness of strangers, he would have a coat to protect him from the fierce cold, and he had access to transportation that would get him up the hill to Foster and whatever she had that Ortega wanted so bad. Albert now had to figure out a way to handle the situation so he didn't have to kill her or any of her companions. Especially the kid. He had never killed a kid.

While he waited for the men and their snow plows to return, he managed to score six Vicodin. He'd need them to get a snowmobile up that hill.

★ ★ ★ ★ ★

Near Fort Collins, Colorado
Saturday, January 25

"Let's get back to the bigger problem," Thomas said after Grace went down the hall to Blue's bedroom. "We need to know what's in the emails you haven't read. The phone messages, too."

"I can listen to the voice mails," Blue said. "I'll take notes." This time Thomas didn't protest.

Lynnette handed her cell to Blue, who took one look at the display and asked, "Do you have the charger? It's almost dead."

"Yeah. In my purse." Lynnette tossed her purse on the counter.

Blue plugged in the phone and accessed Sammy Grick's voice mail as Lynnette opened her emails, beginning with the oldest ones first and dealing with one correspondent at a time. Dave Buchanan, her former boss at *The Indy Reporter,* had tried to contact her as soon as he found out about Carl's death and her disappearance. His most recent attempt had been sent Friday night: *You're scaring me. No matter what you've done, I'll help you. Call me.*

Thomas was reading Dave's emails over her shoulder. Lynnette checked her watch. It was four o'clock Saturday morning in Indiana. Dave probably wouldn't see the message for three or four hours. She hit Reply and typed: *I haven't done anything wrong. I'll call later today.*

After scanning the rest of the emails, including those from her stepmother, Lynnette had the two emails from MGutierrez left. She opened the first one, from Maggie Gutierrez of the Glades Police Department. It read:*It's in your best interest to contact me and no one else, Mrs. Foster. Email me and I'll send you my phone number. We need to talk.*

Lynnette hadn't expected an email from the cops, especially

a female cop. Would she be sympathetic? Or would she be one of those women who had to out-tough the men to prove her worth? Lynnette hit the Reply key and hesitated.

"What are you going to do?" Thomas asked.

"Get the number. I'm not telling her where I am, if that's what you mean." She glanced at the wireless connection icon. It was now covered by a red X. "Nuts, I've lost the connection."

"Lynnette," Blue said. "All of the calls are really scary. These guys want their stuff real bad. The guy with the accent, the one who says he's on his way—"

"Ortega," Lynnette said.

"Yeah. He's called before. But think about it. First it was the fat guy, and you saw him in person. Then there was the guy at the library. We saw him in person. This other guy, Ortega, seems to be the one in charge. Like maybe the other two are working for him. He says he knows where you are, he's coming to pick up his stuff, and he'll help you get away. Dad's got to be right. They're tracking you through this phone. They found out you're here before Dad removed the battery. You should have dumped it a long time ago."

"I know. I was afraid to. I kept thinking I'd make the trade when I got somewhere safe. I needed the phone so they could contact me."

"They won't need to contact you by phone if you stay here," Thomas said. "Whoever these men are, one or more of them will show up as soon as the roads are cleared. This Ortega might do exactly as he promised. On the other hand, he might kill you. He might kill all of us. We don't know what these checks mean, and we don't know what Ortega plans to do with them. We need to involve the authorities, for your safety and for ours."

He was right. She couldn't put Grace and Blue in more danger. Still, she had every intention of talking to Dave before she did anything else. "Okay. As soon as I can get online, I'll email the Glades cop and get her number."

Glades, Florida
Saturday, January 25

Maggie saw Detective Prince walk in the door and felt an immediate urge to duck under her desk. Her worst fears were realized when he stood in the doorway and shouted across the room. "Gutierrez! Have you been sending emails to Lynnette Foster?"

He's such a jerk. Maggie walked across the room to Prince. "Sorry, Detective. I didn't hear you. What did you say?"

Prince looked at his watch. "You've been working on the Foster case since Thursday against my explicit orders. You are in deep trouble . . . unless you can tell me where she is."

Ouch. That does not sound like he gave me unspoken permission to work this case. "I haven't been able to catch any movement since she disappeared from the mall in Denver. Hasn't used her credit cards, no ATM withdrawal, no contact with her friends or her relatives. She has a stepmother in Southern California who's been trying to email her and call her on her cell phone, but Foster isn't answering. I think something happened to her."

"Something like what?"

"Car accident? In the hospital? They're having a blizzard out there. Maybe she's holed up in a motel." *How the hell do I know?*

"Bullshit. Somebody's helping her. You talked to the step-mother?"

"Yes. She says she hasn't talked to her stepdaughter since she married that 'damned son-of-a-bitch cop.' "

Prince raised his eyebrows. "Does this stepmother have an alibi for Wednesday?"

"She says she'd love to claim responsibility but she played in a bridge tournament in Laguna Beach and has a hundred witnesses."

"What about the Denver P.D. You talked to them?"

"Yes. And I asked all the right questions. They don't know any more than they already told us. You want me to check the hospitals?"

"No, I'll have someone else do it. Anything else I ought to know before I ask your supervisor to put you on report for emailing a suspect?"

Maggie glanced across the room toward the computer monitor on her desk before looking at Prince. *Do all of my emails get screened?* "Can't think of anything offhand, sir. I'm sorry, I misunderstood your orders. I'll back off."

"You do that."

"Did you get any word from Miami P.D. about that Ortega killing, sir? Did they locate the husband?"

"He was in L.A. on business. He's on his way back."

Maggie returned to her desk. Prince wouldn't report her. He'd used her to save himself a little time but now he wanted to make sure he controlled his case. She refreshed her screen. Still nothing from Lynnette Foster. Maggie couldn't send any more emails to Foster, but she would sure as hell open anything she received from her.

CHAPTER 32

Near Fort Collins, Colorado
Saturday, January 25

It was seven fifteen in the morning when Lynnette woke to the smell of coffee and bacon. A bright sun reflected off the snow and streamed in the living room windows on the east side of the house. She rose from the couch, drew the afghan around her shoulders, and walked to the windows facing the hills and mountains to the west, where the glare was less intense. She sucked in her breath as she saw the view. A steep hill plunged from the wide deck toward a body of water that stretched to the north and south. Beyond the hill, a notched rock jutted skyward. Snow covered most of the terrain surrounding the water. The edges of the lake were frozen, the water in the center placid. The wind had died. A rabbit hopped along the edge of the ridge by the deck.

"Beautiful, isn't it?" Thomas stood at the entryway between the dining room and kitchen.

"Where are we?"

"West of Fort Collins on the eastern ridge that borders Horsetooth Reservoir. That's Horsetooth Mountain." He pointed toward the rocky growth to the west.

"Yes, it's beautiful." She gestured toward the table where she'd left her laptop open and plugged in. "Is it working?"

"Afraid not," he said. "Not sure why we've lost the connection."

"And the television?"

"Too much snow on the dish. Unfortunately, the south side of the house is where the drifts are the worst. I can't do anything about it now. We shouldn't waste any more time. Let's have breakfast and hit the road. The plows won't make it up here until this afternoon, but I have a blade on my truck, so we'll take that. No one's going to get up here in a rental car, but I don't feel comfortable keeping you and Grace here any longer. I'm willing to see you back to Florida and help you sort out your problems there."

"Thank you. I appreciate that. I should call my stepmother," Lynnette said. "And my friend in Indianapolis."

"Our landline is out, same as our Internet connection. My cell couldn't even pick up a signal this morning."

Lynnette's own phone showed no signal, though the battery was fully charged. "What would cause that?"

"Ice on the tower? Wind damage? I'm not sure."

Lynnette met Thomas's gaze and wondered what he thought about as he studied her face. Without saying anything, he returned to the kitchen. She heard plates and glasses clinking against each other, followed by the sound of bacon sizzling in a frypan.

Grace wandered into the living room from the hall. She stopped when she saw Lynnette, then turned away and went into the kitchen.

"Good morning," Lynnette heard Thomas say. "Bacon? Toast? I'm out of eggs."

She could not decipher Grace's mumbled reply. Thomas handed Lynnette a new toothbrush, still in its store packaging. "Blue's using my shower so you can use the bathroom in the hall. Blue pulled together some clean clothes for you, including a couple of my black T-shirts. She also put a few things in there she thought Grace could use."

When Lynnette returned, her breakfast was on the table. She sat opposite Grace, who had nearly finished.

"Grace and I had a talk," Thomas said. "I'm going to escort her back to Florida and stay there until we've found someone to represent her and help sever her connection with her foster family."

"That's very generous," Lynnette said.

"You would have done the same. The simple fact that you tried to help Grace along the way, even while you were struggling with your own problems, proves the point."

He put four strips of bacon and two pieces of toast on the table seconds before Blue walked in and sat down. "Grace now has a better understanding of the situation," he said. "Don't you, kiddo?"

"Uh-huh. I'm sorry I yelled at you before, Lynnette. And I'm really sorry I told all those lies. It's just, you were nice and all, but I couldn't be sure—"

"I get it, Grace. It's okay." Lynnette leaned back in her chair and watched as Thomas stacked dirty dishes in the sink. He seemed so much like her own father. She felt the empty feeling in her stomach that always accompanied thoughts of her dad and his death. Blue was a lucky young woman to have a father like Thomas. And Grace was a lucky kid to have him willing to advocate on her behalf. She was too old to look to Thomas as a father figure, but that's what she wanted to do. "What now?" she asked. "We need to get ready. How can I help?"

"If you and Grace grab bottled water and something to snack on in case we get stuck in a snowdrift, Teresa and I will pack the truck."

"Where are we going?" Grace asked as she and Lynnette bagged the supplies. "I mean, I know you're going to fly to Fort Lauderdale, but are we going to Denver to the airport? Is Thomas going to take me on the same plane with you?"

"I don't know. We'll see what Thomas has in mind."

It was almost eight before they'd loaded the truck and warmed it up. They squeezed in the oversized interior with Thomas in the driver's seat and Blue beside him. Grace sat behind Thomas. Since Thomas had to lower the blade and plow a path through the snow drifts, it was slow going.

Near Fort Collins, Colorado
Saturday, January 25

It was after eight when Albert left the western edge of Fort Collins and started up the road toward Horsetooth Reservoir on a new snowmobile equipped with a GPS. When he first left the Ski-Ride lot, he had tried to steer the vehicle with his right hand, but found his one-armed approach didn't work. He removed the sling and stuffed it in a pocket, slid his left arm into the sleeve of his jacket, and yelped as he lifted his left hand to the vibrating handlebar.

He knew he would suffer excruciating pain every moment of his ride to the top of the ridge. It was stupid to keep going. He could turn around and walk away from this job, tell Ortega that Foster and her friends were already gone.

But after all he'd been through, he wanted that payoff. He cursed Ortega with every jolt and every bump. As he approached the steep road, he accelerated to avoid stalling at the bottom of the hill.

The sun rose above the storm clouds now menacing the plains to the east. Any other time, Albert would have stopped to admire the scene. Today he focused on the white landscape before him. He moved his left arm about, trying to relieve the strain on his elbow. Moving only made it worse. He replaced his hand on the grip and accelerated a bit more. The snowmobile stayed on track, no skid, no slide.

Halfway up the hill, the outside of the right ski caught the

Patricia Stoltey

edge of a rock poking up through the snow. The impact sent the front of the snowmobile skidding to the left. The rear end slid to the right toward the hillside. Albert killed the engine and slid backward, slowly picking up speed. The snowmobile's rear end rammed into the hill, spinning the front end outward toward the road and the steep downhill drop beyond.

He held his breath as he tried but failed to restart the engine, then glanced at the back end of the skis. One ski stuck in a small leafless bush barely larger than a football. Climbing off the snowmobile might send it careening down the hill, dragging him along with it. He tried to start the engine again. Nothing happened.

He sat still, listening. Another engine. He checked to the left, downhill, and then to the right. The sound came from above. The vibration could dislodge the snowmobile from the bush. He had no choice. He had to climb off the machine. Slow movements, no jerking, no bumping. He slowly lifted his right leg. The snowmobile shifted. The ski broke loose from the bush as if in slow motion. He jumped. The snowmobile slid a few feet and plowed into a snowdrift.

The vehicle drew closer. There was no place for Albert to hide. He tried to scramble toward the snowmobile, thinking he'd have an excuse to fiddle with the machine with his back to the road. The snow was too deep. He was ten feet away when he heard the vehicle behind him.

He could tell when it slowed. Out of the corner of his eye, he saw the driver roll down the window. A girl's voice shrieked from inside. The driver rolled up his window and drove on past, shoving snow to the sides and into Albert, pushing him backward and knocking him off his feet. As the truck passed, the plow completely buried the snowmobile.

CHAPTER 33

Near Fort Collins, Colorado
Saturday, January 25

"That was definitely the same guy," Blue said. "It's a good thing Grace was paying attention."

"No kidding." Lynnette rubbed the fog from the window and tried to see the man and his snowmobile. He was no longer visible. She looked out her own window and saw the pink and orange sun and cloud display to the east. The city of Fort Collins spread out below. In good weather it would only take a few minutes for the Youngs to drive from their house to town. In the deep snow, with the blade down, they crept. Lynnette sighed with relief when Thomas reached Overland Trail and found two lanes had already been plowed. Thomas lifted the blade, drove past Overland, and headed east.

"There's a coffee shop in the truck stop out by the interstate," said Thomas. "Has free Internet access. I'll stop there. If everything is working, we'll make our calls. You can send your email to the cop and tell her you're coming in."

Lynnette nodded, but didn't answer. Thomas was a lawyer and an officer of the court. Harboring a person of interest in a murder case and a runaway kid would land him in big trouble. If the police pulled him over, no matter how hard he tried to convince them otherwise, it would appear that he'd helped Grace run away from foster care and Lynnette run from the cops.

If she didn't turn herself in, what would she do? Her first instinct, as always, was to run. She had always dealt with uncomfortable situations that way. She'd handled her attraction to a very married Dave Buchanan at *The Indy Reporter* by running to a new job in Florida. She'd escaped the grief and overwhelming burden of her father's death by marrying the first guy who seemed protective and safe. It's how she avoided conflict and dealt with fear.

Now she wanted to escape again, escape to the safety of Ramona's home in the middle of Orange County, California. No matter how hard she tried to convince herself of her concern for Thomas and Blue, the truth niggled at her mind and raised a blush of guilt. She hadn't locked the patio door! What if, somehow, the police knew she'd left the door unlocked and turned off the air conditioner? What if they thought her negligence was intentional? Would she be considered an accessory to murder? Or, even worse, a cold-blooded killer?

Lynnette wasn't sure Thomas could help. She couldn't guarantee that any of them could help Grace.

Once on his feet, Albert looked at the buried snowmobile and gave up without trying to dig out.

Now that one lane of the road was plowed, he could walk uphill without a struggle. The snow crunched under his boots, his hands grew numb in spite of the heavy gloves, and his whole body ached, the left elbow worst of all. He pulled the sling from his pocket, fitted it over his head, and maneuvered his left arm into a more comfortable position. The puffy lining of his jacket made the arrangement awkward, but his arm ached less than when it dangled at his side.

He finally made it up the hill and went first to the garage door where he peered through the glass panes. The little black car he'd seen in Denver was there, parked beside a larger sedan.

The steps up to the front door had not been shoveled. Neither had the walkway to the back of the house, although the snow had been packed down in a narrow path around the side of the garage. He tried to raise the garage door, but it was locked.

He waded through the snow and knocked at the front door, in case someone had been left behind. No one answered. He rang the bell three times to be sure. He tried to kick the door in.

"Aw, shit!" He dropped to his knees and leaned his head against the door, tried to take a deep breath but failed. When the pain in his ribs eased, he stood. One of the clay pots near the front door lay on its side, the dirt and dried plant spilling onto the walkway. He heaved it through the nearest window and used his gloved fist to knock the remaining shards of glass free from the pane before climbing through the space.

For the next few minutes he owned the house. He took a hot shower with the drain stopper engaged so his feet would warm up as the tub filled. A search through the closets and bureau drawers produced underwear and socks, jeans, two flannel shirts, and another pair of gloves. At least he'd be dry and warm when he hit the road again. He figured out how to use the fancy coffeemaker on the counter and drank two cups of dark roast while he took a few cold puffs from his pipe. Grabbing ham and cheese from the refrigerator, he slapped together two sandwiches to take with him.

A careful search of the medicine cabinets in all three bathrooms led to the discovery of an expired pill bottle half full of Vicodin. He stuffed the container in his pocket.

Car keys hung from hooks by the door that led from the kitchen into the garage. He grabbed the set that had a key chain logo matching the burgundy sedan. Lights flashed and the car beeped when he pressed the unlock button. He raised the garage door and backed the car into the drive, leaving it there to warm up. Inside, he found a travel mug and filled it with coffee.

He pulled out his cell phone and turned it on. No signal. He left the phone on and shoved it in his pocket.

It took him less than ten minutes to drive down the hill on the plowed road.

As soon as he found a place to pull over, he tried to call Ortega. This time the phone worked fine. "They were gone by the time I got there," he reported. He did not describe his own meeting with the truck and the condition of the new snowmobile. "They live on a big hill, but they have a snowplow. That's how they got out. Where are they now?"

"I can't stand it," Ortega said. "Is there no one in this goddamned country who can carry out a job without screwing it up?"

"Why? What's wrong?"

"The tracker lost the signal," Ortega said.

"How will I find them?"

"How the fuck do I know?" Ortega paused. "Look, I'm on my way to the airport. I have to go to Miami. I'll call the tracker again before the plane leaves."

Albert rubbed his neck, then stretched his head toward each shoulder. He didn't say anything. He had hoped to finish this job and meet with Ortega while he remained in L.A. Flying to Miami meant he'd be on the rich man's turf, surrounded by Ortega's goons.

"I want you to keep looking for Foster," Ortega said, "until I tell you to stop. Understand?"

"She's got people helping her. They could be on the interstate already. They could be heading north to Wyoming, or south to Denver. Without the tracker, it's impossible."

"I'll call you back," Ortega said.

Albert remained by the side of the road, the engine running, and thought about Foster, tried to guess what her next move would be. Would she go to California? Denver? Return to Florida? Whatever she decided, she would most likely start out on I-25. The closer he was to the interstate when Ortega called, the better off he'd be. He remembered the big truck stop on the edge of town, close to the north and south ramps.

Thomas drove around to the back of the station restaurant where he could park the truck in a wide space near the eighteen-wheelers. "Stick together," he said. "No wandering off alone."

Lynnette glanced at him, saw he watched her as he spoke. Her eye felt twitchy and her mouth dry. What was he thinking? Did he expect her to run? Or was he concerned the guy in the tweed jacket would be hot on their trail?

"Better bring your laptop, Lynnette," he said. "You need to get that email off to the police officer in Florida."

She retrieved her laptop, placed the envelope containing the checks into her case, then stowed the case under the dash and followed Thomas into the building. As she slid into the booth next to Grace, she noted that Thomas had elected to sit in an alcove not visible from the front door. She placed her laptop on the table.

"I'll be right back," Thomas said. He headed to the back of the room where a Restrooms sign hung over a swinging door.

"I gotta go, too," Grace said.

"I'll go with you," Blue said.

Grace put her hands on her hips. "Blue, I can go to the bathroom by myself."

"Dad said we were supposed to stick together."

"What about Lynnette? Who's going to watch her?"

"It's not to watch anybody, Grace, it's to protect you."

"I can pee by myself. I've been doing it forever, you know."

"Blue, it's okay," said Lynnette. "Let her be. Go on, Grace. Hurry up."

Lynnette pulled out her own phone and dialed Dave Buchanan's number. The call went to voice mail. She didn't leave a message. She started to punch in the numbers to call Ramona, then changed her mind and hung up.

"You better put my number in there," Blue said. "Dad's, too."

Lynnette decided to check for new messages on the fat man's phone, hoping she'd get some idea where Ortega was. She replaced the battery and accessed the voice mail. There were no new messages, both a relief and a concern. She shut off the phone and removed the battery.

The laptop's charge level was dangerously low. She logged on to her email, opened the most recent communication from the female cop, hit reply, and typed her message:

I didn't kill Carl. I want to come in, but I'm in trouble. A scary guy named Sammy Grick switched our laptop cases in Miami and he was chasing me. Grick had stuff that belonged to a man named Benny Ortega. These two men, and another one who showed up yesterday, threatened to kill me. I'm almost out of—

"Lynnette, Thomas called the FBI and told them where we are!"

Lynnette stared at Grace, unable to clear her mind of the message she was typing. "What?"

"I walked out of the restroom, and he was by a door at the end of the hall with his back turned. I heard him talking to someone he called Agent."

Blue jumped up and started toward the restrooms.

Lynnette hit the Send key and powered off. She grabbed her jacket, purse, and laptop and followed Grace toward the door. Just as Grace reached out to open it, a burgundy sedan cruised past the front of the building. The man in the driver's seat leaned forward, seemed to peer through the windshield at the parking lot beyond, then slowed and drove on. Lynnette grabbed

Grace's shoulder and jerked her back. "Wait," she said. "That car that went by looks like the other car in Blue's garage. Her dad's car."

CHAPTER 34

Glades, Florida
Saturday, January 25

Officer Maggie Gutierrez's email pinged. She opened her mail tab and saw the reply she'd been waiting for. Her excitement quickly changed to disappointment and then to anxiety when she saw that Lynnette had stopped mid-message. She snatched the phone and punched in the extension for computer support.

"Bill, can you tell where an email came from if I give you the email address?"

He typed then said, "It comes up as Sunnyvale, California. Silicon Valley. It could have originated there, but it's more likely the email carries the host IP. Doesn't mean she's in California."

Maggie printed out the email and went to find Detective Prince.

Near Fort Collins, Colorado
Saturday, January 25

Albert steered into the lot of the truck stop, cruised slowly past the gas pumps and the front of the restaurant. As he rounded the side of the building, he spotted the tail end of a truck that resembled the one he'd seen on the hill. He stopped, backed up, and parked around the corner, halfway between the front and back doors.

He left the car running while he called Ortega.

"They got a fix on her five or ten minutes ago," Ortega said.

"She's at the southwest corner of I-25 and—"

"I know. I'm here."

"Do not let her get away," Ortega said.

"She's in a public place. Lots of witnesses."

"Get my stuff, Getz. If you get my stuff, you can let her go."

"Then it's time you told me what she has."

"The most important thing is a mailing envelope with checks inside. Even if you don't get anything else, you must get those checks. And Sammy Grick's phone. I'll call you as soon as my flight lands in Miami."

Los Angeles, California
Saturday, January 25

Benny boarded his plane moments after his conversation with Getz and made one more call to his tracker. Nothing had changed. The cell phone no longer emitted a signal. He retrieved a bottle of scotch and a glass from the galley cupboard. Once buckled in, he poured a generous amount in his glass.

When did everything start to go wrong? Benny leaned his head back and stared out the window. *When the Foster woman got in the way. No. Before that. When Sammy killed Maria.* He paused to think about Maria and pressed his cold glass to his forehead. He wouldn't miss her all that much, but now he had to worry about Sammy being connected to her death. Lots of people knew Sammy did jobs for him all the time. It would look as though he'd hired Sammy to kill his wife. Considering her life insurance payoff, the cops would consider Benny the prime suspect.

Getting the checks posed a completely different problem. If they were ever tied to Sammy or to Benny, the Feds would have his balls in a vise. He couldn't cash the checks now anyway, but even if he'd recovered them sooner, he couldn't have used them while Foster was still alive. What had she seen and how much had she figured out? He had to assume she snooped through his belongings. If the thefts hit the news, she would know he was responsible. Unless he had her killed, and the others with her, he would be exposed. He had to face facts. All their work stealing these checks had been wasted effort. The only reason he needed them now was to shred them.

He was in enough trouble already without inviting the Feds to join the party. Because of his wife's death, everything he'd done in the last month, every trip he'd taken, every shithead he'd ever hired, everything and everyone would be scrutinized. Even if he claimed Sammy Grick had never been in his employ, the cops would still do their best to tie Ortega to his wife's death. Truth was, they already hated his guts because he was Cuban and he was filthy rich. He'd been questioned about his various business interests several times in the past.

He poured himself another drink as he considered the possibility Foster would take the rap for her husband's murder. He wondered if she did it.

He thought about the checks again. The combined forces of the IRS, the FBI, plus every other agency involved with interstate commerce and banking would investigate every nook and cranny of Ortega Enterprises.

His business would bite the dust, and he would go to prison.

Sweat broke out on his forehead. He wiped it off with his sleeve.

CHAPTER 35

Near Fort Collins, Colorado

Saturday, January 25

Thomas walked toward Lynnette with Blue at his side, gesturing and waving her arms. Thomas glanced past Lynnette toward the door, then quickly strode to a side window and peered through the glass. He pointed through the window and Blue placed her hand over her mouth. Lynnette grabbed Grace's hand and ran to the window.

"Is that your car? Do you have another set of keys?"

"Yes," Thomas said. "On the same ring as the truck keys."

Lynnette stuck her hand out. "Give me the keys to the truck. Is there a back door in this place?"

"Yes, but you can't handle the truck—"

"Don't be stupid. When he comes in the front, you take Blue and Grace out the back and make a run for it in the car. He doesn't care about any of you, only me and the stuff Grick stole. I need the truck keys to get my laptop case. That's where I put the checks."

"I think it's better if we all wait in here together."

"Why? Because you called the FBI? What did you tell them?"

"I told them you were being pursued by a couple of thugs because you accidentally came into possession of checks that might expose a major crime. I thought our safety was more important than—"

"You're right. You three should never have become involved

203

in my mess. But you have no right to make decisions for me. You can take the girls and walk away, or you can take your chances and wait for the Feds, but you can't tell me what to do."

"I don't see that you have a choice. I'm not giving you the keys to the car or the truck. It's too crowded in here for this guy to try anything funny. A dozen truck drivers would jump him if he threatened any of us."

"He might have a gun," Grace said.

"That's right, Dad. He could hurt a lot of people before anyone could catch him." Blue held out her hand. "Let me have the keys. I'll help Lynnette get this guy's stuff out of the truck and we'll—"

"No." Thomas stuffed his hands in his pockets and widened his stance. "Sit down in the booth. Everything is going to be okay." He reached for Grace's hand.

"Don't touch me!" she yelled. "If you hurt me or my mom again, I'm telling."

Thomas jerked his hand away and took a step back and stared at Grace. Two burly truck drivers stopped in their tracks and glared at Thomas. They took a few steps in his direction, but Blue held up her hand and smiled. "It's okay," she said. "My little sister has a mental problem."

"I do not!" Grace yelled. "And I'm not your sister!"

"Grace, come on," Blue said. "Don't do this."

Lynnette held out her hand. "Blue, unless you want me to start screaming bloody murder, you'd better make your dad give us the keys."

Thomas fumbled in his pocket for his keychain, removed one key and placed it in her hand.

Grace tugged on Lynnette's jacket sleeve and tried to pull her toward the hallway. Before she could move, she saw Thomas and Blue look toward the front door of the restaurant.

"Mrs. Foster, hello."

The guy from the library edged in her direction. His left arm hung in a sling, and his puffy jacket made him look chubby and off balance.

Her first thought was that he'd walk up to her, they'd chat, and she'd retrieve what Ortega wanted and hand it over.

As soon as the guy began to fish around in his pocket, Lynnette panicked. Maybe Grace was right. Maybe he had a gun. She yanked Grace out of the way, thrust her laptop and purse into Grace's hands, and shoved her toward Blue. Thomas pulled Grace and Blue behind him. He reached for Lynnette, but she jumped away and turned to face Ortega's man. Two steps took her close enough to his left arm to grab hold of the sling and jerk it toward his elbow. As he yelped and jumped away, he clutched his arm closer to his body.

Lynnette plunged her hand into his right pocket, grabbed his middle finger and jerked it upward.

"Son of a bitch!" he yelled as he pulled free from her grip. "Why the fuck did you do that?"

A tall man wearing a Caterpillar baseball cap stomped his feet on the floor mat to loosen the snow from his boots. "Hey, buddy, there's ladies and kids in here. Watch your mouth."

Grace pulled away from Thomas and pointed. "He's got a gun in his pocket."

"I don't have a gun." The guy from the library reached into his pocket, pulled out his pipe and cell phone. "I need a word with Mrs. Foster. She's in no danger from me."

"He has a gun somewhere," Grace said. "Frisk him."

"Damn it, kid, shut the fuck up."

"Hey! What'd I tell ya?" the trucker yelled.

"Right. Sorry. Mrs. Foster, all I need is the contents of the laptop case Sammy Grick had when yours got switched with his. I have a list. If I get everything, Mr. Ortega says that you all walk away and there's no more trouble."

"Lynnette, be careful," Thomas said. He had grabbed hold of Grace's wrist and yanked her behind him. "Let me handle this."

Lynnette ignored him. She didn't know whether to believe Ortega's man or not, but she had to be the one to decide, the one to take a chance. It seemed too simple, especially considering the terror she'd felt when Sammy Grick was after her. Was it any different now? What had changed? Maybe Ortega just wanted his checks and cash. And the checks? Perhaps they were intended for Ortega's companies. If so, she was a thief.

"Okay," Lynnette said. "My case is in the truck. I'll get it. You wait here."

"Not a chance," he said. "I'll go with you."

"Grick's phone is in my purse." She took her purse from Grace, pulled the phone and its battery from an outside pocket, and handed them over.

"We'll go out the rear door," Lynnette told Thomas. "Take care of Grace." She handed her purse to Grace as she passed.

"Are you coming back?" Grace asked.

"She's coming back, kid," the man said. "Don't worry about it."

When Lynnette reached the door leading to the parking lot, she glanced over her shoulder. Ortega's thug followed right on her heels, replacing the battery in Grick's phone as he walked. Grace watched from the other end of the hallway, her pack in place on her back, Lynnette's purse strap over her shoulder and the laptop tucked under one arm. Lynnette smiled, then turned and walked out the door.

Glades, Florida
Saturday, January 25
"This is all we have," Maggie told Detective Prince. "I checked with the techies. It's nothing. She could be anywhere."

"I don't believe this crap she sent you. It's a smoke screen. She's trying to cover her ass because she knows we'll catch up with her sooner or later. Making it sound like she's running because the boogey man scared her. This woman ran because she killed her husband or she hired Grick to kill him."

"What do you want me to do?"

"Follow up. Same stuff. Send her another email that sounds sympathetic. Offer protection."

Maggie returned to her desk and leaned back in her chair with her feet propped on the partially opened bottom drawer. She closed her eyes and rubbed her forehead. Prince wasn't looking at anyone else for Carl Foster's murder. He'd already decided Foster's wife was guilty.

When Maggie opened her eyes, a teenage girl with long, dark hair stood in front of her desk. She wore a white peasant blouse and jeans. Maggie jerked her feet off the drawer and sat up straight. "What can I do for you?"

The girl blushed and shook her head.

Maggie switched to Spanish. "You don't speak English?"

The girl shook her head again.

"Sit there." Maggie motioned toward a chair. She grabbed her clipboard and a pen.

"What's your name?" she asked in Spanish.

"Laura."

"And your last name?"

"It's better if I don't say."

"Why are you here?"

"That cop who was murdered. They're saying his wife did it."

"Who's saying that?"

"A guy I know. Said he saw it on TV."

"Why do you care?"

"She didn't do it."

"How do you know?"

"I know who did it, but if I tell you, they'll kill me."

"They?"

"They're crazy. Make us all look bad."

"Gangs?"

"Yes. That's all I can say." Laura stood up and started to walk away.

"If you can't tell me who did it, why did you come here?"

"I don't want that woman to get blamed for something she didn't do."

Holy shit, what do I do if this girl disappears? "Wait," Maggie said. "If you leave, there's no way I can help Mrs. Foster. I need you to tell my boss what you told me."

Laura shook her head and kept going.

Near Fort Collins, Colorado
Saturday, January 25

Lynnette led Ortega's henchman to the truck. "You got a name?" she called over her shoulder.

"Al."

"Okay, Al. Everything else that belongs to your creepy boss is in my laptop case. You said you had a list, so you'll know you have everything. There's cash. It's all there. You have the phone already. The charger for the phone . . ."

Lynnette paused when she got to the truck and inserted the key. As she opened the door, Al said, "There's also an envelope. It has checks inside."

Damn. She had hoped he didn't know about the checks. "Yep, got those too." She climbed into the truck's cabin and pulled the door partially closed. Al reached up and grabbed the top of the door so it wouldn't close all the way. Lynnette reached for the laptop case and unzipped one side. Her hand reached for the cash. She hesitated.

With one fast movement, she grabbed the door with her left

hand, jerked it shut on Al's fingers, then kicked it open, slamming it hard against the man's chest.

With his left arm in the sling and his right hand bleeding across the knuckles, he had no way to break his fall without hurting himself even more. His feet slipped out from under him as he fell, and the back of his head smacked against the hardpacked snow.

Lynnette tried to fit the truck key into the ignition, but quickly realized she held only a door key. It wouldn't start the engine. She stepped out of the truck with her laptop case. Al lay on the ground. He didn't move. Blood trickled from his nose.

She set the case on the snow and dug through his pockets until she found the keys to Thomas's car. As she ran toward the sedan, parked several yards on the other side of the truck, Grace burst through the back door, the laptop clutched to her chest with one hand and dragging Lynnette's purse across the snow with the other.

"What are you doing out here? Where's your coat?" Lynnette yelled.

"It's in the booth. I didn't have time to get it."

Lynnette grabbed her purse and slung the strap over her shoulder. "Okay, kid, let's get out of here. Might as well add car theft to my list of offenses." Lynnette stripped off her jacket and tossed it on the passenger seat. "Put that jacket on before you fasten your seatbelt." Seconds later, Lynnette drove past the restaurant. Blue stood at one of the windows.

"I'm sorry, Blue," Grace called out, even though Blue could not hear.

Lynnette glanced at Grace as they cruised around the front of the building, past the gas pumps, and onto the frontage road, which led to the interstate's on-ramp. Grace had never looked sadder than she did at that moment.

CHAPTER 36

Near Fort Collins, Colorado
Saturday, January 25
Albert opened his eyes and stared at the sky. *What the hell happened?* He shook from the cold. His face ached, his elbow joint felt as though it had been twisted out of alignment, and he couldn't take a deep breath. The pain in his head was so intense he wanted to puke. As he became more aware, he heard voices. He started to turn his head, but it made him dizzy. He shut his eyes again.

"This is the guy," a man said. "The woman told us he had chased her and she feared for her life. We brought her here and I called you. Then she disappeared."

"You didn't see her leave?"

"Dad didn't." A woman's voice. "But I saw her talking to a trucker and then she walked out with him. They headed over there where the semis are parked."

Albert tried to take a deep breath and moaned. The voices stopped. He felt a hand on his shoulder, shaking him gently.

"Hey, you okay? We called an ambulance. Should be here any minute."

Oh, hell no. Not again. "No, I'm not okay," Albert said. His voice sounded tinny.

"I need to ask you a few questions."

Albert grunted.

"What's your name, sir?"

"I don't know."

"Where's your vehicle, sir?"

"What?"

"Your vehicle. How did you get here?"

Albert shivered and moaned. "I'm cold. I'm really cold."

"Sir, may I check your pockets for a wallet? We need to know your name."

"Who are you?" Albert asked.

"Can you open your eyes, sir? I'm Agent Bailey of the FBI. This is my badge."

Albert opened his eyes a slit, focused on the badge, thought about the contents of his wallet, and decided he had no choice. "Okay."

He closed his eyes again and let the agent check his pockets.

"I have it, sir. It says your name is Albert Getz and you live in Los Angeles. Is that true?"

"I don't know."

"And you don't know how you got here?"

"No. Can you get me a blanket or something?"

"What about you?" the officer said, speaking over Albert's head. "What's your name, sir?"

"Thomas Young. This is my daughter, Teresa."

"And you say this man slipped on the ice and hit his head on your truck?"

"That's what it looks like to me. I didn't actually see it happen."

"Did you see this happen, Miss?"

"No."

"Did anyone else witness the accident?"

"Not that I know of."

An ambulance siren wailed in the distance, getting closer and closer. Albert felt a sinking feeling in his chest. This job had turned into a disaster. He quit. He no longer wanted Ortega's money. Ortega's crime against Albert's brother would not be avenged. Albert wanted only one thing.

He wanted to go home.

"Where are we going?" Grace asked.

Lynnette pulled onto southbound I-25. "I haven't decided."

"We could go to California. My dad will be back tomorrow."

"What do you mean? I thought we were past that story about your dad's body. Didn't you admit you're a runaway from a foster home?"

Grace sighed. "I didn't say that part. Blue did. I got tired of lying and being accused of more lying, so I didn't say anything."

Lynnette kept her eyes on the road. *I can't deal with this and drive at the same time.*

"So we're going to Denver? To the airport?" Grace asked.

"I don't know. I didn't want the FBI hauling me away in handcuffs without me knowing where you were or if Thomas would look out for you. I didn't have time to finish my email to the lady cop in Florida. Maybe she can help me. Maybe she can help both of us."

"A lady cop in Florida isn't going to help me get to my dad's house. She'll call my mom and this whole mess will start all over again."

"I know. But at least you won't have to worry about me and my dumb mistakes. I thought if we found a motel where I could put the car out of sight, I could get on the Internet, make contact with this cop, you know, work something out."

"Lynnette, my dad will get home from Afghanistan tomorrow. He'll call as soon as he arrives in the U.S. Then he'll want to come get me. It would be easier if we were already in L.A. Dad could pick me up at the airport and you could catch a flight to Florida from there. I'll be out of your hair, and you can straighten out your own problems. I know you went to a lot of trouble to help me, and I'm glad you did. If you could do this one more thing, I know my dad would appreciate it."

Grace was telling her story as though talking about someone else. *What the hell? Now she says her dad is alive?* It was obvious Grace had a whole repertoire of alternative life stories to fit the situation.

"So your mom does exist? You're back to the original story?"

"Yeah. I'm sorry. I thought the story about my dad being dead would convince you to take me straight to L.A."

"Is your mom really out of town with her boyfriend?"

"Yeah. She'll get home tomorrow. Then she'll try to call Dad and explain that I'm incorra . . . incorrig—"

"Incorrigible?"

"Yeah. She wants me to live with Dad. She doesn't want me around anymore."

"How do I know you're telling the truth?"

Grace fingered an X on her chest as she said, "Cross my heart and hope to die."

CHAPTER 37

Fort Collins, Colorado
Saturday, January 25

Albert opened his eyes. Fuzzy white ceiling tiles floated overhead. A needle poked out of his arm. Clear liquid dripped through the attached line. He lay on a hospital bed in a curtained cubicle.

From somewhere close by, a phone rang four times. A minute later, it rang again. Four times.

He'd put the battery in Grick's phone and stuffed it in his pocket while he followed the Foster woman to the truck. His fingers closed around something cold and solid. He held it up and found the remote control for the bed. With his thumb on the up button, he raised the head a little at a time. His jacket lay across the end of the bed. He reached for it, but a blinding pain shot through his skull. A wave of nausea turned his stomach upside down.

As soon as he lay still, he felt better. He inched his hand toward his jacket, retrieved the phone, and checked the voice mail. Ortega had left a message for Foster. He sounded drunk.

In the air
Saturday, January 25

Benny downed his third scotch before his co-pilot walked out of the cockpit and handed him a piece of paper. "Your office said it's urgent."

214

Benny looked at his watch. "Where are we?"

"Almost to the Kansas–Missouri state line."

The note said: *The signal is active. Current location is a trauma center just south of Fort Collins, Colorado.*

"Wait," Benny said as the co-pilot walked away. "Is it okay to use my cell phone?"

"It's better to use the flight phone. I'll get it."

When the co-pilot returned to the cockpit, Benny made two calls to Sammy Grick's phone and left a brief message each time. "I will not leave you alone until you have returned everything that belongs to me."

Denver, Colorado
Saturday, January 25

One of the exits off I-70 east of Denver listed a dozen motels on the exit sign. Lynnette took the off-ramp and drove through several of the parking lots until she found a motel advertising free high-speed Internet connection. "We need to get cash," she told Grace. "But not around here."

She took the on ramp to I-70 and drove two exits east, then cruised along the main road until she saw a bank with a walk-up ATM. She parked the car on the far side of a nearby fast-food restaurant lot and left Grace in the car with the doors locked so she could approach the ATM on foot. Hopefully, there would be no camera at the restaurant to document her license plate. Fearing the cops might have closed her account, she held her breath until the machine spit out the requested three hundred dollars and ejected her card. She wasn't so worried about being tracked anymore. By the time they sent someone to the ATM, she'd be long gone.

After they'd returned to the motel, Grace said, "Can we get food now?"

"Sure. Can you handle burgers and fries? I want to use the

drive-through."

"Fine. Get lots. And milkshakes, too. One chocolate and one vanilla."

"Okay. We aren't going out again tonight, so this will be lunch and supper."

Lynnette bought more than she thought they could possibly eat and handed the bags to Grace. Less than ten minutes later, with the car parked behind the motel, she and Grace settled into their room and watched cable news.

There was no mention of a missing child from Florida or a person of interest named Lynnette Foster, aka Hudson.

Lynnette set her food on the coffee table and plugged in her laptop and phone charger.

Fort Collins, Colorado
Saturday, January 25
Albert awoke to the annoying sensation of a woman shaking his shoulder.

"The doctor says you can go home, Mr. Getz. Do you have someone to drive you?"

"Home?"

"You might be a little shaky for a couple of days, but you're fine. A slight concussion. You'll have a few bruises and a headache. I'll be back in a minute to remove that needle for you. You need someone to drive you home and stay with you overnight." She left the cubicle and whipped the curtain closed.

Albert sighed. Until this trip, he'd only been in a hospital two times in his life. Suddenly he was accident-prone. He thought about Sammy Grick. Grick had died on this job.

He was superstitious, but he wondered if Benny Ortega was jinxed. Or maybe the Foster broad was jinxed. Whatever the problem, he'd never had this much bad luck in his whole life.

Thinking about Foster pissed him off. If it turned out she'd murdered her husband, he was going to wish he'd taken her out when he had the chance.

He rubbed his forehead, then felt the sore spot on the back of his head. He didn't like the idea of leaving the hospital on his own. What if he blacked out while driving? Hey, he didn't even have a car. He'd have to rent one.

He'd take a cab to a motel and hole up for a day or two, make sure he could drive safely. He was fed up with Ortega's job. Fed up with the Foster woman. Sammy's laptop was the only thing he'd retrieved so far, and he didn't know where the hell it was. He dialed Ortega's number and left a message that he'd retrieved Sammy Grick's phone but nothing else because he'd had another accident and got sent to the hospital.

In the air
Saturday, January 25
Benny redialed every half hour and left messages for Lynnette Foster on Sammy's phone. After three hours, he staggered to the restroom, peed a river of scotch, and returned to his seat. He rang for the co-pilot and demanded a meal and a bottle of wine.

Glades, Florida
Saturday, January 25
Detective Prince looked around the room, even stepped aside and peered behind Maggie's back. "Where is she?" he said.

"She left. I asked her to stay and talk to you, but she walked out."

"You got her name, right? Send a car to pick her up."

"She just gave me her first name. She's scared."

"Not good enough, Gutierrez. I like Foster's wife for this killing. If you want to get her off the hook, you'll have to do a lot more than come up with a flimsy story you can't prove. Think about it. You're saying a police officer let a bunch of punks inside his house, no sign of forced entry. If she didn't do it herself, she set it up."

"What about the Internal Affairs investigation? Carl Foster was in trouble. That's the reason my partner and I went to Foster's house in the first place. We were supposed to pick him up because he blew off the preliminary hearing. Couldn't that have something to do with his murder?"

Prince's jaw clenched and unclenched.

"Didn't you read my report?" Maggie tried to keep a straight face, tried not to let her expression show her shock and dismay that Prince had set himself up as judge and jury.

He glared at her. "Stick to the tasks I give you and leave the rest of the case to me. See if you can find that girl. Check mug shots, the surveillance recording, you know the drill."

After he'd left, Maggie checked her email. Still nothing new from Foster. She grabbed a notebook and pen and headed downstairs to the reception desk.

CHAPTER 38

Denver, Colorado
Saturday, January 25
Lynnette needed to make a decision before she and Grace left Denver the next morning. Were they going to L.A. or Florida? A lot would depend on what Maggie Gutierrez had to say.

First, however, Lynnette had to let Ramona know she was okay. She'd contact her by email again to save time. If she called, she would be forced to tell her stepmother the whole story. That would only make matters worse. And she still couldn't tell Ramona her exact location or that she had a young girl with her. That would put Ramona in the bad position of keeping information from the police or the FBI.

Lynnette sighed at the hundreds of unread emails. She looked for mail from Ramona. There were two, both referring to phone calls from the Glades Police Department. Lynnette hit Reply on the most recent message and wrote that she was okay and would be in touch with Officer Maggie Gutierrez about returning to Florida.

The car. How could she have dithered around the room and wasted time without calling Thomas about his car? The way things had been going, he might have reported it stolen by now. She found her phone and dialed his number. He answered on the first ring.

"Thomas, I'm sorry. I didn't know what else to do. When you

called the FBI, I was afraid they'd take me out of there in handcuffs."

"It wasn't like that, Lynnette. I told them you were in trouble, that you'd accidentally came into possession of an envelope that contained several very large checks and were scared of the people chasing you. I hoped that getting rid of the checks would get this Ortega guy and his thugs off your trail."

"Or make them furious."

"Yeah, or make them furious. Where are you?"

"Did you report your car stolen?"

"No, of course not. As far as they know, we came in the truck and planned to leave in the truck. Which, by the way, is the truth."

"But you didn't have the checks. What did the FBI agents say?"

"When they first got there, we were outside by the truck. They checked out the guy on the ground and saw him off in the ambulance. After that, I told them about you getting scared when this guy came into the restaurant. You ran and he chased after you. When I turned to the window and saw this guy sprawled on the ice by my truck, I ran outside to see if he was okay. By then, you'd disappeared."

"Thanks, Thomas. I don't know how I can ever repay you and Blue for everything, especially after Grace's outburst at the truck stop."

"For starters I'd like to get my car back. What are your plans?"

"I'm working on that. I need to talk to the police officer in Glades. I want to help Grace at the same time I'm getting myself out of this mess, but she's changed her story again, back to the original about her dad returning to the U.S. tomorrow . . . alive. I need to sort this out myself. If I can keep your car overnight, it would help. I'll let you know where it is tomorrow morning."

With a sigh of relief, Lynnette dialed Dave Buchanan's

number. Her call went to voice mail. She left a message asking him to call her. The least she could do before checking in with the police was tell Dave she'd done nothing wrong and that she'd be fine. She didn't want him back in her life, but she did want to know if she had a story worth taking to the press. Maybe it was dumb, but one part of her still hoped to turn this fiasco into a coup.

"What did Thomas say?" Grace asked.

"He said everything would be okay. I'm supposed to call him tomorrow morning and let him know where we leave the car."

Grace picked up the TV remote, and began clicking furiously through the channels.

"What's wrong?" Lynnette asked.

"I'm worried."

"About what."

"Everything, Lynnette. What if my dad doesn't get back on schedule? What if you get arrested? What if my mom finds out where I've been all this time?"

"Me too, Grace. I'm worried about all those things, too."

Fort Collins, Colorado
Saturday, January 25

Albert left the hospital and took a cab to a nearby motel. He used his credit card to check in and had long distance activated on the phone. When he dialed Benny Ortega's number from the room, his call went directly to voice mail.

"I quit," he said. "I will never work for you again. Don't ever call me."

He thumbed through the motel handbook until he located a pizza joint that advertised delivery and placed his order. While waiting for the food, he took two aspirin from the bottle he'd purchased at the front desk. He soaked a washcloth in cold water and pressed it against his forehead. When the cloth turned warm, he wet it again, this time holding it to the back of his head. He continued this treatment until a knock on the door signaled the arrival of his order.

The smell of warm pizza permeated the room in seconds. After turning on the TV, he stared at the food spread out before him and wondered how long it had been since anything had looked and smelled this good. His headache eased. The tense muscles in his neck and shoulders seemed to melt as he leaned back.

Pizza first. He pulled a slice from the carton and took a bite. He was still savoring the first taste when a sharp rap sounded at his door. A pain shot through his head as he jumped to his feet. He threw the pizza slice back in the carton and grabbed a napkin to wipe his mouth.

"Who is it?" he called.

"FBI, Mr. Getz. We need to ask you a couple more questions."

Albert stared at the door. Why were they here? He slipped on the ice at a truck stop and he went to the hospital. Unless the guy and his daughter had told the FBI something different after the ambulance took him away. How would he play it? Pretend he still couldn't remember what happened?

He opened the door and stared at the two men who stood in the hall.

"Do you remember me, Mr. Getz? Agent Bailey? I talked to you at the truck stop." He waved toward the other man. "This is Agent Drake."

"I remember the name. I wasn't seeing too straight. Why are you here?"

"We have a couple more questions. Something happened and we're wondering if you know anything about it. Could we come in?"

"Oh. Sure." *Like I can do anything to stop you.*

The two agents followed him to the table where his pizza cooled, spilled cheese congealing in clumps on the cardboard container. He sat and retrieved the slice he'd been eating.

Agent Bailey sat on the only other chair in the room. Drake sat on the end of the bed and took a notepad and pen from his pocket. Albert chewed, swallowed, and said, "Didn't you have questions?"

"Yes, sir. A woman was supposed to be at the truck stop with a package of checks for us. The woman and the package have disappeared. Do you know anything about that?"

"She had the checks?"

Agent Bailey raised his eyebrows. "You said 'the checks.' You seem surprised that Mrs. Foster had them. Where did you think the checks were?"

"I meant to say 'she had checks?' "

"That's what Mr. Young told us. Is that why you chased her out of the restaurant?"

"Why would I do that?"

"That's what we'd like to know."

Albert wiped the grease from his mouth with a napkin and opened the container of salad. He tried to think while he pretended to concentrate on removing the cellophane top on the salad dressing and spreading it across the greens.

"How did you find me?"

"We have our ways, Mr. Getz," Bailey said. "We went to the hospital to talk to you and found you had been released. The receptionist saw you leave in a City Cab and she knew what time. One call to the dispatcher, and here we are."

"I didn't see a package at the truck stop. I didn't take one with me when I left."

"Where were you going?"

"I beg your pardon?"

"When you walked out the door of the truck stop. Where

were you going?"

Albert rubbed his forehead as though trying to massage the fog away. "I . . . don't . . ."

"Come now, Mr. Getz. You have a minor concussion. The doctor told us your memory should not be impaired. Please tell us where you were going when you left the truck stop."

Think. Why not tell the truth? Maybe this is the way to nail Ortega. Albert thought about his story, realized he could be in the clear. He just ran an errand, right? He was a courier. He didn't carry a weapon, he didn't do anything wrong. Breaking into the house on the hill and stealing a car didn't count. After all, he'd been stuck in a damn snowdrift.

What did he know? He knew Benny Ortega hired Fat Ass Sammy Grick, who was definitely a killer. And he knew about Lynnette Foster, who might be a killer. And he knew Foster had things that belonged to Ortega, even if he didn't know why Foster had them. *Sounds like a mess. Maybe I don't know very much after all.*

"Mr. Getz?"

"Yeah, uh, what was the question?"

"Where were you going when you slipped on the ice and fell?"

Albert sighed. "Okay . . . I didn't slip on the ice."

The FBI agents exchanged a glance.

"Do you want some pizza?" Albert said. "It's a very long story."

By the time he got to the part where Lynnette Foster knocked him off his feet, Drake had taken several pages of notes. The two agents knocked off two slices of pizza and were now chewing antacid tablets.

"Let me get this straight," Bailey said. "Mrs. Foster still has Mr. Ortega's property, which was originally in Sammy Grick's possession? And as far as you know, she has the checks?"

"That's what she told me. She gave me Grick's cell phone inside the building. I followed her out to the truck to get an envelope from her laptop case. Mr. Ortega said she had a brown envelope containing six checks, and if she turned over everything, I should let her go."

"And if she didn't turn over everything?"

"I'd have to talk her into it."

Bailey said, "I'll bet."

"Nothing happened to her. I waited outside the door of the truck and she got inside to get the stuff. The driver's door all of a sudden closes on my hand and then flies open, whacking me in the chest. My head hits the ground so hard it feels like it's splitting open. The next thing I know, I hear voices. That's all hazy. Then the ambulance siren." Albert rubbed his head. "I do have a concussion." He held his hand over his mouth and belched. "Feel like puking."

Bailey ignored Albert's distress. "Where did the Foster woman go after she knocked you down?"

"Didn't you hear what I said? I was out cold."

"The car you drove to the truck stop, you say that belonged to Mr. Young?"

Albert sighed. "Yeah."

"So you stole it?"

"Borrowed."

"Did you have Mr. Young's permission to borrow his car?"

"Not exactly."

"What does that mean?" Bailey asked.

"It means, they buried me and my snowmobile under a pile of snow and left me there to die. Loaning me his car was the least Young could do to make amends."

"Is the car still at the truck stop?"

"That's where it was the last time I saw it. Unless . . . how did the Foster woman get away? Oh, hell!" He thrust his hand in his pants pocket. Nothing. He stood up slowly and walked across the room to the closet, pulled out his jacket and felt in all the pockets. No sedan keys.

"I'll bet Foster stole the keys out of my pants," he said. "I don't have the car. She has it. And if she has it, I'll bet Young hasn't reported it stolen. And if he hasn't reported it stolen, I'll bet he's talked to her. I bet she still has the checks. Frankly, gentlemen, I think you're talking to the wrong guy."

CHAPTER 39

Denver, Colorado
Saturday, January 25
Less than thirty minutes after she'd placed the call to Dave, Lynnette's cell phone rang.

"What the hell is going on, Lynnette? You're all over the news. I've had three calls from a policewoman in Florida and two from your stepmother. Did you kill a cop?"

"No, Dave. The cop is . . . was my husband. He punched me in the face and I walked out. And someone killed him. That's all I know. The police left email messages for me, but I didn't have a chance to answer before now. I'm going to call them, but I wanted to talk to you first."

"They told me to call if I heard from you."

"That's okay. Wait an hour, okay? In the Miami airport my laptop case got switched with one carried by a thug named Sammy Grick. From everything I can tell, he worked as a courier for a Cuban businessman from Florida named Benito Ortega."

"What was in the case? Something illegal? Drugs?"

"No drugs. But the other stuff, well, it included an envelope containing a few very big checks from several different companies. I suspect they're stolen."

"So what? You turn them over to the cops."

"You don't think there's a story in this?"

"Lynnette, the story doesn't matter. You're in trouble. You

227

need to get your priorities straight."

"If I go to Florida and still have this stuff in my possession, the police will take it. We won't have the checks anymore. We need them to investigate."

"What do you suggest?"

"Should I mail you the checks before I call the Florida cop?" There was a long silence.

"Dave, are you still there?"

"Yeah. I did a quick search on Benito Ortega, Lynnie. He's a powerful and very scary guy. I got kids—"

"Okay." She tried to ignore Dave's use of the nickname he'd given her. Their relationship had always been professional until the day Lynnette's father died. Dave rushed to her side, took her in his arms, and held her while she cried. He also kissed her. But Dave had a wife and three kids.

When Lynnette resigned from her job, he continued to call her Lynnie and begged her to stay. At one point, he even offered to get a divorce.

Lynnette handled this crisis the way she tended to handle all crises. She ran away. And because this crisis was two-pronged— her father's death and the temptation of a married man's comfort and love—she ran all the way to South Florida.

And we know what kind of trouble I got into there.

"Tell you what, Dave. Call me Lynnette and treat me like a reporter."

"Okay. What do you think the checks mean?"

"A check theft conspiracy. Steal them in Florida, launder them in California. These are big checks. One is over half a million dollars."

"You can't withhold evidence. It would be better if the Feds handled this one. Turn Ortega's stuff over to the FBI."

"Dave, are you afraid to look at the checks?"

"No. I'm afraid to even have the checks in my possession.

You should also be afraid."

"This is crazy. I've been chased all over Denver and points north by the guys working for this Ortega guy, but I hung in there, hoping to get the story. Ortega won't know anything about you. He won't know you have the evidence."

"He'll know if I break the story."

"That's it then. We probably won't be talking again."

"Lynnie, please—"

"Lynnette. My name is Lynnette."

Miami, Florida
Saturday, January 25

The moment Benny's plane landed in Miami, he checked his cell phone for messages. When he heard Getz tell him he didn't want to work for Benny ever again, he laughed. Why would he want to hire the guy for anything else? He was accident-prone. A klutz.

"Mr. Ortega?" The co-pilot stood in the doorway to the cockpit. "We have instructions from the tower to hold a position near the police hangar and remain in the airplane until further notice."

"Why?"

"They didn't say, sir."

Benny looked at his cell phone and thought about the whole mess with Sammy Grick, Lynnette Foster, and Albert Getz. He wondered where his money was. He thought about the checks that his wife had painstakingly collected from clerks on the take at six different companies. Maria had made all the contacts, she had all the names. He'd have to start from scratch.

Did Getz have the checks? Or the Foster woman? What did it matter now? It was too late to launder them through one of his bank connections without getting caught. His life was over.

★ ★ ★ ★ ★

Denver, Colorado
Saturday, January 25

Grace looked up from the television. "Your boss didn't want the checks?"

"No."

"What are you going to do with them?"

"Turn them over to the FBI."

"That guy still wants them back."

"I know."

"What are we going to do now?"

"I'm going to call Officer Maggie Gutierrez of the Glades Police Department in Florida."

CHAPTER 40

Glades, Florida
Saturday, January 25
Maggie sprawled on the couch in her apartment, too tired to cook and almost too tired to call for Chinese take-out. She wanted to stay awake, go over her notes on the Foster case, check on Carl's background and see why he was under investigation at the time of his death.

She groaned as she rolled to her side and sat up. *Crappy-looking room.* She needed to get new furniture. Maybe something red or orange. Brighten up the place. She'd moved in eight months ago and had only a couch, a bed and cheap dresser, and a small kitchen table with two chairs. Books were stacked on the floor by the couch. One floor lamp lit the living room. *At least I could get a TV. And maybe a cat. A cat would be good company.*

When her cell phone rang, Maggie jumped off the couch and hurried to the table.

"Gutierrez," she said.

"Officer Gutierrez, this is Lynnette Foster."

"Hey, thanks for calling in. Where are you?" Maggie inwardly groaned at her own cheery, conversational tone. She was talking to a suspected killer, for God's sake.

"I didn't kill my husband."

Foster's first five words were exactly what Maggie had expected to hear. "Okay," she said. "Are you still in Denver?"

"We'll get to that. First I want to tell you a long story, start-

231

ing with last Wednesday when I walked out on my husband. Do you have time?"

"I have all the time you need." Maggie sat at her little table, pulled out her notebook and grabbed a pen.

It took Lynnette Foster nearly an hour to tell her story. Maggie doubted she'd left out anything. She had even mentioned the possibility that she'd left the patio door in their home unlocked when she left. If that was true, whoever killed Carl Foster would have had easy access to the house, which would explain why there was no sign of forcible entry. If Foster's actions had eased the way for a killer to get at her husband, it would explain her getting choked up when she talked about it, even though she'd walked out on the guy.

Wanting a person out of your life didn't necessarily mean you wanted the person dead. Detective Prince, for instance. It wouldn't break Maggie's heart if she never had to work with Prince again. But if he were killed, it would be a tragedy.

Foster explained why her husband had been called to an Internal Affairs hearing. Beating up an unarmed kid for loitering, even if the kid belonged to a gang, was frowned upon by the public as well as the IAD. Bad press for the cops.

"How long had you been married?" Maggie asked.

"Just a few days."

"And you didn't know he liked to beat up people?"

"I thought I knew him. I was wrong."

Another good lesson learned. Don't marry a guy unless you've known him so long he couldn't possibly have any secrets left. Maggie figured ten years would do it. Better yet, don't get married. If you must have company, get a cat.

The references Foster made to Sammy Grick, Benito Ortega, the guy in Denver, and the switched laptop cases were inconclusive, but clearly the men were after Foster for a reason. Whatever she had was important. "Mrs. Foster . . . Lynnette

. . . what was in the laptop case you found in your possession after the switch?"

"A cell phone and a laptop. The guy in the tweed jacket has those now."

"Anything else?"

"Yeah. A big wad of cash. I still have all of it."

Foster hesitated, then said, "There was also an unsealed brown envelope. I looked inside. It contained six checks drawn on South Florida companies. Big checks. I'm sure that's what Ortega wants back the most."

"Maybe the checks belonged to Ortega and he thought you were stealing them."

"All he had to do was tell me that. Instead, he threatened to kill me. He clearly did not want me to turn the case over to the cops—"

"Which is exactly what you should have done."

"That fat man screamed at me and said he'd kill me. I think the checks were stolen and Sammy Grick was a courier."

"Where did you get an idea like that?"

"I'm a reporter. I keep up on the news. I read a lot. I know. More than one business has been tripped up by a check theft ring and had to sue a bank or the bank's insurance company to get their money back."

Lynnette Foster told Maggie everything she'd learned about the death of Ortega's wife, the relationship between Grick and Ortega, Grick's death, and what little she knew about the third man—the one who'd shown up at the library, the snowbound road to the house on the hill, and the truck stop.

"A man and his daughter helped you?"

"Yes."

"What are their names?" When Lynnette didn't reply, Maggie said, "It doesn't matter. Ortega isn't my case. Miami P.D. is working it. I'll tell them about the connection between you and

Grick—the laptop case and its contents. They'll want whatever you still have in your possession. It might help make a case against Ortega. We need *you* to return to Florida so we can clear this up. I'll give you twenty-four hours to come in on your own. After that, you'll be the target of a nationwide manhunt."

"I'm in Denver. Will I be able to use my driver's license and credit card at the airport without getting arrested?"

"We have a watch on your credit cards, but that only results in an alert to our email here in Florida. We'll know when you buy your ticket, but the Denver police won't have that information unless we call them."

Maggie waited through another long silence. Finally, Foster agreed to come in on her own. When Maggie hung up, she felt a mixture of relief and anxiety. If Foster came in as she'd promised to do, Maggie would meet her at the airport and take her into custody. She'd find out for sure if Foster was guilty or not.

On the other hand, if Detective Prince found out about Maggie's actions and Foster reneged on her promise, Maggie's career in law enforcement would probably be over.

Denver, Colorado
Saturday, January 25
"I have to go to Florida within twenty-four hours or the Florida cops will alert Denver's police department," Lynnette told Grace. "State police too. I can't leave you here, and I can't put you on a plane to L.A. unless I talk to your dad first. It would be better if you'd go to Miami with me. I'll work it out so Thomas can come down to Florida and help you like he said."

Grace nodded, although she kept her eyes on the television.

Lynnette let her thoughts drift to the stolen checks. It was interesting that Sammy Grick had been taking those checks from Florida to California, especially since Ortega's home and business were in Miami. She wondered if Ortega had been in L.A. all along, perhaps to establish an alibi for the time his wife was murdered and to oversee transfer of the stolen funds. It wouldn't take the cops long to figure it out. She had a feeling Benny Ortega would be in the news again real soon.

She turned to her computer and booked an early-morning flight to Fort Lauderdale for herself and for Grace.

After that, she wrote a long email to Ramona, explaining everything that had happened with Carl and the two thugs who had chased her around Denver, the unexpected appearance of Grace, and the help they had received from Blue and her father. She added a postscript to her message: *If I could do one thing over in my life, Ramona, I'd listen to you and not marry Carl.*

Miami, Florida
Saturday, January 25

Benny sat on the plane, waiting. It had been thirty minutes since they'd landed, and they still had received no communication from the tower or the police. He called his tracker.

"Did you get another signal?"

"Hang on, I haven't checked since your plane took off."

Benny sighed. Nobody had any initiative anymore. If you didn't tell the help to do something, it didn't get done. If you didn't tell them exactly how to do it, it might get done but it wouldn't get done right. And if the going got tough, they quit.

"Hey!" Benny yelled into the phone. "I don't have all day, you stupid asshole."

The co-pilot appeared in the cabin doorway, his eyebrows raised. "Sir?"

Benny pointed to his cell phone and waved him away.

"Mr. Ortega," the tracker said, "the phone has been reactivated."

"Where is she? Is she still in Denver?"

"The phone's in Denver, sir."

Maybe Getz has it. Maybe Getz has it all. Is it possible he has my checks and is going into business for himself?

"Do you have a fix on the phone's location?" Benny asked.

"Yeah, but you're not going to like it."

"Just tell me where the phone is!"

"Downtown Denver. FBI Building."

Benny's vision blurred. He dropped the phone in his lap. *It's over. I might as well be dead.* He picked up the phone and dialed his lawyer.

When Benny exited the plane, two Miami police detectives stood at the bottom of the steps. One said, "Mr. Ortega, we're taking you in for questioning in the murder of your wife, Maria Ortega."

"I have nothing to say. I'd like to speak to my lawyer."

Shoved into an interrogation room in a downtown Miami station, Benny tried not to cringe when two FBI agents appeared.

Where was his damned lawyer?

One agent sat in a chair on the other side of the table. The second leaned against the wall near the door, out of Benny's sight. Benny didn't like anyone standing behind him. He liked to sit with his back to the wall.

Where was his fucking lawyer?

The room was too cold. He was accustomed to tropical heat and humidity. He rubbed his arms, then blew warm breath on his hands. Walking around the room would have helped, but his ankle was chained to a table leg.

He didn't know how long he'd been in the room. The cops had taken his watch along with his belt and shoelaces. He jiggled his legs, tapped his fingers, blew on his hands again.

The Fed across the table was staring at him. Sweat broke out on Benny's forehead.

"Mr. Ortega," the Fed said. "I need to ask you a few questions."

Getz talked. When I get out of this mess, I'll find him and rip him apart. Benny crossed his arms over his chest and stared at the table.

"Two of our agents had an interesting conversation with a Mr. Albert Getz in Denver," the Fed continued. "Do you know Mr. Getz?"

Benny shook his head.

"Mr. Getz spoke of you, also a Mr. Sammy Grick. Do you know Mr. Grick?"

Benny shook his head again.

"What about a woman named Lynnette Foster? Do you know Mrs. Foster?"

Holy shit, did Getz tell them everything? "No," Benny said.

"Mr. Getz told our agents that Mrs. Foster had an envelope full of checks he wanted to recover on your behalf. Is that true?"

"I have no idea what you're talking about. Who is this Getz guy, anyway?"

Hours later Benny was locked in a holding cell with half a dozen low-life crooks. The cops hadn't charged him with one single crime, nor had the Feds. It was Saturday. They didn't have to do anything with him until Monday. Even his lawyer couldn't do anything before Monday. Benny sat down in the corner of the cell, his back pressed against the wall. He pulled up his knees and, with an occasional quick glance around the room, checked out his cellmates.

Fort Collins, Colorado
Saturday, January 25
Albert felt pretty damned smug as he closed the door behind the two FBI agents. In exchange for Grick's phone, Ortega's phone number, and the name of the car rental company where

he'd rented the now demolished car that might still contain Grick's laptop, the agents let Albert go. He had been ordered to return to his home in California and remain there in case the FBI had further questions.

He knew they wouldn't. They had bigger fish to fry. They thought he was a courier, at worst an enforcer. He didn't think it had crossed their mind that he was a hit man. The word would get around, though. He'd screwed up, and no one would hire him. If the FBI did nail Ortega, they'd probably subpoena Albert and make him testify about his involvement. After that exposure, his anonymity would be down the toilet.

He'd have to live on his savings. At least he had the $250,000 down payment. He wouldn't collect anything else from Ortega. He had no more jobs lined up. If Benny Ortega had been in the room at that moment, Albert would have crushed his windpipe and happily watched him struggle for the breath that would never come.

CHAPTER 41

Denver, Colorado
Sunday, January 26
As soon as Lynnette and Grace had passed through Security at the Denver airport, Lynnette called Thomas and told him where she'd parked his car. She listened with growing anxiety as Thomas told her about the two FBI agents who'd questioned him and Blue again. He cautioned her to treat them with respect if they stopped her at the airport, to tell the truth and to turn over the checks immediately. With fifty minutes left before they needed to board their flight, Lynnette took Grace to a restaurant on the edge of the food court and picked a table that gave her a good view of the concourse.

"What am I supposed to do when we get to Florida?" Grace asked as she poked at her scrambled eggs with her fork.

"We're going to take a chance on the lady cop from Glades."

"If I don't like her looks, I'm taking off."

"Grace, don't do that. Please."

"You don't know what it's like living with my mom, Lynnette. And if the cops have to call her back from her vacation, she's going to be so pissed off at me."

"That's true. I don't know what it's like. I want to make your life better, honest. It's just that I can't do much until I get my own problems straightened out."

"I should have stayed with Blue and her dad."

"It wouldn't have been fair to them. They could get in big

trouble. I know you're worried. So am I. But we'll do our best to work it out."

"Who's 'we'?"

"Me, the cops, and I'm sure your mom—"

"Wait!" Grace grabbed her backpack and unzipped the side pocket. The muted melody of "Oh, My Papa" came from inside Grace's pack. Lynnette watched with confusion as Grace pulled her cell phone from the pocket and said, "Daddy?"

Grace listened for a couple of minutes, then said, "She's not dangerous, Daddy. But she's making me go to Florida with her."

Lynnette's mind raced as she watched Grace listen to whatever her dad told her, assuming Grace's father really was on the other end of the call.

"Yes, we're at the airport. How did you know?" Grace pulled the phone away from her ear and said, "This phone has a GPS tracker too, Lynnette. Daddy already knows where I am." She put the phone to her ear. "You can spy on me?" She listened then said, "We're in Terminal A, in a restaurant right by the escalators." Grace handed the phone to Lynnette. "My dad wants to talk to you."

Lynnette took the phone. "This is Lynnette Foster, Mr. McCoy. I'm so—"

"I can't even imagine what kind of explanation my ex-wife, my daughter, and you have for this bizarre situation. Right now, I don't care. I want Grace to be safe, and I think the best way to insure that is to get her into the custody of the FBI in Denver. They'll take care of her until I arrive . . . which should be in about three hours. The agents will arrive within thirty minutes. They'll come directly to the restaurant, so you're to wait there with Grace. Do not leave. Do you understand?"

"I can't miss my flight."

"Don't worry about your flight."

Grace's father ended the call before Lynnette could explain.

Grace bounced up and down in her chair and grinned at Lynnette. "You didn't believe me, did you? That I even had a dad and that he's an FBI agent? You should have called him Agent McCoy, not Mr. McCoy. He's going to be here in three hours and then take me home."

"Home to Florida?"

Grace stopped bouncing and sat still, her face suddenly less animated.

"Don't worry, honey. I could tell your dad loves you a lot, so I'm sure he's going to do what's best for you."

Lynnette felt she had no choice but to follow Agent McCoy's orders and wait. She tried to relax, rolling her shoulders to relieve the tension in her neck. As she sipped her coffee, she looked through the window and focused on the concourse traffic.

Albert stood in the center of Terminal A's food court and studied his options. He had a full hour before his flight to L.A. He needed coffee. Good coffee. The one sit-down restaurant appeared far more comfortable than the packed seating area in the midst of the fast-food counters. As he took a step toward the restaurant, he glanced inside. Lynnette Foster and the kid were seated at a high table by the front window. Both were looking in his direction. The girl pointed. Foster nodded. The girl slid off her chair and turned toward the door, but Foster grabbed the girl's arm and pulled her back to the table. Albert made eye contact with Foster. She shook her head.

It was an odd feeling, but Albert had the impression she was warning him off. From what? He glanced around, uneasy, now certain he should leave the area as fast as possible. His foot slipped on the marble floor as he turned away. Struggling to recover, he tried to stop his backward momentum. His knee struck a woman's wheeled carry-on as he fell to the side, jerking her off balance. Unable to break his own fall with one arm still confined by the sling, he landed on his left arm and hip. The woman tumbled hard, the full weight of her body on Albert's right knee. He screeched in pain, shoved her to the side, and grabbed his knee with both hands, whimpering when new pain seized his injured elbow.

"Mr. Getz, airport medics are on their way."

The voice sounded familiar. Albert opened his eye and found FBI Agent Bailey kneeling beside him, one hand on his shoulder. The other agent knelt by the lady who had landed on his knee.

"What are you two doing here?" Albert glanced toward the restaurant window where Foster and the kid were watching everything that had happened. If the woman still had Ortega's checks, she was about to get busted. Albert sighed. Was there any reason he shouldn't rat out the Foster woman? Did she know that her goose was cooked if she told even the tiniest lie to the FBI? What about the kid? Maybe the FBI didn't know about her. The last thing he wanted to do was make trouble for a little kid.

He grabbed Bailey's hand and held on. "Just get me some help," he said. "And don't leave me." He moaned and closed his eyes, but maintained his iron grip on Bailey's hand.

"We can't stay here and wait for the FBI," Lynnette said. "If those guys work for Ortega—"

"But Dad said to wait."

Lynnette grabbed Grace's hand. "He wouldn't want me to keep you here if you might get hurt. Get your pack."

"But, Lynnette, I—"

"Wait until we get on the plane. You can call him before we take off."

They hurried past the gurney and EMTs while everyone's attention was focused on the passengers still sprawled on the floor. Lynnette glanced back and saw the two men stand up and head toward the restaurant. It seemed too soon for them to be the agents McCoy had sent for Grace, but they could have talked to Thomas and already been on their way. On the other hand, they had clearly recognized the guy in the tweed jacket and talked to him as though they knew him. No way could she take a chance, not after seeing Ortega's man right here at the airport.

The plane was already boarding when they arrived at the gate. Shortly after Lynnette and Grace were in their seats, the flight attendants closed the door. Grace did not have time to call her father before the attendant instructed passengers to turn off their phones.

Glades, Florida
Sunday, January 26

Maggie knew when Lynnette bought her ticket. But two tickets? She did a search on the passenger's name, Grace Foster, and found nothing helpful.

Since Foster's flight wouldn't arrive in Fort Lauderdale until Sunday afternoon, Maggie still had time to look for the girl, Laura, who claimed she knew Mrs. Foster did not kill her husband. Maggie decided to start by talking to the kid who was still in a Miami hospital, most likely a safer place to visit than the kid's home. She didn't take anyone with her, and she didn't tell Detective Prince.

Maggie tried to hide her surprise when she walked into the hospital room and found Prince sitting in a chair by one of the two beds in the room. He chatted with the kid who seemed in good spirits in spite of the I.V. in his left arm, the cast on his right arm, and the bruises and lacerations that covered the visible parts of his body. There was a bandage over his left eye.

The room was packed with Latinos, most milling about the tiny space, talking and laughing. A heavy-set woman in a flowered dress sat at the end of the bed, one hand on the injured kid's foot. She listened to the conversation between the kid and the detective.

Prince looked up when Maggie walked into the room. If he was surprised, he didn't show it. He merely said, "Come here. I want you to meet Eduardo."

Maggie crossed the room, shook hands with the boy's mother and winked at Eduardo when they were introduced.

"Eddie's one of my P.A.L. club boxers," Prince said. "He's also a straight-A student. He and his younger sister are going to college."

Eddie's mother didn't say anything, but she looked away from the detective and scanned the room as though searching for someone.

"He's not here," Prince said. "He left when I walked in." He looked at Maggie. "Eddie's brother. He used to be one of my kids, but he got away from me. He's a gang man now."

"You can't get him back?"

"I tried. He won't listen." Prince stood, patted Eddie on the shoulder and shook hands with Eddie's mom, then joined Maggie at the foot of the bed. "What are you doing here?" he asked. "Looking for the girl?"

"Sort of. I thought this kid might know something."

Prince took hold of Maggie's elbow. Instead of moving her toward the exit, he guided her to a door that stood ajar. When he took hold of the doorknob and pulled it open, the girl inside the bathroom covered her face and began to cry.

"Laura?" Maggie looked at Prince. "You know Laura?"

He looked around to make sure nobody stood within earshot. "This is Eddie's sister, the one I said was college bound. She's one of my kids."

"Did you tell her to come to me?"

"We need to talk." He pulled Maggie out of the doorway as he said, "Laura, you stay safe. You're going to be fine. Officer Gutierrez has everything under control."

"Where's your car?" he asked when they were in the hall.

"Parking garage. What's the deal? What does Laura know about Carl Foster's murder?"

"She knows her brother did it, along with two of his buddies. Carl Foster hurt Eddie and Eddie's brother was honor-bound to get revenge."

"Why did they kill Foster? Why didn't they just beat the crap out of him?"

"That will be one of the questions we ask when we pick him up."

"Is Foster's wife completely off the hook then? Do we even need to talk to her?"

"Haven't you found her yet?"

"Not exactly."

"We need to ask her a few questions. Have her come on in for a chat. No need to go to Fort Lauderdale this afternoon and meet her, though. There's no arrest warrant."

Maggie stopped in her tracks. "You know she's flying into Fort Lauderdale? How did you know that?"

"You honestly think I'd turn something like this over to a rookie? Not a chance."

Maggie didn't know what to say. She stared daggers at the detective as he walked away. The last thing he said before he walked through the sliding glass doors was, "By the way, Gutierrez. You did a good job. Keep it up and you'll make detective someday."

★ ★ ★ ★ ★

Miami, Florida
Sunday, January 26
Benny's lawyer accomplished one thing on Sunday. He arranged for Benny to move to a private cell after his cellmates beat him up.

Denver, Colorado
Sunday, January 26
"My dad's going to be mad," Grace said.

"I know. I'll talk to him and explain what happened when we get to Florida."

"What's going to happen to me if the police arrest you when we get there?"

"I don't know. But you'll be safer with the police than you've been with me. And if they know your dad is on his way to get you, they won't call Social Services or anything like that."

"They'll call my mom."

"Maybe not." She reached over and patted Grace's arm. "Don't worry. All this will be over soon. You'll be fine."

Grace said very little until they landed in Fort Lauderdale and were given permission to use their phones. When she called her father's number, she listened for a long time before she finally spoke. "We saw one of the bad guys who chased us—"

Lynnette could hear Agent McCoy's voice from Grace's phone but couldn't understand what he said.

"Lynnette was afraid—"

Lynnette took a deep breath when Grace handed over the phone. "Dad wants to talk to you."

"Agent McCoy, I—"

"I'm in the airport in Denver, Mrs. Foster. I'm catching the next flight to Fort Lauderdale. You and my daughter will be met at the gate and you will be taken into custody by the FBI. Do not try to run again."

"I wasn't—"

"If anything happens to Grace, I will hold you personally responsible."

CHAPTER 42

Fort Lauderdale, Florida
Sunday, January 26

Maggie sat near the arrival gate for Lynnette Foster's flight. A couple of minutes after the plane pulled up to the jetway, two men strode into the waiting area and spoke to the man at the desk.

Suits. She wondered who they were after.

The man at the desk picked up his phone and spoke into it briefly, then beckoned the two men to follow him through the door and down the jetway. A few minutes later, the agents returned, one walking beside Lynnette Foster and the other holding the hand of a young girl.

Maggie jumped up and hurried toward the men, pulling out her badge as she went. "Wait," she said. "I need to speak to Mrs. Foster."

The men stopped and looked at Maggie's badge. "We're taking her in," said one.

"Who are you?"

The two agents displayed their identification. FBI.

Feds. She was right. "I need to tell her something," Maggie said. "Mrs. Foster, we've apprehended the gang members who killed your husband. There's no warrant out for your arrest. But we do need to ask you a few questions." She shifted her attention to the agent at Foster's side. "Where are you taking her? Why? Who's the girl?"

Lynnette pulled away from the agent. "It's true?" she said. "I'm not a suspect?"

"It's true. Why are they taking you in? Who's the kid?"

"It's a long story. For now, I need to make sure this little girl gets back to her dad."

"When can we talk to her?" Maggie asked the Fed.

"It'll be a while, I'm afraid." He handed Maggie a card. "Call that number in a couple of hours and I'll see what I can do."

West Palm Beach, Florida
Sunday, January 26

As soon as Lynnette and Grace entered the FBI resident agency office in West Palm Beach, the second agent took Grace away in spite of her protests. The man who introduced himself as Agent Samuels guided Lynnette into an office and assisted her into a chair. He placed her purse and laptop case on a desk and asked her permission to examine the contents.

"I guess Thomas told you everything," she said. "What you're looking for is in the laptop case. Inside the brown envelope."

Samuels went through everything in Lynnette's case before removing the envelope and examining the checks. "Where did you get these?"

Lynnette told him the whole story, starting with Carl's assault and ending with her flight from the man in the tweed jacket at the Denver airport.

"Stay here," Samuels ordered.

When he returned he carried a laptop. "We're going to the field office in Miami," he said.

"Why?"

"Benito Ortega is in police custody in Miami. I need to talk to him."

"What about Grace?"

"She's coming with us."

When they met by the front door, Lynnette hugged Grace to her side. "Everything okay?"

"Yeah," Grace said. "He gave me a soda and a candy bar. And we called my dad again. He's going to meet us in Miami."

Miami, Florida
Sunday, January 26

Benny had been stuck in the interrogation room at the FBI field office in Miami for over three hours before the FBI agent named Samuels returned with a laptop.

It only took a couple of minutes for him to open the computer and power it on, tap a few keys, wait a couple of seconds, then type something else. He turned the computer around so Benny could see the screen.

The image of a check for over $500,000 appeared. Benny reached out and used the touch pad to scroll down, examining the six checks one by one. They would have been worth more than three million dollars if all had gone as planned. Maria had done a fine job putting contacts in the company's accounts payable departments and then timing the thefts. "I've never seen these before," Benny said.

Samuels tapped a few more keys, then let Benny see the screen again. "There were three more checks inside the front pocket of your wife's day calendar. They turned up during the search conducted by the FBI after Mr. Getz talked to agents in Denver. Does that surprise you?"

Benny could have sworn his hair stood up on the top of his head. Maria held out on him? He wondered how long that had been going on. Maybe she deserved to die. He tried to look dumfounded, but he couldn't control his facial muscles. He figured shock and surprise showed all over his face. He began to laugh—stupid uncontrollable laughter.

"There was also considerable cash in Sammy Grick's laptop

case. Do you know anything about that?"

"No," Benny said, almost choking on the word. He covered his face with his hands and bit his lip in an effort to stop laughing. When he finally took his hands down, he avoided making eye contact with the agent.

"I have to leave for a while, Mr. Ortega, but I'll be back. You'll be busy though. Officials are lining up to talk to you this afternoon. The Internal Revenue Service. Maybe Homeland Security since one of these checks is drawn on a company based in Havana. Alcohol, Tobacco and Firearms, because one of the payees is a distillery. Can you think of anyone else who might want to talk to you, Mr. Ortega?"

Benny shook his head.

"Oh, yeah," Samuels added as he shoved back his chair and stood. "There's a homicide detective who's anxious to have a crack at you. He says they found a Luger in Mr. Grick's car at the airport."

Benny's shoulders began to shake.

Samuels frowned. "This is no laughing matter, Mr. Ortega."

Benny placed his elbows on the table and cradled his forehead in his hands. There had to be a way he could hang this whole mess on his wife and that big-mouth bastard, Albert Getz.

Denver, Colorado
Sunday, January 26
Albert watched the two FBI agents who looked on with interest as the doctors examined the X-rays of his knee.

"Looks broken, Getz," Agent Bailey said. "Bad luck."

"What happened to the woman and the kid? Did you get them?" Albert asked.

"Nope. They got picked up when they arrived in Florida. Mrs. Foster told agents there how you tried to chase her down in Denver and again in Fort Collins. And Mr. Ortega says you must have been in cahoots with his wife to steal those checks. He says Sammy Grick worked for the two of you. He also said he heard his wife mention you were a hit man. Is that true?"

Ignoring Bailey's question, Albert shook the rails of his hospital bed. "It's been hours since I had a shot for this pain! I can't stand it!"

"Looks like you need surgery on that knee," Agent Bailey said, his voice oozing fake sympathy. "After the docs are done with you, we'll be back for a nice long chat. There are at least three police departments that want their turn at you, too. Denver P.D. sent someone to sit outside your door and make sure you don't hobble off on your own."

CHAPTER 43

Miami, Florida
Sunday, January 26

Lynnette sat inside the Miami FBI field offices and waited. Grace had been whisked away again, this time by a female agent. The first visitors to show up were Officer Maggie Gutierrez and Detective Mark Prince from Glades. The good news? They weren't there to arrest her. The bad news? They filled her in on everything that had happened to Carl. When they finished, she felt drained. She put her head in her hands and wondered why she wasn't sobbing her heart out. Was she in shock? Would she fall apart later?

"You don't want to go in there by yourself," Maggie said. "There are services that clean up crime scenes. We can send someone."

"I'd appreciate that. What about Carl's body?"

"His mother said she'd arrange a funeral. She's waiting for the coroner to release the body."

"Did she say anything about me?"

"No."

Carl's mother would grieve for a long time over her only son. She would have no sympathy for the daughter-in-law who had walked out on Carl and left him to face his killers alone. Lynnette rubbed her forehead. She'd still have to go to the funeral. Facing Carl's mother would be one more test of her resolve never to run away from a problem again.

After Officer Gutierrez left, Agent Bob McCoy paid Lynnette a visit. He didn't have Grace with him.

In spite of her exhaustion and apprehension, she paid close attention to Grace's dad, trying to figure out if he was the good guy Grace said he was. He seemed nice enough, although a bit on the stern side, until Lynnette had told him more than half of her story. At the point she described Grace's threat to run away in downtown Denver and her fear of Social Services and foster homes, McCoy's shoulders visibly relaxed and he leaned back in his chair.

"I know I blew it," Lynnette said, "but I was scared for myself and worried that Grace would take off on her own and something bad would happen to her. At the time I didn't know Carl was dead. I thought he had put the Denver police on my trail. I figured if they caught me and I had Grace with me, I'd be charged with kidnapping. She got caught up in my paranoia . . . well, you know the rest."

"Grace said there were people who helped you in Colorado. Thomas Young and his daughter . . . Blue?"

"Yes. I think Thomas has already been in touch with the FBI in Colorado. He wanted to help us by getting the checks to the authorities without telling them about Grace. Thomas's plan got messed up when that guy showed up at the truck stop in Fort Collins and I took off with Grace."

"Yes, she told me how you put the guy out of commission. To tell the truth, before talking to Grace this morning I intended to file kidnapping charges against you. After hearing her version, however, and then talking to you, I reconsidered. You didn't make the best decisions along the way, but I'll concede that you tried to protect Grace in spite of her tall tales and willfulness and in spite of your own fear. Thank you for that."

"What happens to Grace now?"

"Her mother gets back tomorrow. I'll meet with her and see

what she intended when she took Grace to the airport. We already have a joint custody arrangement, so we might be able to work it out without going to court. I'd love to have Grace live with me. She's a great kid and I love her like crazy."

"Do you have to travel a lot?"

"I do now, but I can change that."

"If Grace's mother lets her go, when will you and Grace go to California?"

"Tuesday at the latest."

"I'll miss Grace very much, Agent McCoy. After I get my life together, would it be okay if I called to see how she's doing? Or come out to see her?"

"Get your affairs straightened out first, and then call me."

He stood up and walked out of the room. Ten minutes later the door opened again. McCoy stood aside to let Grace into the room.

She ran to Lynnette and threw her arms around her neck. "We're going to be okay now, Lynnette. My dad promised."

Lynnette hugged Grace and whispered, "I know. You take care of yourself, okay?"

"I will."

"Come on, Grace," McCoy said. "The agents need to talk to Mrs. Foster." As he ushered Grace out of the room, he looked back and said, "You'll be okay. I wish you the best of luck."

CHAPTER 44

Sunday, January 26

Agent Samuels rejoined Lynnette and told her she needed to tell her story one more time, beginning to end. A second agent came in to man the digital camera and record the interview. Samuels asked an occasional question but mostly listened.

When Lynnette finished, she glanced at her watch and realized she'd been sitting in that chair for more than four hours. "Okay if I stand up and stretch?" she asked.

"Sure. Actually, you're free to go, Mrs. Foster. Where will you be staying?"

"In a motel. I won't be able to live in my . . . Carl's . . . that house."

Samuels handed her a business card. "Whenever you change your address, please call me. You're a witness in this case. Eventually you'll need to testify in a federal court. You'll receive a subpoena when that time comes."

"A case against Benito Ortega?"

"And possibly against Albert Getz, the man you call the 'guy in the tweed jacket.' "

"He worked for Ortega, right?"

"We have reason to believe Mr. Getz is a hit man, Mrs. Foster."

Startled, Lynnette gasped. She couldn't think of anything to say.

Samuels placed Lynnette's laptop case on the table. "We're keeping the checks and the cash, of course." He leveled a stern gaze at her and added, "Keep an eye on your possessions when you travel. You're lucky you didn't have your identity and your savings stolen while your papers were in the possession of Sammy Grick or Albert Getz."

Lynnette caught her breath but didn't say anything. As events spiraled out of control before the weekend, she'd forgotten about her investments and bank accounts. She hadn't contacted the banks or changed her passwords. Now she was anxious to get away from the FBI building and find a motel with an Internet connection.

As soon as she checked in to her motel room, she logged on to her accounts, checked the balances, and changed her passwords. With a sigh of relief, she acknowledged her close call. The fat man had died, so he'd never be a threat again. But the guy in the tweed coat had been in possession of her case and her important papers for several hours.

She drove to a nearby restaurant where she enjoyed her first leisurely dinner in nearly five days. Then she returned to her room and worked her way through her email. She'd received one more email from Dave, this one pleading with her to return to Indianapolis and promising to take care of her. Lynnette deleted it without answering.

The most recent note from Ramona said she was on her way to Florida to help Lynnette sort out her troubles.

Lynnette glanced at her watch, saw that Ramona's red-eye flight had taken off more than an hour ago, and smiled. It was too late to stop her, and that was fine. Lynnette needed all the moral support she could get.

Running away was no longer an option.

ABOUT THE AUTHOR

Patricia Stoltey grew up on a farm in central Illinois and has also lived in Oklahoma, Indiana, the south of France, and Florida. A retired accounts payable and inventory control manager, she currently resides in northern Colorado with her husband and precious Katie Cat. Her blog (http://patricia stoltey.blogspot.com) explores the writing life and regularly features guest authors from a variety of genres. Patricia is also the author of the Sylvia and Willie mystery series, including *The Prairie Grass Murders* and *The Desert Hedge Murders*. *Dead Wrong* is her first standalone novel. She is a member of Northern Colorado Writers, Rocky Mountain Fiction Writers, Sisters in Crime, and Mystery Writers of America.